MURDER AT THE COLLEGE LIBRARY

Also by Con Lehane

Bartender Brian McNulty mysteries

BEWARE THE SOLITARY DRINKER
WHAT GOES AROUND COMES AROUND
DEATH AT THE OLD HOTEL

42nd Street Library mysteries

MURDER AT THE 42ND STREET LIBRARY
MURDER IN THE MANUSCRIPT ROOM
MURDER OFF THE PAGE
MURDER BY DEFINITION *

* *available from Severn House*

MURDER AT THE COLLEGE LIBRARY

Con Lehane

SEVERN
HOUSE

First world edition published in Great Britain and the USA in 2024
by Severn House, an imprint of Canongate Books Ltd,
14 High Street, Edinburgh EH1 1TE.

severnhouse.com

British Library Cataloguing-in-Publication Data
A CIP catalogue record for this title is available from the British Library.

ISBN-13: 978-0-7278-2305-2 (cased)
ISBN-13: 978-1-4483-1330-3 (e-book)

All Severn House titles are printed on acid-free paper.

Typeset by Palimpsest Book Production Ltd.,
Falkirk, Stirlingshire, Scotland.
Printed and bound in Great Britain by
TJ Books, Padstow, Cornwall.

Praise for the 42nd Street Library mysteries

'Draws us in and keeps us firmly glued to the page'
Booklist on *Murder by Definition*

'Intriguing'
Publishers Weekly on *Murder by Definition*

'A treat'
Booklist on *Murder by Definition*

'An apt choice for bibliophiles'
Booklist on *Murder off the Page*

'Atmospheric setting . . . Those who love
New York City and libraries will be rewarded'
Publishers Weekly on *Murder off the Page*

'Intense, thought-provoking'
Library Journal on *Murder in the Manuscript Room*

'Plot twists and multiple points of view add to a gritty,
complex tale that weaves details of library work and
references to crime novels throughout the story'
Booklist on *Murder in the Manuscript Room*

'A fun read for mystery buffs and librarians alike'
Library Journal on *Murder at the 42nd Street Library*

About the author

Con Lehane is a mystery writer, living in Washington, DC. He is the author of the 42nd Street Library mysteries, featuring Raymond Ambler, curator of the library's (fictional) crime fiction collection. He's also the author of three mysteries featuring New York City bartender Brian McNulty and has published short stories in *Ellery Queen Mystery Magazine* and *Alfred Hitchcock Mystery Magazine*.

Over the years, he has been a college professor, union organizer and labor journalist, and has tended bar at two-dozen or so drinking establishments. He holds a Master of Fine Arts degree in fiction writing from Columbia University School of the Arts and teaches writing at The Writer's Center in Bethesda, Maryland.

conlehane.com

To the American Library Association

for its unwavering commitment to protecting the right of all readers to read the books they want to read, and their right to freedom from unreasonable intrusion into or surveillance of their lawful library use.

AUTHOR'S NOTE

Raymond Ambler, the main character in my 42nd Street Library mysteries, is of course fictional as is his crime fiction collection and the crime fiction reading room at the renowned 42nd Street Library. Trinity College of the Bronx and its college library, which provide a setting for the events that take place in this story are—as you would expect—fictional also, as is the The New York Mystery Writers collection and its curator.

However, there exists at least one crime fiction collection and its curator that are not fictional. I owe a special thanks this time around to Randal Brandt, Head of Cataloging at The Bancroft Library, University of California, Berkeley. Mr. Brandt in addition to his cataloging duties is Curator of the California Detective Fiction Collection at The Bancroft Library. His impressive collection served as an inspiration for *Murder at the College Library*.

You can read about the California Detective Fiction Collection here: https://www.lib.berkeley.edu/about/news mystery-murder-mayhem-meet-man-behind-librarys-detective-fiction-collection, as well as a conversation I had with the real-life curator here: https://crimereads.com/randal-brandt-crime-archives/.

ONE

T he Woodlawn section of the Bronx, tucked away between Van Cortland Park and the city of Yonkers, is the home to a small, not especially well-known, liberal arts institution, Trinity College of the Bronx. Ray Ambler, curator of the New York Public Library's crime fiction collection, housed at the 42nd Street Library, had never been to Woodlawn or Trinity College of the Bronx until he was invited one early spring afternoon to evaluate the college library's collection of mystery novels.

An assistant something-or-other in the college president's office had called to tell him the collection was for sale and the college president wanted the 42nd Street Library to buy it. Setting out for the far reaches of the northern Bronx on that chilly spring afternoon, Ambler had no idea that awaiting him within the ivy-covered, hallowed halls of academe would be greed, betrayal, fierce rivalry, intrigue, and what might well turn out to be an unsolvable murder.

He knew the Trinity College mystery collection existed because he'd met its curator a half-decade ago at an exhibit Ambler had put on at the 42nd Street Library – *A Century-and-a-Half of Murder and Mystery in New York.*

Since that first meeting, they'd run into one another a number of times at book conferences, auctions and such events, and they'd become friends of a sort – book-world friends-enjoying one another's company at whatever conference or meeting they were attending but not much in touch otherwise. Sam Abernathy was proud of the college's collection of New York Mystery Writers, a project he'd been assembling for decades. Ambler had meant to take him up on his offers to visit the collection but had never gotten around to it.

Now it looked like the collection was headed for the auction block. Small and not especially well-endowed liberal arts colleges had been suffering financially for a decade or longer, many of them forced to shut down programs and not infrequently eliminate entire departments, as well as replace full-time tenure-line faculty with poorly paid adjuncts.

The fact was that there was little chance the 42nd Street Library would purchase the Trinity College collection anyway. With the usual financial crunch for the New York Public Library system, Ambler wasn't sure the Manuscript and Archives Division would come up with the crime fiction collection's operating budget for the coming year, much less provide funds to expand the collection.

The Trinity campus could as easily have been in a small town in Iowa or Indiana instead of the North Bronx, with its well-tended lawns, stately trees, shrubs, and flower beds with budding daffodils and tulips in front of the low-rise classroom buildings. A pattern of sidewalks crisscrossed a central quad-rangle of manicured lawns, beneath a canopy of budding trees, traversed by backpack-wearing, hurrying students, one of whom – a tall, thin, black-bearded young man with a rainbow flag on his backpack – Ambler flagged down and asked for directions to the library. The boy pointed to a stone structure, much like a chapel, attached to a more modern brick-and-glass building that was probably more functional than the stone building but had as much character as a strip mall.

When he tried to enter the stone building, he found the thick ornate wooden door locked, so he followed a sign pointing to an entrance in the newer brick building. He gave the young woman at the information desk in the modern, brightly lit, antiseptic main-floor reference room the name of the person he was to meet, and she directed him to a conference room behind the reference desk.

A small group awaited him, all of them stone-faced, as if they awaited the bearer of bad news. He expected someone to welcome him. Since no one said a word, he introduced himself and added, 'Am I in the right place? I was invited to look at a collection of mystery novels. I was hoping to see Professor Abernathy.'

For a moment no one responded, until a sharp-featured woman, her grey hair pulled back in a tight bun, said in a voice cultivated by years of admonishing young scholars to shush, 'The college is not selling the collection. Professor Abernathy is in class at the moment. He would tell you what I just told you.'

The rest of the assemblage – two tweedy, salt-and-pepper-bearded men, and a young, blonde-haired woman, whose delicately sculpted face, with porcelain skin, ruby lips, and wide, deeply blue eyes, wouldn't be out of place on the cover of a fashion magazine – made clear their agreement with nods and a slight hardening of their expressions.

Ambler was surprised by the hostility of the group facing him. At least they weren't carrying torches and pitchforks. He told them about the call he'd received from the president's office and said he was sorry if he'd misunderstood what he'd been told.

'You're not mistaken,' the spokeswoman said. 'Dr Barnes thinks he can rule by fiat, forgetting the faculty has a meaningful say about what happens at the college. We haven't been consulted on this proposal because he knows we would vote it down, which we plan to do at an emergency meeting of the faculty senate executive committee later this afternoon.'

'I see,' Ambler said. He didn't like that he'd been dropped into the middle of a dispute between the faculty and the college president. Neither did he like being confronted by a self-appointed vigilante group acting as if he'd created the problem. He wasn't going to argue with them. He was invited by the president, so he'd talk to him. And he wanted to see Sam Abernathy. 'I'm an innocent outsider here,' he told the group. 'I thought I was meeting Edward Barnes, and I hoped to see Sam. I've known him for years.'

After another moment of heavy silence, during which Ambler and his interlocutors glared at one another, a well-dressed, well-groomed man banged through the conference room door.

'Mr Ambler, I presume.' He held out his hand and gripped Ambler's with a firm businessman's grip, looking him steadily in the eye. 'Edward Barnes . . . I see you've met some of our faculty . . . very proud of them. Professor Randolph, I hope you've made Mr Ambler welcome. His crime collection at the 42nd Street Library, I've been told, is among the most well-regarded collection of its kind.'

Actually, it was probably one of the only ones of its kind. But Ambler let the president pontificate because that was what college presidents were supposed to do.

Professor Randolph's visage, if anything, became more stone-like. 'I told Mr Ambler the faculty senate hadn't yet acted on your proposal and that we were unlikely to approve an action that would diminish the library's collections.'

Barnes addressed Ambler. 'Professor Randolph is mistaken.'

He turned to Randolph, whose face had reddened and whose eyes were bulging. 'I've discussed this with Dr Stuart. You might want to speak with him. My understanding is the faculty senate supports the effort.'

He turned back to Ambler. 'Dr Stuart is the president of the faculty senate. Professor Randolph and some of the older faculty are the not-always-loyal opposition, naysayers who provide the foot-dragging opposition to changes needed to bring the college into the twenty-first century.'

His modulated tone and condescending expression conveyed disdain better than if he'd spat out a barrage of vulgar curse words. Dressed in a tailored business suit, his hair styled, eyewear with designer frames, he looked like a hotshot private equity investor on the rise, not at all Ambler's image of a college president.

'College faculty can't stop themselves from engaging in prolonged debate before taking any action. The more insignificant the action, the more ruthless and brutal the debate.' He addressed Ambler with a smug smile. 'We'll get it sorted out.'

He turned to Professor Randolph again. 'I hope you'll have the courtesy to show Mr Ambler the detective novel collection.' He smirked as he said, 'I asked Professor Abernathy to dust it off since I don't think anyone's looked at it in years.'

Randolph stared daggers at Barnes and said, 'Professor Hastings will,' before stomping out of the office.

Hastings made an effort to keep up her hostility and aloofness, but after a frosty moment or two her naturally open and friendly manner and her love of books and the library overcame her borrowed ill will, and she became quite enthusiastic and utterly charming as she escorted Ambler to the New York

Mystery Writers reading room and introduced him to the collection.

By the time Ambler did a quick browse through the shelves, Professor Hastings, who asked to be called Sarah, had warmed considerably to him. 'The collection is Sam Abernathy's passion,' she said, as they sat together later at a small table in the relatively subdued student union drinking coffee. She slipped quite easily into sharing faculty gossip, though without any malice, as if she'd judged Ambler to be one of them, an attitude Ambler found appealing.

The president who preceded Barnes had been at the college nearly forty years, and got along wonderfully with the faculty, she said. He believed in shared governance and supported faculty members in their scholarly work, whatever it was.

Barnes came in to shake things up, changing the emphasis from liberal arts to a new business model, catering to students. She waved at her surroundings – refurbishing the student union, for example, and emphasizing readying students for the corporate world and the more practical fields, de-emphasizing the humanities.

'Whatever scholarship a faculty member might be doing was irrelevant if it wasn't important to the business world or likely to draw grant money. That's where the trouble comes from. You wouldn't think disagreements among scholars would be as nasty as these are. There's so much rancor, you'd almost think the sides would take up arms.'

Ambler, too, was surprised by the hostility he'd been met with. The collection was interesting, though its aim was fairly modest, or at least contained. Sam had collected what he could find – and afford – of mysteries either set or written in New York.

He focused on first editions and later on acquired the papers of some contemporary mystery writers. Since he'd been doing this for thirty years or so, he'd put together more significant holdings than one might expect to find in a small library at a relatively undistinguished college.

He didn't have a Poeana collection nearly as impressive as the one at the Harry Ransom Center at the University of Texas, or even on a par with the Poe collection in Manuscripts and

Archives at the 42nd Street Library. But Sam's collection did include letters and copies of magazine articles by Poe, written during his time in New York, some of which might be originals.

He'd also found a first edition of *Life and Letters of Edgar Allan Poe*, two volumes, by James Harrison, as well as both the Mabbott and Pollin *Collected Works of Edgar Allan Poe*, as well as the James Albert Harrison, seventeen-volume *The Complete Works of Edgar Allan Poe*, which – though not one-of-a-kind, occasionally inaccurate, and hardly complete – would catch the eye of a Poe collector.

Overall, the value of the collection wasn't its depth so much as its breadth, including a few writers Ambler wasn't familiar with, which meant Trinity College of the Bronx might be in possession of unique copies of some materials. He'd need to go through the collection more carefully to see if there were any gems; that was the fun part of evaluating a more-or-less obscure collection.

He and Sarah Hastings were waiting for Professor Abernathy's class to finish. She looked at the clock for the fourth or fifth time. 'He should be in his office by now. His class finished up a few minutes ago and he always goes to his office directly afterward.'

'That's why he wasn't at the library to meet you.' She frowned, as if to apologize for her earlier behavior. 'He wouldn't miss a class.'

They walked across the campus, at ease and comfortable together, as if they'd become friends.

'I know it's against your interest. Yet I feel you're an understanding man.' Her tone was earnest. In the short time they'd been together, he'd come to feel kindly toward her, and toward the college as well. The campus was what he'd always imagined a liberal arts college would look like, the kind of place where he'd once hoped to spend his working life, a college devoted to the search for knowledge for no purpose other than the intrinsic value of the search itself. Adrift in his own thoughts, he only caught up with what she was saying as she was finishing.

'. . . if you could see your way to recommend the collection stay with the college, you'd do us a great favor. It would break Sam's heart to lose it.'

He of course understood what a collection meant to its curator. 'I'll have to give Dr Barnes an honest assessment of the collection's value. But you should know I don't have the funding to purchase Professor Abernathy's collection, and I'm not likely to come up with it.'

She began to thank him but he stopped her.

'That doesn't mean that if the collection is valuable, or has valuable pieces, another institution with better funding wouldn't buy it.'

Her smile faded. 'The bastard.' Presumably she was referring to Dr Barnes. 'He should be running a supermarket. He doesn't care a thing about the academy.'

TWO

With his mane of white hair, quick movements, lively expression, and slight Eastern European accent, Sam Abernathy could play the role of a shoemaker in a Hans Christian Andersen tale. Taking in his surroundings, Ambler wasn't at all surprised when Sam said he'd been in his office for four decades. You could bet some of the books and paraphernalia on his shelves had been there since the day he moved in.

Abernathy greeted him like an old friend. 'You finally made it up here to the outpost of civilization.' He chuckled. 'What'd you think? Not the New York Public Library, but not too bad a collection for a small college and no endowment.'

They talked comfortably about what Ambler had noticed in the collection and what Sam told him was there that he hadn't noticed. Sam spoke modestly, but without hiding that he knew what he was doing as a collector.

He'd gathered a good deal of Chester Himes's detective fiction. Besides the French and US first editions of the Coffin Ed Johnson and Grave Digger Jones Harlem series, he had original copies of *Abbott's Monthly* magazine from 1932 and 1933, in which Himes published his first crime fiction stories, written while he was in prison, one of which featured a pair of detectives who were the forerunners of Coffin Ed and Grave Digger.

After a student stopped in to drop off a research paper and chat for a few moments (Sam was teaching a seminar on Poe and the origins of detective fiction that semester), he folded his hands on his desk and directed a mournful, searching gaze at Ambler, the expression he might have when telling an unfortunate student he'd received an F on his paper.

'I understand from Dr Barnes you might buy my humble enterprise for the 42nd Street Library.' He paused for a long moment before continuing in measured words. 'I'm flattered that you're interested in my life's work. Yet your acquisition feels akin to the big corporate powers gobbling up the mom-and-pop store – CVS wiping out the local drug store, Home Depot burying the local hardware store, Amazon driving independent bookstores out of business.'

His voice rose dramatically. 'So, nothing personal in this, but I plan to fight you tooth and nail to hold on to my assemblage of mystery novels.'

Ambler hadn't thought of his tiny piece of the 42nd Street Library's Manuscripts and Archives Division as a colossus gobbling up anything. It was more likely his collection could get gobbled up by the likes of Beinecke Library at Yale or the Ransom Center at the University of Texas. Still, he supposed, everything was relative.

'I didn't know there was a controversy,' Ambler said. 'When the college president's office called, I thought I'd come take a look and have a friendly chat with you. Instead, I come up here and I'm treated like I'm the repo man.

'I've run into enough controversy in my life; I'm not looking for more. From the little I've seen and from what you've told me about the collection, I'd expect the college to be supportive of the work you're doing. I don't know why they'd want to get rid of it.'

As Sam started to respond, he was interrupted by a pounding on the still-open office door. Ambler watched Sam's eyes widen and turned to see a scholarly type middle-aged man, slight of build, with an unruly head of black hair and a bushy mustache, standing in the doorway, breathing like a smoke-spewing dragon. The man ignored Ambler and directed his wrath at Abernathy.

'Who the hell are you to think you should be senate president? If Doug wanted to step aside, I'm next in line. And let me tell you, Doug won't be stepping aside. Why would you try to take him on? Only the oddballs and malcontents would vote against him. What the hell is the matter with you, Sam?'

Abernathy was unruffled by the barrage directed against him. 'Nice to see you, too, George.' His tone was mild, if not chummy. 'Meet my friend Ray Ambler from the New York Public Library. Pull up a chair if you'd like. We're discussing the underhanded plan to wreck the special collection at the library, which Barnes came up with and Doug agreed to. Your partner's gotten too big for his britches. He's forgotten he serves at the pleasure of the faculty.'

Sam's words and his gentle manner had a calming effect on the intruder, who walked in and held out his hand to shake Ambler's, his handshake not nearly as firm nor his gaze as direct as the college president's. He pulled up a chair, and now spoke as calmly as Sam had, as if he were an actor who'd joined them offstage after playing a part. 'Doug was fit to be tied when he found out. I said I'd have a word with you before he came after you.'

'Doesn't like having his boat rocked,' Sam said matter-of-factly. He addressed Ambler. 'Doug Stuart has been the self-appointed – and self-deluded – leader of the faculty for years. The faculty senate is his fiefdom. Most of the time, he's been a benevolent dictator – and no one else really wanted the job.

'He's been in bed with the administration for years, never stands up for us when things get tough, but lords it over the faculty, who are either afraid of him because he controls the promotion and tenure committee or beholden to him for travel and research grants and other perks. Everyone else, like me, is too engrossed in their own scholarly work to give a good damn about the senate.'

'You're being unfair, Sam,' said the intruder, whom Sam introduced formally as Professor George Olson, chair of the biology department and vice-president of the faculty senate. George turned to Ambler. 'Sam is justly proud of his collection of detective fiction, though many in the faculty agree with Dr Barnes that it's not of the same level of scholarship as other collections . . . such as the early utilitarians.'

Sam laughed. 'That's Stuart's line,' he said to Ambler. 'George wouldn't know an early utilitarian from mid-twentieth-century beatnik. It's Doug's argument to justify Barnes's money-grubbing approach to college leadership. No one would pay a nickel for the other collections in the library. Barnes found out from his cronies that a few of the mystery first editions, as well as some original copies of pulp magazines and early paperbacks I've picked up along the way, might be worth a pretty penny to collectors.'

The two old friends argued over the merits of the college selling the mystery novel collection and then the wisdom of Sam's challenge to Doug Stuart. They argued without enmity; the kind of reasoned and civil debate you'd hope for from colleagues on a college campus.

'If you run against Doug, you should know you'll be running against me too. He asked me to be his running mate again. I hope you weren't thinking you could turn me against him.'

Sam chuckled. 'I intend to do just that.'

George made ready to leave. 'Think it over, Sam. Dividing the campus, turning colleagues against one another, it will be perceived you're doing it for your own self-serving purposes.'

Sam spoke sharply for the first time. 'You know that's not true. My purpose is to rescue the faculty from years of unaccountable, autocratic dictatorship. Doug thinks he rules by divine right.'

Ambler thought George looked somewhat sheepish. He and Sam sounded like children who knew they were really friends but had had a fight and didn't know how to make up afterward.

'I'm sorry you've decided to run,' George said. 'I have my reasons for sticking with Doug. You know I owe him a large debt . . . You should know also he sees what you're doing as a betrayal. He doesn't like to be challenged, so he'll do what he has to do to win.'

Sam spoke softly again, but the expression in his eyes was rock hard; what you might expect in the gaze of a Marine drill instructor. 'Don't underestimate me, George. I grew up here in the Bronx. I won't run from a fight.'

'Jesus,' Ambler said, a minute after George Olson had left. 'You two were doing so well, a calm, reasoned discussion of a disagreement. Then, poof; it all fell apart. And I was watching two street-gang leaders fighting over turf. What happened to two professors at an ivy-covered campus discussing an upcoming faculty senate election?'

Sam chuckled but mirthlessly. 'George isn't a street fighter.

Stuart is. George is actually saintly – a hut by the side of the road and be a friend to man, that's George.

'But his sticking with Stuart is a problem. George isn't a wheeler and dealer like Stuart. Everyone trusts him. I hadn't talked to him, but I thought he'd support me. We've been friends a long time. More important, I need him on my side. I don't think I can win without him.'

Sam was preoccupied for a moment, as if he'd forgotten Ambler was there and what they'd been talking about before Olson stopped by.

'I'll lean on him,' he said, as if the faculty senate election were Ambler's primary concern also. 'George is an ethical person. It's difficult for him not to do the right thing . . . And he knows as well as I do, Doug Stuart is the wrong thing, not the moral person he pretends to be.

'The problem is – I probably shouldn't tell you this but it's not like you would or even could do anything about it – he's beholden to Stuart. When George went up for tenure years ago, his promotion portfolio wasn't strong. The dean let him know informally he was going to deny his tenure application, despite the promotion and tenure committee recommendation, so George went to Stuart.

'Doug had an "in" with the president and undoubtedly had some dirt on the dean. He pulled strings. The biology department was lukewarm about George, but he was a good teacher, everyone liked him, and he did the scut work in the department no one else wanted to do, so the department approved his promotion.

'The senate promotion and tenure committee was under Stuart's thumb and rubber-stamped the application. That left the dean. Doug did something with the senate travel and conference fund that made it look like the dean allocated funding from the college budget that the senate never received.

'The dean was ambitious. He was in the running for a provost position at a research university and couldn't afford scandal. He knew what Doug wanted, so George's tenure application sailed through to the president's office. George got tenure, and Doug found the dean's misplaced funds after all.'

Ambler found the tale astonishing. Intrigue, blackmail and

chicanery at an idyllic monument to liberal learning? 'How
do you know all this?'

Sam chuckled, this time mirthfully. 'I'm not the curator of
a detective fiction collection for nothing.'

Before Ambler left, he told Sam the 42nd Street Library
didn't have the funding to make a bid on the Trinity College
collection, which he and Sam together estimated could be
worth $200,000 if the first editions were in fine condition and
some of them had author signatures.

He might have come up with the funding if he put his mind
to it. He kept a list of a few donors he could call on in a pinch,
who believed – as he did – that crime fiction deserved a place
on library shelves alongside the rest of humankind's literary
endeavors.

'If another institution makes a bid, we might reconsider,'
he told Sam.

The Trinity College mystery collection would make a fine
addition to the 42nd Street Library's holdings, but he didn't
think it right to take the collection away from his friend who
had so painstakingly put it together.

THREE

A week later, Ambler had all but forgotten about Trinity College and Sam Abernathy's collection of New York Mystery Writers when he was reminded of it by his supervisor, Harry Larkin, the director of the Manuscript and Archives Division, who called him into his office, a rare occurrence, to talk about the crime fiction collection, an even rarer occurrence. Even more remarkable was what Harry told him.

'We may be getting an unexpected supplement to our acquisitions budget.' Harry, as guileless as a baby, watched from under his eyebrows for Ambler's reaction.

Ambler had no reaction. Good for them. Harry husbanded the division's funds like an elderly woman keeping watch over her change purse. So the surplus wasn't that big a surprise, and there was little chance it would have anything to do with the crime fiction collection. Except he was wrong.

'What?' he asked, though he'd heard perfectly what Harry had said; he couldn't believe what he heard. Harry didn't repeat himself, instead watched Ambler like he were about to do a dance step or a magic trick.

'Two hundred thousand dollars for the crime fiction collection?' Ambler was incredulous. 'Did I hear you right? . . . That's not possible. Did you rob a bank?' He was slowly getting his mind around what he'd heard and running through about a dozen acquisitions that kind of windfall would make possible when Harry dropped the other shoe.

Harry, a one-time Jesuit, lacked the ability to speak anything but the truth. He tried his best to keep to the administration line, which at times meant he had to try to sell a plan he didn't believe in, an undertaking that required the skill of a snake-oil salesman, a skill Harry didn't have. This time he hemmed and hawed before he blurted out. 'It doesn't come without strings.'

Ambler swallowed his dreams. He should have known.

'An anonymous donor is promising a donation for the

express purpose of enhancing the crime fiction holdings in New York writers. I'm told you're familiar with a collection housed at the Trinity College of the Bronx library now on the market that would do just that.'

'Jesus,' Ambler moaned. 'How did this happen?' He told Harry about Sam Abernathy's collection, the internecine struggle over the collection and the faculty senate. 'You can see why I thought better of bidding on the collection. Having to part with it would crush Abernathy. Why doesn't the benefactor make the donation to Trinity College instead so they don't have to sell their mystery holdings?'

Harry's expression was pained. 'First, I'm surprised you wouldn't jump at the chance. On the other hand, I understand why you'd be hesitant to deprive the poor man of his life's work.' Confronted with an ethical dilemma or a moral choice, Harry became mournful.

This happened now; he took on the gloomy aspect of Eeyore. 'I don't think it's unethical for the college to take possession of something a faculty member created at the college.' He paused for a long moment – the moral philosophy of Thomas Aquinas weighing in, no doubt. 'I'm afraid your suggestion that the library forgo a sizable bequest and bestow it instead on Trinity College wouldn't go over well with President Ledyard or the Board of Trustees.'

Ambler fumed. Harry was right. Ledyard would give away his eye teeth before he'd let another institution have money earmarked for his library; asking him to give up a donation was like asking a dog not to sniff.

'I'll need to appraise the collection before I agree. I made a wild guess as to its value. It may only be worth half that. Sam Abernathy didn't build the collection based on market value. His purpose was academic. A lot of the writers he collected no one has ever heard of. They don't have monetary value. They have value to scholars.'

'It's not your money.' Harry, as much as he was capable of, had geared up for battle. 'If this is how the donor wants to spend their money, who are you to say they can't?'

'I'm the curator of the collection.' Ambler was already furious about the monetization of books and the arts. 'The collection has value other than what it's worth in dollars. Ask your pals Aristotle and Thomas Aquinas about intrinsic good.'

Harry was trying his best to bring Ambler around. 'Think of how much more the president and the Board will value the crime fiction collection if it receives this donation. They'll think of it on the level of some of the true literary collect . . .' Harry froze; his eyes widened; watching Ambler's reaction, he realized he'd stepped in it this time.

'That isn't what I mean. Not to say your crime fiction isn't on the same level of literary value as other holdings,' he said lamely. 'It's a valuable collection that will be more valuable with the new addition.'

Ambler arrived home that evening to a lively apartment; perhaps 'jumpin' would better describe it, given the hip-hop blaring from speakers his son John had somehow hooked up to his new iPhone. The kitchen table and counters were crowded with plates and bowls, utensils and kitchen equipment, enough paraphernalia to prepare a banquet rather than a simple supper.

'Adele is coming for dinner,' his grandson Johnny announced.

It was hard to tell who was in charge of the dinner preparations. Neither his son, who'd recently gotten out of prison, nor his nine-year-old grandson were what anyone would think of as accomplished cooks, though Johnny – under the tutelage of his maternal grandmother's live-in cook – was learning the trade and considered himself a budding chef.

Johnny's father had been living with Ambler and Johnny since his release. The boy had been living with Ambler since his mother's tragic death a few years before. He hadn't known his father, who'd been in jail almost as long as Johnny had been alive, until after his mother's death. Now, they were making up for lost time, getting to know each other.

Two men and a boy in a one-bedroom apartment made for tight quarters. For Ambler, who'd lived a good part of his life alone until Johnny came along, the living conditions were unsettling, but he was happy to put up with the crowding and the inconvenience to have his son home. John, after his years in prison, hardly noticed the crowding; to him, the crowded apartment was the lap of luxury. Johnny with his dad home was in heaven; he'd live in a telephone booth if it was with his dad.

Adele arrived a few minutes after Ambler. Bustling into the apartment with her arms full – a box of fruit tarts from a neighborhood bakery, a bottle of wine, a baguette and who-knew-what else – Adele kissed Ambler and Johnny and awkwardly shook hands with John.

John tried to hide that he was uncomfortable around her, as he was uncomfortable around everyone except Ambler and Johnny. He hated telling anyone he was recently out of prison. The outside world was foreign to him, as if – like Rip Van Winkle – he'd awakened from a long sleep. Nothing around him was familiar, nothing as he remembered it. So he carried himself – though he was polite and quiet – with a chip on his shoulder, on guard against the world, expecting to be challenged by everyone he met.

Acutely aware of his unease around her, Adele wasn't sure how to act around him, worried about him accepting her as much as she worried about her accepting him. Because she was closer to John in age than she was to Ambler, she thought John wouldn't approve of her relationship with his father. They hadn't told John yet that she was pregnant with Ambler's child.

To avoid the hubbub in the kitchen, Ambler parked himself in an easy chair in his smallish living room with Lola, the dog – who'd grown to be the size of a small horse – nuzzling him until he patted her; she then lay down at his feet. From where he sat, he could watch the kitchen and, not for the first time, wonder about the changes the last few years had brought to his life.

What he realized at that moment was that despite the mammoth changes, especially over the last year or so, he was happier than he'd ever been; contented – his world at peace and everything in its place – in a way he hadn't been since he was a child.

Up until a few years ago, he'd lived alone after his divorce from John's mother when John was a boy. He forever regretted that he'd left John to grow up with his alcoholic and unstable mother. Never more so than when John – because of an unintentional shooting in which he'd killed a man – was sentenced to prison. Ambler did stay in touch with his son then, visiting him religiously in prison and working for years to get him a new trial and a reduced sentence, which finally happened a short time ago.

He was delighted his son and his grandson had taken so easily to each other; it was as if they'd never been apart. John, who was wary of everyone and uncomfortable everywhere, became totally at ease when he was with his son.

During the time John was in prison, Adele Morgan came to work at the library and, for reasons Ambler never understood, took Ambler under her wing, became his best friend, and later . . . more than a friend. This development came about under the strangest circumstances of all, when Adele found a little shoeshine boy haunting the gentrified bars on Ninth Avenue. The tragic circumstances that followed her meeting the boy led to Ambler discovering that the boy, by then essentially an orphan, was his grandson.

Now here they were, gathered in his cramped, rent-stabilized apartment, Ambler's son reunited with his own son, and Ambler expecting in a few months to become a father again, thirty-some years after he first became a father. He was having a difficult time adjusting to the idea that he'd soon have a child younger than his own grandson – something he thought should be mathematically impossible. Yet he had come to believe he and Adele were in love.

The cloud hanging over these tranquil and happy times, what worried Ambler, was the effect prison had had on John. Despite the unthinkable reality that he'd killed another man, John had been a gentle boy, never a fighter, nothing close to a gangbanger. He devoted himself to poetry and music. He taught himself how to play the guitar, later took lessons, and became enough of a musician that he made his living playing with a traveling band and as a studio musician when he was home in the city.

This was what John hoped to do again . . . but he'd been out of circulation for almost a decade and was having a tough time finding a gig. Ambler had bought him a guitar after he was sentenced and he kept up his practice in the prison, so he played as good as ever if not better, and he'd kept up with changes in music, adding country and jazz and even classical to his repertoire. The problem – the unspoken difficulty – was being an ex-con. No one spoke the words. But everyone knew, certainly John.

So with this resentment and the chip on his shoulder, his son was too easily provoked. Ambler had already witnessed a couple of almost-confrontations, when John had reacted more defensively and potentially more violently to encounters that most people would let pass: one with a cab driver, who stopped just short of running into him as he was crossing the street, who fortunately for him saw the fury rising in John and backed off. There could have been other encounters that Ambler hadn't witnessed. He knew how easily an ex-felon could run afoul of the law and find himself back in prison.

He'd shaken these scary thoughts out of his head and was heading to the dinner table when the phone rang. He hesitated, thinking he wouldn't answer, when he recognized the 917 area code. Many of the faculty at Trinity College, including Sam Abernathy, lived in the Bronx, so he answered. It was Sam. Ambler was sure he'd called because he'd gotten wind of the donation that would enable Ambler to buy the Trinity College crime fiction holdings. But he was wrong.

'What's up?' He braced himself for an uncomfortable conversation.

'Well,' said Sam. 'I don't know how to say this. I'm still in shock. Despite my obsession with murder mysteries, I never thought I'd find myself talking about the real thing.'

Ambler was slow to catch on. Or perhaps he did catch on, but was slow to admit to himself what he'd caught on to. 'I beg your pardon . . .'

'I hesitate to say . . . You see, there's been a murder.'

Ambler, in spite of himself, knew before Sam uttered the words that this was what he would say. There'd been something in the tone of the speaker's voice that – if you've encountered as many murders in your life as Ambler had – tips you off. 'I'm sorry to hear that,' he said, hoping without hope that the murder would prove to have nothing to do with him.

'Yes . . . It's terrible. You'd want to think something like that would never have anything to do with you.'

Ambler's ears pricked. 'Does it?'

'I'm afraid so.'

Ambler pictured the verdant and peaceful campus, a refuge from the hustle and bustle of the city, a place for serene reflection, contemplation, and learning, as Sam told him that George Olson, the man Ambler had met and chatted with on his visit to the college, a longtime friend of Sam's, had been killed: shot by a sniper as he sat in his office.

'The police knew that right away.' Sam's voice shook, even though he spoke matter-of-factly. 'The bullets came through the window, most likely from the roof of the library. I can't believe someone would kill George. He never hurt a soul.'

'Suspects?' Ambler immediately thought of the far-too-many recent shootings at schools and colleges. The country had gone crazy. These were insane times. Once more, a gunman victimized a college campus. If the police hadn't apprehended the shooter, or at least had a suspect they were tracking, the campus would be in turmoil, locked down until the police turned up someone.

Sam's voice became strained and he spoke hesitantly. 'I don't know how to say this either. This is why I called you. *I'm the suspect* and may be arrested . . . for killing my friend of more than thirty years. How could anyone think that?'

Sam wasn't thinking straight and Ambler couldn't blame him. His world had been turned upside down. He was looking for sympathy, for someone – Ambler at the moment – to help him understand what was happening to him. But he also needed to be practical. 'Do you have a lawyer?'

'I don't think I need one. There are incriminating circumstances . . . but I can easily explain that I didn't kill anyone. No one in their right mind would seriously think I killed George.'

Ambler calmly told Sam he absolutely needed an attorney, whether he killed anyone or not. He didn't want Sam hauled off to the Bronx House of Correction, even if he was innocent. The poor guy had no idea of the fix he was in, no idea of how to find an attorney. He thought the world of criminal justice

was reasonable and sane. He would tell the police he didn't
do it. And that would be that. Fat chance.

'Wouldn't the court appoint a lawyer?' he asked.

'Eventually.' Ambler was exasperated. 'Do you want to
spend a few nights in jail waiting?'

'They'd put me in jail?' Sam was incredulous. 'Surely, no
reasonable person . . . George was my best friend.'

'Reason has nothing to do with what happened, nor what's
going to happen to you if you're a suspect.' Since he didn't
know how much trouble Sam was in, or what the evidence
against him was, the incriminating circumstances Sam had
casually mentioned, he demanded Sam call David Levinson,
the attorney who'd won a new trial for Ambler's son, as soon
as he hung up the phone.

'Who needs a lawyer?' John asked, when a flustered and
out-of-sorts Ambler sat down to dinner. He'd noticed while
he was on the phone that conversation had stopped around the
dinner table. All eyes had been on him, as they were now
when John asked the question. Ambler told them with as few
details as possible about the call.

'Why's he a suspect?' Johnny asked. The boy was far too
interested in anything that had to do with a murder investigation, and had much more experience of murder than any child
should have. Ambler's discovering he had a grandson had been
the result of a murder investigation.

At one time in his life, he'd been eager to attempt to unravel
the complex matters of guilt or innocence in a homicide investigation – and at times, he'd done some good. Other times, he
wished he'd left well alone: people had died who might not
have died if he had not uncovered past wrongdoing.

FOUR

The next morning David Levinson called shortly after ten. Ambler heard his voice on the other end of the phone, as if he'd been expecting to hear it.

'Thanks for the referral,' David said. 'Maybe one day you or McNulty can find me a client well-off enough financially to afford my fee.' When he was talking, which was most of the time in any conversation Ambler had had with him, David wasn't inclined to let anyone else get a word in. 'My new client has gotten himself in a world of trouble: "up shit's creek without a paddle" as we used to say.

'The crux of the matter is that I need you to do some legwork for me because I don't think my client can swing the extra cost of my hiring a private investigator – which will be a pretty hefty nut in his case. I thought your son might do some of the work – I'll put him on the clock as an investigative intern – but he'll need to be careful. He can't do anything approaching illegal. And, since you have experience uncovering secrets and dispelling lies, you might have to give him a hand.'

'Nice way to put it; I'm flattered. Why is Sam Abernathy in trouble? He's one of the most unassuming and sweet-tempered people I know. Compared to him, Caspar Milquetoast looks like a braggart and a bully.'

'My impression, too. But I've learned you can't judge people by their covers.'

'That's books you can't judge by their covers.'

'Actually, a lot of times you can judge a book by its cover. Try it sometime.'

'You're telling me about books?'

'What I'm telling you is your friend, Mr Milquetoast, is in trouble. Do you know how the victim was killed?'

'Shot. Sam told me.'

'Correct. Shot from quite a distance . . . by a sniper.'

'Yes. He told me that.'

'Did he tell you he served as a sniper in the army?'

Ambler took a moment, 'No.'

'That's problem one. Do you know how many trained snipers you find on your average college campus on a given day?'

Ambler thought back to the Texas tower sniper, Charles Whitman – the first mass shooting on a campus in his lifetime. 'What do the police say? Isn't it more likely a random shooting than someone out to get George Olson? Besides, what motive would Sam have for shooting his friend?'

'You might think it was random. The police say targeted, not an indiscriminate shooting. Abernathy is their suspect . . . At the moment they're not ready to arrest him. But it may not be long. Unless he can clear up a couple of disagreeable matters.'

Levinson paused and Ambler waited.

'He owns a Remington Model 700 rifle, a fitting possession for an expert marksman, one of the most accurate long-range rifles ever made.'

Levinson paused again and Ambler waited again. David went in for theatrics and liked his listener to grow impatient and ask him questions. Ambler didn't want to fall for that. But this time he did. 'And? Do the police have the gun? Was that the gun used in the shooting?'

'Good questions,' David said in his self-satisfied lawyerly voice. 'The rifle in question is missing. Abernathy says he hasn't used it or seen it in years. He stored it in the basement of his house not far from the campus. He went to look for it when the police asked and couldn't find it.'

'Someone could have stolen it and used it.'

'Yeh. And Abernathy could have used it and got rid of it. Or someone could have stolen it and not used it. Someone entirely unknown to us could have used a different rifle. Which scenario do you think a detective would find to be most likely?'

'It doesn't make any difference. The fact he had a rifle and it's missing isn't evidence that he killed George Olson.'

'Well said.'

Ambler could picture David with his cell phone pressed to his ear, in a cab on his way to court, in a hallway outside the

courtroom, or charging along a city sidewalk at a pace a man
would use when his train was leaving the platform. He
reminded Ambler of the irritating child who couldn't sit still.
'That's problem one, or maybe problems one and two. We
have others. An unidentified witness places Abernathy in the
library around the time of the shooting. He denies he was in
the library but can't account for his whereabouts. When I told
him he had to, he said he was in his office. One of your tasks
would be to find someone who saw him there.'
   'Why is the witness unidentified?'
   'He or she prefers to remain anonymous. At some point the
person will need to come forward but we might not know until
discovery. Or there might not be a witness. The cops could
have made it up to put pressure on Abernathy. Finding this
person or proving he or she doesn't exist is another task for
you . . . One more thing, the cops asked Abernathy about his
threatening the victim.'
   'That's ridiculous. They were friends. When I was on the
campus, I heard them discuss – argue would be too strong a
word – a significant disagreement in a perfectly civil way.
Some people can still have discussions about serious disagreements without animosity.'
   'On that one, you're wrong. Abernathy told me he had an
argument with Olson. He said it was the other way around.
Olson threatened him.'
   'With violence?'
   'Blackmail, not to put too fine a point on it.'
   'Blackmail? . . . Over what?'
   'He wouldn't say.' Levinson continued in his obnoxious
lawyerly tone. 'Blackmail, as you know, is the threat to reveal
something the target of the blackmail very much doesn't want
revealed . . . It's happened that blackmailers have been killed
because the person being blackmailed can't allow the black-
mailer to live having possession of such damaging knowledge.
Part of your assignment, I'm afraid, might require you to
uncover Professor Abernathy's secret.'
   'Jesus,' Ambler said. 'People are allowed to have secrets.'
   'Jesus is your business,' said Levinson. 'We have our own
God to contend with.'

'I don't like the idea of exposing something a person doesn't want revealed.' Ambler heard himself whining.

'Spending the rest of one's life in prison isn't such a great idea either. It's easier to stay out than to get out once you're in. Ask your son.' Levinson's tone softened; he sounded almost sympathetic; perhaps he had a heart after all.

'It's happened before. Someone holds back information because they're embarrassed, believing that because they're innocent, the truth will come out; they'll be exonerated without having to reveal something they consider shameful. When they find out how slippery the truth is, it's too late. Innocence doesn't always protect you.

'Revealing someone's secrets might be a moral question for you. What's moral for me is to get my client off without violating the law, to keep him on the street. Go talk to your friend and let me know what you decide . . . I gotta run.'

After the phone call, Ambler went about his business, his thoughts mostly on the murder at Trinity College and Sam Abernathy, whom he thought of as a friend; though he really didn't know him that well, he liked him.

After too much thinking, he decided to go to lunch at the Library Tavern, something he rarely did because the lunch crowd was different than the after-work crowd, and his friend McNulty the bartender was grumpy and taciturn because everyone who came in at lunchtime was in a rush, too many people who sat at the bar didn't drink, and he had to serve the food himself. In the evenings, people weren't in a hurry, the folks who sat at the bar drank, and the servers took care of food at the bar.

Ambler went this time because he wanted time to think, and he went late enough so the lunch rush would be pretty much over and he might get a chance to talk with McNulty. This turned out to be the case. He ate a chicken salad sandwich with pineapple, which he'd never noticed on the menu before, and told McNulty about Levinson's proposition.

McNulty was enthusiastic; his eyes lit up. 'You'll be a real PI . . . a gumshoe . . . a shamus. That's cool. You'll be doing what you've done in the past more than once but now you'll be official, almost legitimate.'

'It's not official. I'm not getting paid, although my son might be, at a reduced rate.'

McNulty didn't miss a beat. 'That's David, the cheap prick. Tell him I said he should pay you and your son the going rate, or I'll tell my pop to tell his pop he's an exploiter of labor.' McNulty was alluding to the background he and Levinson shared; red diaper babies, the offspring of Communist fathers.

'If I tell him that, he'll point out he never charged you when he represented you.'

McNulty grumbled. 'He didn't do much.' The representation they were talking about had to do with a murder rap the police hung on McNulty not so long ago. It was complicated. David had given Ambler a break also, charging him for only the bare essentials when he took on the appeal of his son John's sentence.

McNulty went off to put Ambler's dishes in a bus pan at the end of the bar, so Ambler turned to look out the window at the city passing by. When he did so, he caught a glimpse of a man in the doorway and did a double take. On the second take, he recognized the rumpled, bemused and bewildered gnome-like man, entirely out of place among the fashionable, business-casual-attired lunchtime crowd bustling past the Library Tavern. He beheld Sam Abernathy, whose face brightened when he saw Ambler; he made a beeline toward him.

'They told me I'd find you here . . . I could use a little something myself.' He signaled to McNulty, who, having watched Abernathy come in as he watched everyone who came through the door, rolled his eyes, finished the drink he was making, and sauntered over.

'You know,' he said to Abernathy, who watched him eagerly. 'When you came in and sat at the bar, I said to myself, I wonder why this man came in and sat down at my bar. If you hadn't gestured to me, I'd have never known you wanted to order something.'

Abernathy stared at McNulty, his mouth gaping open.

'He means you didn't need to signal to him,' Ambler explained. 'He knew you wanted to order something – that's his job.' Ambler smiled at McNulty, who didn't smile back.

'Of course,' Abernathy said, making a conciliatory gesture

with his hands. 'I should know better. A Scotch on the rocks, please.'

Ambler raised an eyebrow. He didn't think of college professors as daytime drinkers. Sam did seem shaken, so a midday Scotch might be something out of the ordinary for him. Not every day do you find yourself named a suspect in a murder.

'Are you in the city to see David?'

Sam took a healthy slug of the drink McNulty put in front of him. 'I wanted to let you know,' he glanced at the few lunchtime stragglers at the bar and lowered his voice, 'I've taken it on the lam . . . as they say.'

Both Ambler's and McNulty's eyebrows went up. McNulty didn't say anything, but his antenna was waving. The obvious question would be, 'Why?' But Ambler had a pretty good idea what the answer to that was, so he asked instead, 'Why are you telling me?'

Sam didn't answer right away, so Ambler tried a follow-up question. 'Does David know about this?'

Abernathy squirmed like one of his students might under questioning from his professor. 'Yes and no . . . He, perhaps unwittingly, gave me the idea. His actual directive was to turn myself in at the Pelham Police Department. He'd try to get me held there, if I was charged, until I was arraigned, so I didn't have to go to jail in the Bronx.'

Ambler wasn't surprised. 'So you're what they call "a person of interest". I think any lawyer would advise you to turn yourself in if the police want to talk to you. If you don't, the NYPD might get the warrant and you'll be a fugitive.' Ambler turned to McNulty – once a fugitive himself – hoping for a couple of words of support. McNulty's expression was that of a man waiting for a bus, yet Ambler knew he was listening.

Sam looked at McNulty when Ambler did, and then back at Ambler.

'Why would you abscond?' Ambler's tone made his questions sound like an accusation. 'Why are you going against David's advice? He's a good lawyer; you shouldn't second guess him. And back to my original question: Why are you telling me?'

Sam's expression was sheepish, if not guilty. 'I thought,

since you've had experience with criminal activity, you might give me some tips on how to hide, tell me where criminals go when they "take a powder".' He smiled shyly.

They went back and forth for a while until Ambler became convinced he wasn't going to change Sam's mind. Already Sam, in his heart, had 'taken a powder'.

'I'll turn myself in when they arrest whoever killed George and realize I'm innocent.'

McNulty, who'd listened in to most of the back-and-forth, finally joined in with some advice based on experience. 'The first thing you don't do when you take it on the lam is tell anyone where you're going. No one who knows you should know where you are, and you can't get in touch with anyone you know once you get there. You gotta be on your own.'

'I've got to get back to work,' Ambler said. 'The best thing is for our conversation to stop here so when the police ask me what I know about your disappearance, which they quite likely will, I can tell them truthfully I don't know where you went.' He left then. McNulty might give Sam some advice or he might not. It was better for Ambler not to know. The police might track Sam to him but probably not to McNulty.

The question he should be asking himself was whether Sam's decision to disappear was based on his innocence or his guilt. Running and hiding, the thinking goes, is an indication of guilt. If you're innocent, we're told, you have nothing to fear . . . Ambler had long before disabused himself of the notion that an innocent man had nothing to fear from the law.

Later that afternoon, he caught up with Adele and told her about the developments since his phone call from Sam Abernathy the night before.

'I suppose you'll try to track down another murderer now.'

He started to say he hadn't said that, or even thought it, but realized that wasn't exactly true. He'd agreed to gather some information for Levinson and sign his son up to help. He was already knee-deep in a new investigation.

Adele looked at him for a long moment – sadly, he thought – before dropping her gaze. 'I hoped you'd take a break. Now all I hope is this one is less dangerous than some of your past escapades.'

Ambler wasn't anxious to get involved; she was wrong about that. But he felt he had to. He told her about the call from Levinson. 'The lawyer wanted John to do some of the legwork – as an intern so he wouldn't cost Sam as much as paying for a private detective. John has to be really careful not to violate his probation, not to get involved with anything criminal. Things can go wrong in an investigation, so I thought I should take the lead, bring him along slowly, and take over if anything untoward comes up.'

'I don't know why it's a good idea for *you* to get involved in anything criminal.' Her eyes glistened in an unusual way, and he realized she was close to tears. 'You're not a spring chicken, and you have other responsibilities . . .' She put her hand to her mouth and then spoke hurriedly. 'Forget I said that. I didn't mean it the way you think . . . You're not responsible for me.'

He knew what she meant all right. He did have other responsibilities and he was responsible for her whether she wanted him to be or not. But he didn't argue.

'I need to appraise the collection anyway.' He tried to sound nonchalant. 'That's a reason for me to be on campus. I've met some of the faculty, so I'll ask a few questions and see where that leads. Maybe I'll find out Sam is guilty and I can let the police take it from there.'

Adele harrumphed. 'You don't think that. You want to help your friend. You think you know what you're doing.' Her voice became small. 'And you do, dammit . . . That's how you are. I knew that. If you don't go out looking for trouble, it comes looking for you.

'This time might be different, though. The police in the Bronx are a tough, no-nonsense bunch. They aren't going to like you snooping around. You won't have your friend Mike watching out for you.'

Ambler knew Mike would tell him the same thing – life was closer to the edge for cops in the Bronx, so he'd planned to leave Mike out of things for the time being. But after talking with Adele, he thought better of that, and decided to let his friend know what he was up to, in case the cops in the Bronx did object to his snooping around. Mike might know someone in homicide up there and might be able to pave his way and perhaps find out what the deal was with Sam. He called him and they met, as they often did, at the Oyster Bar.

He told Mike what he knew.

'Murders from long range with a rifle aren't that common,' Mike said, 'especially not in the city. Too many things can get in the way of a clean shot. I know a couple of guys up in the five seven; I can ask. They won't tell me much, or not much I can tell you.

'Your friend had opportunity, motive – and means . . . if he's lying about the theft of his rifle. Add that to his being a sniper in the army, and the killer being a marksman, makes him a person of interest. I'm sure they'd have liked to chat with him for a while without a lawyer breathing down their necks.'

They finished their oyster pan roasts at the same time. 'Delicious,' Ambler said. 'I can't believe I've never ordered it before.'

'It's been on the menu for a hundred years.' Mike, something of a gourmand, shook his head. 'I've been telling you try it almost that long.'

That evening, Ambler called Harry at home and said he wouldn't be in the library the next day; he was going to the Bronx to begin an appraisal of the Trinity College collection.

Harry was skeptical. 'You're going up there to see about that murder.' He dismissed any disavowal Ambler planned to make. 'Don't try to tell me you're not.'

'Murder or no murder,' Ambler said. 'Unless you want to give up on acquiring that crime fiction collection, I've got to see what it's worth. If you want to pass on the acquisition, I'd be happy to go along.'

Harry sighed. He knew Ambler was right; the collection had to be appraised. And he knew Ambler was going to get tangled up in another murder investigation. 'We could hire someone to appraise the collection. You're not the only one who knows about collecting crime fiction.'

'I'm the only one on the payroll that does.'

Harry sighed again, louder this time, as if the sigh carried a message. 'You may not be on the payroll for much longer

if President Ledyard finds out what you're doing. You know
what he thinks about the library being associated with a murder
. . . It's uncanny; it's as if every collection you acquire brings
a murder along with it.'

Ambler thought to point out that the crime fiction collection
had the papers of more than a hundred mystery writers, and
only a couple had anything to do with an actual murder, but
he chose not to pursue the point. 'This murder is Trinity
College's problem. I didn't ask for this.'

Despite his misgivings, Harry was intrigued. 'Is it true the
curator of the crime fiction collection there, the man you told
me about, is the murderer?'

'That remains to be seen. He may be a suspect, but he's
innocent until proven guilty.'

Ambler pictured Harry in his easy chair, a glass of wine on
the end table beside him. 'I expect that you will appraise the
college's New York Mystery Writers collection and not
the guilt or innocence of its curator.'

FIVE

I n the morning, Ambler called the president's office at Trinity to make arrangements for his visit. It took a couple of tries to get things straightened out because the person he spoke to said Sam Abernathy would need to guide him through the appraisal. Ambler knew she wasn't going to find Abernathy. But she didn't know that, so convincing her to find someone else took some maneuvering.

Finally, after a long session on hold, she told him Sarah Hastings would be his campus contact. This was fine. He'd gotten along well with her when she first showed him the collection. More important she was a chatterbox, and the best person he could think of to find out what the campus scuttlebutt was surrounding the murder.

She greeted him in front of the library with a big smile and a hearty handshake. Her looks were deceiving; not the pulled-back hair, tortoiseshell-framed glasses and severe expression of a no-nonsense scholar, but long, thick blonde hair, a broad peaches-and-cream face, and the cheerful, exuberant energy you might expect to find in a Lithuanian peasant girl.

'I don't know where Sam is.' Her eyes narrowed with worry. 'He missed his classes today. He never does that. The other day – the day poor George was killed – Sam missed an appointment with me in his office. He never does that either.'

What she said struck a chord; Ambler's ears perked up. 'Was the appointment for near the time of the shooting?'

'It was at 3:00. What time was the shooting?'

Levinson had told him Sam said he was in his office from 3:00 until 3:30. George Olson was killed shortly after 3:00. David had asked him to find someone who could help prove Sam was in his office when he said he was. Now he'd gone and proved the opposite.

'Around that time,' Ambler said.

Sarah's pretty face wrinkled with displeasure. She shot an irritated glance at him. 'That doesn't mean anything, does it?' Ambler was deep in thought. 'I don't know.'

She stared at the faculty office building across the common for a moment, as if he might somehow emerge from it, before turning back to Ambler. 'I hope nothing's happened to him.' She waited expectantly for Ambler to tell her something. Her sincere expression and her concern made him feel he was being devious, which he was.

'So you're familiar with the collection?' he asked to change the subject.

She chuckled and her pretty cheeks turned red. 'I'm a mystery fan, so I like to poke around in there. Sometimes, I curl up in a corner in the reading room with a book and hide from the world. Some of the obscure detective novels I've found turned out to be really good.' She glanced over her shoulder and then lowered her voice. 'Don't tell anyone I told you. They would've denied me tenure if they found out I read mysteries.' She threw back her head and laughed heartily.

Wearing a peasant dress and hoop earrings, with straight blonde hair cascading over her shoulders, her earnestness and unpretentiousness brought back memories of certain flower child, hippie girls of his youth. He liked her immensely and was again tempted to take her into his confidence and tell her Sam Abernathy had gone into hiding. But it was better for her sake for her not to know that. Better for her, too, not to know he lied to his lawyer about where he was at the time of the murder. Instead, he asked her to tell him about the missing disingenuous professor.

She took the question seriously and spent some time thinking about her answer. 'He's an excellent teacher; his students adore him.' She hesitated before continuing. 'Especially the girls . . . I should say, "young women". He knows how to talk to women, how to make you feel understood, appreciated – and not uncomfortable. You might consider him a ladies' man, but honorably so, quaint and gentlemanly.'

She caught on to something in Ambler's expression. 'Nothing inappropriate . . . Or nothing *very* inappropriate. He doesn't *hit on* students.' She paused. 'That wouldn't happen. They like his attention and he's safe, avuncular.'

Something in the way she said this made Ambler wonder if anything romantic might have gone on between Sarah Hastings and Sam. But this wasn't a question he would ask her. He also believed, though without good reason, that if there *had* been something between them, she would have told him. Because she hadn't mentioned it, he began to wonder if she knew yet that Sam was a suspect in George Olson's murder.

'I've been helping him create a database of the material in the collection, though his student assistants over the past few years have done most of the work. Rebecca – Rebecca Dawson – his current assistant is fantastic.'

'Is that for the collection?' Ambler gestured to a couple of ancient, free-standing, blond wood card catalogs against a wall near the first row of shelves. Most libraries hadn't used card catalogs in years, but here they seemed appropriate: the cabinets were five feet high, three feet wide, with rows of drawers six inches wide by three inches deep, but about a foot and a half long, designed to hold three-by-five-inch cards.

The catalogs would have one set of cards by author and another set by title. Another catalog might hold finding aids for the collections of authors' papers. The Manuscript and Archives Division had similar card catalogs for materials that hadn't been digitized yet – entries for names, subjects, geographic locations and types of documents, such as diaries, notebooks, logbooks, typescripts, and such.

Appraising the Trinity collection wouldn't be accomplished in a day. He could use an assistant himself and wondered if he could find a way to get Abernathy's student assistant assigned to give him a hand; Sam wouldn't be needing her for a while. He wasn't sure who to ask about that, so he started with Sarah, who had no idea.

'You can ask Rebecca . . .' She didn't finish the thought. 'The poor kid is totally devoted to Sam and devastated that he's suspected of killing George.'

'So you know he's—'

'Everyone knows and no one believes it . . .' Her voice rose. 'Except for the haters in the administration who'd like nothing

better than to destroy Sam and the few people like him who
dare to oppose their attempts to turn the college into a trade
school for corporate America.'

He was surprised by her vehemence. 'Who else might have
killed George Olson?'

She looked mystified. 'No one. George didn't have enemies.
He was determined to get along with everyone . . . perhaps
at a cost.'

Ambler wanted to know what the cost was, but Sarah hesitated to criticize. 'I couldn't say a word against George . . .
Perhaps some of us wished he was more on our side in the
battles with the administration, and wasn't such a lapdog for
Doug Stuart.'

'Lapdog?'

She grimaced. 'That was unkind. I shouldn't have said it.
George tried to have an ameliorating effect on Doug and on
the senate . . . And Doug's not an easy person to stand up to.
He's super smart, sure of himself, charming when he wants
to be, and he knows what he wants.'

'But he won't stand up to Barnes?'

'He does when it's in his interest, but he won't get himself
into Quixotic battles.'

Sarah came across as smart and sure of herself, too, like
her description of Stuart. You'd wonder how she'd come to
know him so well. Of course, a small college might be its
own version of *Peyton Place*, where everyone knew everyone
else's business, with its share of secrets and scandals and feuds,
and now its own murder mystery.

Was this how he'd do what David Levinson sent him out
to do: listen to everyone's gripes about everyone else; pay
attention to the campus gossip; ask impertinent and intrusive
questions; dig up folks' secrets? It would be a messy and
unpleasant business.

Sarah wasn't finished. 'Doug caught on pretty quickly to
what Barnes was hired to do and how much power he had
to do it – the power coming from the Board of Trustees and
the alumni who matter.' She glanced at Ambler significantly:
'The ones who fuel the endowment. You'll see their names
engraved on the facades of some of the newer buildings.

'Change was coming. We all knew that. Doug was ahead of the curve in adapting. No illusions. Sentimentality be damned. Tradition sacrificed on the altar of expediency, so be it. He would give Barnes the changes he wanted – programs cut, departments combined or eliminated, graduation requirements weakened, full-time faculty lines not filled; no more sacred cows – as long as Barnes didn't interfere with his fiefdom, the senate. That worked because Barnes doesn't care about the faculty senate's domain – retention, tenure, promotion, course approval, academic standards, travel and conference funding. Barnes has never cut or even threatened to cut the faculty senate budget.'

'What does Barnes care about?'

'Donations,' she shot back. 'College presidents raise money. We're a stepping stone for Barnes; he's aiming to be a research university president. To get there, he needs to show he's an ace fundraiser, that he can bring in large donations. And he has. That's good for Trinity if you care about endowments, luxury dorms, high tech computer labs; modern recreation facilities, winning sports teams, even if it is Division III. Not so good if you care about education or scholarship.' She glanced around. Dusty volumes of obscure detective novels, the collected papers of forgotten pulp writers weren't going to make the cut.

Ambler understood the dilemma. Institutions needed money. The 42nd Street Library was under that sort of pressure too: the need to provide what was popular, to attract crowds because this was what brought donations.

For the college's new owners, Sarah went on, the important thing was to entertain the students – state-of-the-art recreation center; a trendy student union; a winning football team; star professors who dazzle students with popular profundity and ask little of them in return. No prizes for finding your own way amongst dusty volumes of philosophy and literature. Who cares about the ancients? They're old.

Ambler moved on. 'And Doug Stuart? An ogre?'

'Far from it. Students love him. His classes fill as soon as they open. His "Introduction to Human Geography" is so popular that it uses the auditorium instead of a lecture hall.

His scholarship is impressive; he has a national reputation in his field. Environmental Studies is a big draw, so the administration and the Board love him.'

'And the faculty?'

'If you ask anyone, except for Sam's small cohort, they'll tell you he's done a great job for the faculty.' She managed to say this in a way that Ambler understood her to mean the complete opposite.

'What they're really saying is they're afraid of him. He's done favors for almost everyone, and everyone else needs him for something. Retention, tenure and promotion are all in the province of the faculty senate, and anything that happens in the senate goes through Doug.'

She studied the shelves of mystery novels for a moment, pulled one down, glanced through it, and put it back. 'It's not like it used to be, like it's supposed to be, when the faculty did run the college. Someone might take a couple of years off and serve as dean or provost, and then go back to their department and their teaching – the important things. Over the past few decades, a new breed of administrators have taken all the power from the faculty. What's left are odds and ends, the vestiges of faculty governance. But it's something, and that's what Doug's glommed on to.'

Ambler noticed again how well versed she was on Doug Stuart; she knew him and his approach to the college's government better than one would have expected. 'Would you mind my asking how you know so much about Professor Stuart?'

'As a matter of fact, I would.' Her cheeks colored and she turned away to busy herself with the bookshelves again, pulling down another book to glance through. They were quiet for a moment.

'*The Hot Rock*.' She handed it to him. 'The first Dortmunder. First edition. Dust jacket. Signed by Donald Westlake.'

He glanced at the signature, flipped through a few pages, examined the dust jacket. The book was in fine or near fine condition. It would be worth something to a collector; probably not thousands but quite a bit. He handed the book back.

She smiled at him uneasily. 'I'm sorry to speak so sharply . . . It's because I'm embarrassed.' She hesitated. 'I might as well tell you. Someone else undoubtedly will. Doug is my ex-husband . . . I'm in the category of those for whom he's done a big favor. I owe my teaching position here to him.'

This time Ambler decided to busy himself so he wouldn't have to share her embarrassment. He wandered over and opened one of the card catalog drawers and browsed through the index cards. She understood right away what he had wrongly inferred from what she'd said.

She spoke bluntly. 'It's not that I slept my way to success . . . Doug and I married very young while we were in college. We were both oddballs, the first in our families to go to college, so as social misfits we clung to one another. After we graduated, I supported him through grad school and, once he had his PhD, he supported me so I could get my degree. He's a brilliant guy and his PhD is from an ivy league school, so he had a choice of jobs. He took this one when he could have done better, so I could get an MFA here in the city.

'With an MFA it's difficult to get a teaching job, no matter where your degree is from. Poets looking for work are a dime a dozen.' She laughed. 'Sorry for the cliché; I should know better. Anyway, it was tough finding a teaching job. Doug got me in here on a tenure-line. Fortunately, I published a chapbook that was well reviewed and won an award, so I received tenure before our marriage fell apart.'

She'd regained her composure. 'There. That wasn't so hard. I'll skip the gory details. They aren't scurrilous, nor are they interesting. Doug is too self-absorbed to have a wife, and I'm better alone with my pens and notebooks, cups of tea, and my poems.'

Well, Ambler said to himself, after Sarah left to teach her creative writing class and he was alone with the shelves of detective novels, I'm already deep in secrets I'd rather not know about. An hour or so later, having gotten a better sense of the collection, he headed to the student union for a cup of coffee. As he crossed the college common, a man he didn't recognize hailed him.

SIX

The man who called to him, wearing a designer sweatsuit and running shoes, waved and trotted over. Slim, wiry, athletic, he breathed easily as he pulled up beside Ambler, his smile bright and engaging. 'You must be Mr Ambler. I saw you coming from the library.' He held out his hand. 'Doug Stuart.' Ambler shook his hand unenthusiastically. He hated extra-firm handshakes.

'I'm the president of the faculty senate, and I've been hoping to talk with you.'

'I know who you are.' Ambler heard the chill in his voice. If Stuart caught it, he didn't let on. 'Do you have a few minutes?'

Ambler sized him up. Youthful vigor, glowing with health, a mop of curly black hair, an unblemished face; the only thing that said he was older than he appeared on first glance were the crow's feet around his eyes and lines around his mouth. The determination lurking behind his winning smile made clear he wasn't a patsy.

'I was on my way to get a cup of coffee.'

'Mind if I join you? I'll take a quick shower and meet you in the student union in twenty minutes.'

Ambler was about to make the same suggestion. He'd have dragged Stuart along if he could; he wanted to grill him, as Mike Cosgrove might say. How could he turn down a chance to spend some time with the center of the storm? 'I'd be pleased,' he said, and watched out of the side of his eye as Stuart trotted off toward the gym.

A section of the casual cafe was portioned off and decorated with large paintings of Black jazz musicians, bearded white men, and slim, long-haired, bewitching white women, decor Ambler surmised meant to replicate the coffee houses of the beatnik era, a time Ambler remembered quite well, though he doubted anyone around him did. He got his coffee from the counter.

A few minutes later, Stuart, carrying an herbal tea, joined him at a small table under a large poster of a saxophonist at the Bitter End. Stuart began the conversation by talking about how fond he was of the 42nd Street Library. This neither surprised nor interested Ambler. Whenever someone learned where he worked, they told him how much they loved the building.

If they were native New Yorkers or if they went to college in the city, they'd tell him about the first time they visited the library on a research project. If they were from out of town, they told how they always tried to visit the building with the lions out front whenever they came to the city.

After a few minutes, Stuart got around to talking about Trinity College's library and the crime fiction collection that was the reason Ambler was there, the source of controversy on campus, and that may or may not have a connection to a recent murder.

'To be honest, I was surprised such a thing as a crime fiction collection existed. I've been here eight years and never heard of it.'

'Not really trendy,' Ambler said facetiously. Stuart, oblivious to Ambler's sarcasm, continued to belittle Abernathy's – and Ambler's – life work. Like many college professors, he was accustomed to being listened to and blithely unaware when his audience had stopped listening. Ambler let him run on.

'I found it hard to believe it would be worth anything to collectors other than Sam. I guess the New York Public Library has the kind of endowment that allows it to buy anything it wants.'

'Would that were true,' Ambler said. He didn't know what Stuart wanted to talk about, but he knew what *he* wanted to talk about: the murder of George Olson. He wanted to know what Stuart knew about that, what he thought of Sam Abernathy as a suspect, what George Olson might have been doing that could have led to his murder – and he intended to ask a couple of off-the-wall questions on the chance Stuart knew more about the murder than he should.

This was unlikely. It wasn't as if he was going to drag guilty knowledge out of the guy, but asking questions can reveal uneasiness, a hesitancy to answer. Stuart might be evasive, make assertions that later proved to be false or inconsistent, might not be able to account for himself at the time of the murder. He wasn't a suspect. Yet for no good reason – except perhaps that he'd done wrong by Sarah Hastings – Ambler didn't like him.

Because he was thinking his own thoughts and because Stuart had been talking pretty much nonstop, Ambler was only half-listening, so unintentionally interrupted him in the middle of a discourse about whether the college library of the future would even have physical copies of books.

'I want to offer my condolences on the loss of your colleague,' Ambler said. 'I'm told you were close friends.'

Stuart's reaction wasn't what he expected. 'George was a longtime colleague. He was easy to get along with, inoffensive, and we worked well together, but we weren't friends. He and Sam Abernathy were good friends. As one of the old guard, George – and Sam, too – had the kind of intellectual snobbishness that made them standoffish. That's not to say George and I didn't work well together. We saw eye-to-eye on serving the college and made a good team, much to Abernathy's disappointment. I'm shocked and saddened by his death.'

The response was straightforward, despite it striking Ambler as strange that Stuart would criticize Olson so soon after his death – damning with faint praise. Sam had said Olson tried to be a bridge between the old-guard faculty and the 'new owners', such as Stuart, Barnes the college president, and some of the junior faculty in the STEM disciplines.

If he were to reinterpret what Stuart said about Olson, it would be that he needed Olson to keep the old guard faculty in line and maintain his power. People with power, Ambler believed, were single-minded in their determination to keep it. Often, because of this, they were unaware of their narcissism or the effect their words or actions had on other people. Stuart, for instance, was probably unaware of demeaning Ambler's scholarly work with crime fiction, or of his callousness when he spoke about Olson's death.

For a brief moment, Ambler thought of Sarah and felt disappointed. Why on earth had she married such a self-absorbed man? Stuart was sure of himself; that was something women found attractive in men, at least until they became confident in themselves. Without meaning to, he compared her to Adele, who wouldn't get mixed up with someone as egotistical as Stuart. Adele was more sure of herself than anyone he knew, including him.

He probably should have more confidence in himself. But Adele found him confident, so that was enough. Power was obviously important to Stuart. Ambler had known other men for whom power or dominance was of the utmost importance. But why? Why did they need it? Why did Stuart need to have power and why did he work so hard for it? And why had he and Sam and George Olson, if Sarah was right about him, and many others never sought power and never thought they needed it?

The moment of silence after they'd spoken of the dead seemed appropriate. But even as Stuart kept silent, he glanced about restlessly and gave the impression his time was being wasted, reminding Ambler of Edward Barnes's mannerism that suggested he had more important things to do and had lost interest in the conversation he was part of. Ambler still didn't know why Stuart wanted to talk to him. He didn't ask anything. He did most of the talking, about not much of anything.

'What made you think George and I were friends?' Stuart ended the silence. His tone was accusatory, as if Ambler had intruded on his privacy, stuck his nose in where he wasn't wanted.

'I talked with Sam on my first visit here, and I met George when he came to Sam's office. Their conversation was about Sam's plan to challenge you for faculty senate president. I got the impression from what George said that you and he were friends. I guess I was wrong.'

'George supported me because I've done a great deal for the faculty.' He hesitated. 'Because I'm the best person for the position . . . Sometimes, I wish I wasn't.' He laughed.

'It's a position where you can't win. You do one thing, you anger half the faculty. You do the other thing, you anger the other half of the faculty, so you make enemies. I asked George to be my vice president, frankly, because he had influence with a cohort of the faculty where my support wasn't so strong.' He laughed quietly, the laugh producing wrinkles around his eyes and softening his expression, so he seemed friendly and likable.

Stuart didn't dress professorially, no worn tweed jacket with elbow patches, no horn-rimmed glasses, no beard, no frown, no absent-minded expression. He dressed like the Silicon Valley whiz kids who were brainy enough to get away with not following convention, who could wear T-shirts and tennis shoes to the office instead of suits and dress shoes.

This afternoon Stuart wore jeans and a blue work shirt, accented with a patterned neckerchief like trainmen used to wear, looking like he'd be more at home kayaking down a river in the Catskills or paddling a canoe on a placid lake in the Adirondacks than lecturing in a college classroom.

His easygoing friendliness and warm smile gave you to think he didn't have many worries and it would take a lot to get him angry. Still, there was nothing frivolous about him. You got the sense he was used to being the smartest person in the room and used to those around him being aware of that.

Every few minutes as they talked, a student, sometimes a couple of students together – a few of them young and shyly flirty women reflecting the ethnic diversity of the Bronx – passed their table, perhaps making a detour to do so, to say hello to their professor.

They said, 'Hi Doug', saying his name like they were trying it on for size, this informality with their professor, and hesitated after they spoke as if waiting to see if he might say something other than 'Hi' back. Ambler was impressed that he made some casual remark to each of them and called each one by name.

The one guy who passed by nodded to Stuart but didn't say anything. He was older than the women students, tall and gangly, longish, shaggy, off-blond hair, a scraggly beard, wearing faded army fatigues and an expression that was borderline surly.

Stuart watched him, still smiling, and said, 'Stop by my office after class, Walt, if you don't mind. I'd like to talk to you about your paper.'

Walt, without altering his stony stare or slowing his pace, somehow acknowledged and accepted the invitation.

'You have a nice rapport with your students.' Ambler gestured toward a table where a group of them had gathered, a couple of the young women, Walt, and a couple of other men, a bit older like him, guys you'd more likely find in a shot-and-beer bar with a string of Harleys parked out front.

Stuart waved his hand dismissively. 'It's superficial; they're not sure what to make of me because I connect to them on their level. They call me by my first name. I joke with them in class, especially the upper-level classes, and encourage them to question what I say, to argue with me and each other. They're not accustomed to that here.' The 'here' sounded contemptuous, as if meant to convey 'second-rate college'.

'Most of the senior faculty joined the higher education enterprise at a different time. They see themselves as necessarily distant from the students.' He raised his eyebrows to form a pious expression and raised his hand above his head as if measuring a height. 'Distant, as in "above them". Founts of knowledge pouring out wisdom with the students as receptacles. Sometimes I think I've been shanghaied into a reenactment of *Goodbye, Mr Chips* or *The Halls of Ivy*.'

He laughed at himself. 'You shouldn't have gotten me started. Really I'm not being fair to my colleagues. Most of them, with a few exceptions, are dedicated teachers and scholars. Today's approaches to learning aren't anything like they experienced or expected. They came into an academy that was mostly white and mostly male and an enclave of the elite.' He gestured at the tables around the student union that had filled up while they were talking with a cross-section of America – Latin, Asian, Black, more young women than young men, more persons of color than white. 'It's a brave new world.

'It's not that my colleagues are consciously prejudiced. They'd be horrified at the suggestion. But most of them are on a different wavelength than the students and don't understand the students as the students don't understand them. Everybody's trying but not much clicks, so the faculty feel they're not respected and the students feel the faculty looks down on them.'

Stuart talked easily, sharing his opinions as someone extremely confident he was right and his opinions would be acknowledged. 'We talk about students as if they're all the same, a flock of birds, a school of fish, yet each is the hero of his or her own story. They need to express themselves, find meaning for themselves. They don't want to be spoon-fed accepted wisdom from those who went before them.' He paused.

'I suppose that's true of the faculty also,' he continued, sounding less assertive. 'We're not a monolith either. Lots of differences. Still, we of all people should model a process of discussion and argument, disagreement without rancor. Our job as scholars is to find truth, however relative, not to prove their side wrong or our side right.

'Barnes and the administration want a more student-centered environment – computer-assisted learning, smart classrooms, interactive approaches to teaching. The older faculty are skeptical and because they're skeptical they're resistant. They see student-centered learning strategies as an attempt to cater to the students' whims. The administration refers to students as consumers, and this drives those faculty members right up a wall. They think this means that students, with the administration as their agents, get to call the shots; not the faculty.' He laughed.

'You remember the old cowboy movies where the innovators in town are bringing in the railroad and the old-timers are standing around leaning on a buckboard giving one reason after another why the train could never replace the stagecoach? That's what our departmental meetings look like these days.'

Stuart ended with a look of smug satisfaction, a professor concluding a successful lecture, awaiting the accolades. Like most of the professorate Ambler had known – and Ambler had spent a good amount of time in higher education himself – Stuart liked to hear himself talk and was used to his listeners recognizing they'd been enlightened by listening to him. That he'd just provided an example of the kind of pedantic lecture he was proselytizing against, he seemed blissfully unaware.

With his hand tented in front of his face, his index fingers pressed to his chin, the professor regarded Ambler for a long moment with a serious, puzzled, and you'd almost say alarmed expression, an expression he might use with a student whose paper had been plagiarized. Ambler sensed they would now get down to business. Everything that went before had been preliminary, setting Ambler up for what Stuart had on his mind, the real purpose of this encounter.

'I understand,' Stuart, no longer smiling, his tone sober, said, 'that in addition to your librarian work, you're also something of a detective.'

'Not a librarian, a curator.'

'But a detective.' His tone was decisive.

Ambler objected. 'I've never thought of myself as a detective.'

'Are you investigating George Olson's murder?' Something in his tone suggested more than casual interest.

Since Ambler planned to ask Stuart what he knew about the murder, he had little reason not to be truthful, although it would be better for his little investigation to be carried out without fanfare.

'As a matter of fact, Sam's attorney asked me to keep my ears open, ask around, get a sense of what folks on campus thought about the murder, as long as I'd be on campus anyway. I wouldn't say I was investigating the murder. The police will take care of that.'

'I thought the matter was pretty well settled. Sam's lawyer has his work cut out for him.' Stuart's eyebrows narrowed into an almost cartoonish expression of concern worthy of Pogo's friend Howland Owl. 'I'm told Sam has disappeared.'

This provided Ambler the opening to ask the questions he'd been waiting to ask, so he asked them, pretending ignorance. 'Disappeared? Are you sure? His lawyer didn't think he was in as much trouble as you seem to. Do you know something the lawyer doesn't?'

'I'm afraid everyone knows Sam had it in for George. They had a falling-out. Maybe he didn't tell his attorney this.' Stuart looked over his shoulder before leaning conspiratorially closer to Ambler. 'George was shot at long range by a rifle. The police determined the shot came from the roof of the library, probably five hundred feet away. Did you know Sam was a sniper in Vietnam?' Stuart sat back, you might say triumphantly.

Ambler put aside Stuart's gloating. 'That's a coincidence the police would take note of, not evidence to convict or even charge someone. His attorney would have told me if the police had charged Sam with anything. And if he hasn't been charged, I don't see why he'd disappear, as you say.'

'There's more.' Stuart used the tone he might use when taking a student to task for a blatantly wrong answer. 'Sam didn't teach his class today. No one has seen him since shortly after George was killed. He hasn't been in his office, isn't at home, doesn't answer his phone . . .' Stuart lowered his voice. 'And he was at the library at the time of the shooting.'

'Someone saw him?'

Stuart nodded.

'Can you tell me who?'

'I could but I won't. The police know but the person doesn't want to be identified at this time.'

Stuart was too eager to pin the crime on Sam, which irritated Ambler. Plus, he sounded so self-satisfied Ambler felt an urge to slap him, an urge he might have felt as a boy with a smug classmate who always knew the answer when you didn't, not an urge he was used to having as an adult. Because of his petulance, he challenged Stuart, hoping to point out the pompous scholar's shoddy thinking.

'It's true murder victims often know their murderers. It's also true, certainly in recent years, that someone can be shot and killed at random. I'm sure you're aware of examples of this. It's more likely a killing is random when the victim is shot from long range.

'My guess, since we're both guessing, would be it's too early to rule out an aggrieved student or former student or aggrieved former employee shooting random victims who have a connection to the campus. It might also be a former student of George's who bore a grudge.'

Stuart nodded, as if granting Ambler his point. 'But Sam is the obvious suspect. He felt betrayed by George. And betrayal by someone you thought a friend is hard to take.' He looked at Ambler curiously for a moment. 'Who knows what lurks in the hearts of men? Wouldn't you expect that someone with such an obsession with murder – building an entire library collection of books about murder – would be likely to one day murder?'

Ambler stared at him – *Did he really say that?* – then laughed. 'I don't think anyone's ever found a correlation between curating a collection of murder mysteries and committing a murder. At least, I hope no one has.'

SEVEN

After his coffee break and a couple more hours in the quiet-as-a-grave, bland, fluorescent-lit, tiny reading room – probably a one-time utility closet – deep within the Trinity College of the Bronx Library stacks, Ambler called it a day. He'd spent most of his time aimlessly browsing through the actual books on the shelves. The books, rather than their listing on a file card, or worse in a database, gave him a better sense of the collection as a real thing. And the physical condition of the books would determine if any of the first editions were collectibles.

A surprising proportion of the collection was mass-market paperbacks. Surprising because libraries tended to acquire hardcover books. Unsurprising, on the other hand, because so many detective novels in the 1940s and well into the 1960s and beyond were paperback originals, never published in hardcover.

The collection also included a number of hardcovers without their dust jackets; even if first editions, without the dust jacket they weren't worth much to collectors. Most private collectors, unlike libraries, tended to look at their books as objects – like figurines – not as something to read.

In addition, a number of the first editions were duplicates of first editions Ambler already had in the 42nd Street Library collection, and books by well-known authors published in large print runs, so not especially rare and not valuable. There was also the problem that a few of what might be rare first editions with cards in the catalog weren't on the shelves. They may have been mis-shelved or borrowed, or they might be missing. He'd need to ask Sam about that.

On the plus side, Sam had first American editions of Chester Himes's Coffin Ed Johnson and Grave Digger Jones Harlem books – police procedurals? urban noir? Or novels of the absurd, as Himes thought them to be, the 'absurd' of Camus and the French Existentialists.

In addition, tucked away in a box on the shelf next to the US editions were a few original Série Noire first editions of the Harlem series, from Marcel Duhamel at Gallimard. *Il pleut des coups durs (If Trouble Was Money* aka *Real Cool Killers)* was one of them. *La reine des pommes (For Love of Imabelle* and later *A Rage in Harlem)* was another.

Himes, an expatriate living mostly in France – who, as far as Ambler knew, never lived in Harlem – wrote the books in English, and Duhamel and Gallimard translated them into French and published them as part of Série Noire. They weren't published in the US until later.

As Ambler was leaving the library, an incident on the quadrangle caught his attention. A group of students, three, maybe four, Asian and Latin young men – Ambler wasn't paying that close attention – had stopped to chat where two sidewalks intersected in the middle of the quad. Two burly men, one of whom Ambler recognized as Doug Stuart's student Walt, came from behind them and pushed through the group, muscling their way through so that a couple of the kids were pushed off the sidewalk on to the grass.

The younger students seemed stunned by what happened and stared after Walt and his pal. One of the kids must have said something, because Walt and his friend turned, took on what looked like menacing stances, and shouted something back. Ambler couldn't make out the words but there was no doubting the challenging tone. The small group of younger students stared for a moment and then walked away, stoop-shouldered and hurrying, without looking back.

On his way home on the train, Ambler thought about Sam Abernathy, Sarah Hastings, Doug Stuart, and the late George Olson. He also thought about the aggrieved student theory he'd expounded to Doug Stuart. Perhaps because of this, the image of this Walt and his thuggish pal stayed with him. Something about what happened on the path through the quadrangle suggested a propensity to violence that should be out of place on the quiet campus.

His reaction to what hadn't really amounted to even a shoving match was prejudice he realized – young white men wearing fatigues, carrying themselves with a swagger and surly expressions, these days suggested anti-government, racist, right-wing militia types. It had gotten increasingly difficult to look at anyone without slotting them into some type of stereotype.

The next morning, with Adele's help, he spent a couple of hours on a computer in the reading room going through the library's online databases looking for random college shootings. He remembered the Charles Whitman shooting at the University of Texas in the mid-Sixties, but not the details. Information was easy to find in ProQuest.

In August of 1966, Whitman, then 25, a former altar boy, eagle scout, and US Marine, shot fourteen people dead and wounded thirty-one from the observation tower of the main University of Texas building after earlier stabbing his mother and his wife to death and killing three people on his way to the observation tower. He was shot to death by police. For a couple of years before the killings, he'd complained of violent thoughts and urges he couldn't control, and a later autopsy found he had a brain tumor that might have contributed to the violence.

In a more recent horrific shooting, at Virginia Tech University in 2007, a twenty-three-year-old student killed thirty-two people and injured twenty-six others on the campus. The perpetrator this time, who had a history of mental health issues, committed suicide.

Between 2012 and 2015, there was a shooting, resulting in multiple deaths, at a US college every year: seven killed at Oikos University, a Korean Christian college in Oakland, California, in 2012; six dead, including the killer shot by police, at Santa Monica College in 2013; another six murdered near the University of California, Santa Barbara, in 2014; this time, the killer, Elliot Rodger, stabbed three people to death at home before his shooting spree; he shot himself to death in his car as police closed in. In 2015, a student enrolled at Umpqua Community College in Oregon killed a professor and eight students and wounded eight other students before killing himself after being wounded in a shootout with police.

Another statistic that stood out was from *Campus Safety*

Magazine. Between the 2001–2002 and 2015–2016 school years, 437 people were shot in 190 college campus shooting incidents. The good folks at Trinity College might be shocked that a murder took place on their campus, telling themselves, 'Murders happen in the barrios of the South Bronx, shootings don't happen on a college campus.' They'd be surprised to discover that they were far from alone in their horror at their campus being visited by sudden, violent death.

Given that somewhere around 15,000 people are murdered in an average year in the United States, thirty or so shootings, not all of them fatal, on college campuses each year wouldn't be exceptional, except that shootings aren't supposed to happen on a college campus.

Still, statistics didn't tell you everything. The data say the most probable suspect in George Olson's murder would be an alienated young – in his twenties – white male, a student or ex-student, most likely suffering from mental illness, most certainly a social misfit, possibly an incel. That this was the most likely suspect didn't eliminate the possibility that the killer was a disgruntled elderly English professor.

Ambler had met Rebecca Dawson, Sam's student assistant, briefly before he left campus the previous evening and made plans to see her again after her classes, during her usual work-study working hours, when he went back this afternoon. Sam had told her about Ambler, she said, and asked her to assist him with the appraisal. Ambler found her waiting for him when he arrived at the college library in the early afternoon.

For some reason, he felt he made her nervous, or perhaps she was always anxious. Dark, sad eyes, shiny black hair pulled back so tightly into a ponytail that it stretched smooth the white skin of her forehead and pulled her eyes open wider. Diffident and solicitous, she reminded him of girls he knew growing up who were always determined to do everything perfectly to please the teacher, or anyone else in authority, and would descend into misery bordering on heartache when they realized they'd done something wrong or were corrected, however gently, by the teacher.

Rebecca was an odd combination of confidence in her eagerness to show him how everything worked on the database, and timidity and diffidence when he tried to go deeper into an entry. When he mistakenly asked her for information that didn't exist in the database, she apologized as if the omission were her fault.

She answered questions about herself, which Ambler had no business asking, with perfunctory, apologetic answers, rather than brushing them off. In a way, she reminded him of his son John when he was young, shrugging off questions about him as if there wasn't much to tell because he wasn't worth very much.

Ambler asked some arguably unseemly questions about Rebecca Dawson's personal life (the kinds of questions older men, assuming a sort of privilege, ask young women), making her uncomfortable and creating this awkward and clumsy exchange between them, because he hoped it would serve as a preamble to get her to talk about Sam Abernathy and the murder of George Olson. Despite her mumbled and courteous but unforthcoming answers, he persisted.

'Do you choose the faculty member you work with, or are you assigned one by the financial aid office or whoever gives you the job?'

'It's work-study money from the government. Financial aid doesn't care what kind of job you have. They have some you can choose from. But if you come up with a particular job or a professor comes up with a job, it's fine with them as long as it fits some weird work-study rules.'

'When I qualified for the aid, I asked Sam . . .' She blushed and both her mouth and her eyes opened wider, as if she'd said something embarrassingly indiscreet. 'I mean Professor Abernathy . . . I asked Professor Abernathy if he needed a student assistant.'

Appearing to feel on firmer footing, she managed a little laugh. 'He hadn't put in a request, he said, because he thought the work he needed done was too complex for a student. But since it was me . . .' She blushed again. 'He felt I could do the job, so he put in the request and I applied for it.'

She stood up straighter. 'I'm older than most of the students. I have two children, and I'm married.' She made this last statement curtly, as if to make clear it was something she wouldn't want to discuss, wouldn't want Ambler to ask about. 'I'm more mature so I'm more serious about my courses and the work with Sam.' She didn't correct herself this time.

Ambler thought it interesting that Doug Stuart bragged about students calling him by his first name. And when Rebecca called Sam by his first name, it was as if it had slipped out and she should more properly have called him by the honorific 'Professor'.

'Do you read mystery novels?' Ambler's experience was that not many young people did. If they read anything for fun, it was fantasy, romance, science fiction, or horror.

'With my kids, my classes, and my job.' She gestured toward the bookshelves and the card catalog. 'I don't have time to read for pleasure. I've read some books Sam suggested, and I liked them. Do you know who Dorothy Sayers is? She's a mystery writer and was kind of a feminist before her time.'

'I do,' Ambler said. 'I'm well acquainted with Lord Peter Wimsey and Harriet Vane.'

'She wrote an essay, "Are Women Human?" Do you know about that?' She said this with fierceness in her tone, a challenge to let on she was ready for a fight. The fierceness Ambler thought out of character for her until he realized maybe it wasn't. He knew about the essay but hadn't read it. He told her this.

She nodded. The boldness didn't last. 'Dr Abernathy is the only man I've ever known who recognizes male supremacy without being told about it.' Her tone was timid again. She seemed to shrink as she spoke. 'He opened my eyes to a lot of things.' She'd glanced shyly at Ambler as she said this, held his gaze for a quick second before looking away as if perhaps she shouldn't have said what she said.

Eventually he brought her around to talking about the murder. She was sure Sam didn't kill George Olson. 'The only reason anyone even thinks he did is because *certain people* have it in for him and took something that happened and made it into something it couldn't possibly be.' She spoke convincingly, which meant to Ambler that she was convinced of what she said, not that what she said would convince anyone else that Sam was innocent.

Despite her certainty regarding Sam Abernathy's innocence, her tone and her mannerisms had become agitated. She spoke quickly, correcting herself when she didn't need to, words tripping over words, as if she might, if she weren't careful, reveal something to Ambler she didn't want him to know about.

Something about Sam? Something about her? He wasn't sure. Because of her nervousness, her determination and certainty about his innocence ended up having the opposite effect, causing Ambler to think she might be afraid Sam was guilty. If she thought that, Ambler got the strong sense she wouldn't say so; she'd cover for her professor.

Sarah Hastings had said Rebecca was devoted to Sam. Listening to her, you felt she idolized the man. Sometimes that happened between a professor and a student. The teacher makes a profound impression on the student, changes his or her life. He remembered an article he'd read when he was a teaching assistant in the time before the 42nd Street Library. "Eros and Education", *eros* in this case referring to a Platonic philosophical concept, the love of truth and beauty, desire beyond the sexual, a passion for learning that is in its way erotic.

Sarah had made clear she wasn't talking about sexual desire when she told him about the relationship between Sam and his student Rebecca. You wouldn't think of Sam as much of a Don Juan anyway. But Rebecca's eyes sparkled when she spoke about him. Their shared love of beauty and truth, or whatever it was, had an effect on her, something going on not just on the intellectual level.

Ambler hoped she'd have an alibi for her professor, but she didn't. Nor did she have anyone else in mind for the murderer. She was intrigued by the possibility of an alienated student as the killer, but didn't know of any student who she thought alienated enough to commit murder. 'Don't deranged people like that kill a bunch of people all at the same time, like commit mass murders?'

She had a point. This was what happened in most of the campus or school killings. But you could look at it another way. 'In recent years, we've suffered through too many horror stories like that,' he told her. 'But other killers have operated differently; I suppose you call them serial killers, rather than mass murderers, Ted Bundy, John Wayne Gacy, a bunch of others. Then there was the DC sniper, John Allen Muhammad and his young disciple. Those sniper killings weren't at all like this one, but they did take place over a period of time, two or three weeks, not all at once.'

A student or former student might have had a grudge against Olson and no one else. But this was Ambler's conjecture, and he had no real basis for it. He had no reason to believe Olson was shot by a serial killer either, no reason to believe anyone else was in danger of being shot by a sniper. The police had discounted that possibility. They called it a targeted shooting and they were zeroing in on their suspect. Nonetheless, there was a heavy police presence in and around the campus.

Rebecca didn't know George Olson. She knew who he was but had never taken a class with him. She'd taken a class with Doug Stuart and said it was great. 'He's a brilliant teacher. The course wasn't easy. But he was spellbinding. You had a lot of work to do – a big research project with a team. Mine was on grocery stores and plastic.'

She gave Ambler a stern look. 'Do you know how much plastic a grocery store uses – not only plastic bags to carry groceries but plastic jars, plastic bottles, plastic wrappings; plastic everywhere you look, everything you touch?'

She took a breath. 'That was the best thing about him. Dr Stuart made you feel passionate about what he was teaching. What you learned was important enough that you had to do something with it. That's why the course was so great.'

Her enthusiasm made Ambler almost regret his antipathy toward Stuart . . . almost. 'Do students compare older professors like Sam Abernathy or George Olson unfavorably to Stuart?'

She didn't know what he meant. 'Some professors are boring. Most of them aren't. As far as I can tell, they're all really smart.' She smiled. 'Smarter than me anyway. I'm lucky to be here; I'm getting a second chance. I take in everything I can. Soak it all up.'

When she talked about the college or her courses, she was

bright-eyed and bushy-tailed. When she talked about herself, anything about her life beyond school, she was more reticent than you'd imagine someone that young would be.

Still trying to force the issue, he asked her what she wanted to get out of college.

'I want to be a teacher.'

'Like Professor Abernathy?'

She demurred. 'Oh no. I'd never be that smart. He wrote a book on Edgar Allan Poe. A book they still use in college courses. I could never do that.'

'Maybe you will,' Ambler said. 'Once upon a time, Sam might not have believed he'd write a book or be a college professor.'

'I guess,' she said dubiously.

Ambler liked talking with Rebecca Dawson, though he wished she was more forthcoming. Though really it was unrealistic to expect her, or any student, to have 'inside baseball' knowledge of the workings of the college. Students had their own take on college life, which had little to do with campus politics or campus intrigues, or campus scandals. Whether they had their own take on a campus murder was yet to be determined.

EIGHT

After Rebecca left to pick up her kids, Ambler spent another couple of hours wrestling with the database she'd created for the collection. She'd listed the author, title, publisher, but not the date of publication or the edition, so when he found a book that looked interesting, he had to go into the stacks to find it. This shouldn't have been that difficult, but was, because Sam – rather than simply shelving the books according to the author's last name – had created categories based on some kind of designation known only to him and shelved the books alphabetically by author last name in various categories.

Ambler was wandering through the stacks grumbling to himself when a serious-looking owl-eyed student with a massive amount of wildly curly dark hair asked if he was Mr Ambler and told him President Barnes wished to see him before he left campus for the day if this could be arranged.

Sure, said Ambler, and asked the young man to show him the way to Barnes's office; the college was a kind of maze and he didn't want to spend the time looking for the administration building. The president's office, like the library and Sam's office, was in one of the campus's original buildings: the kind of Gothic structure – with massive rough-hewn stone walls, flying buttresses, spires and gargoyles – adopted by colleges and universities, most of them connected to a religion, that were founded in the early centuries of the nation.

The style was ponderous, solemn, dignified, and, whether meant to be or not, forbidding. Yet Ambler liked the buildings, as he liked the Beaux-Arts architecture of the 42nd Street Library. He liked buildings that were old, built of stone, and had stood the test of time.

Inside the stone building, the exposed beams, staircase, pillars and wainscoting were of dark wood, Ambler guessed mahogany, giving the hallways a medieval feel, an aura of

ancient wisdom. Yet behind the massive wooden doors, the
modern world flourished: fluorescent lights, buzzing computers,
fax machines, printers, and every other electronic device a
college ran on reminded him they were deep into the space
age; ancient elms and marble and granite buildings notwithstanding. As Doug Stuart had told him in no uncertain terms,
the college kept up with the times.

The young woman at the reception desk, another student
aide Ambler guessed, stared at him as if he'd dropped from
the ceiling and seemed bewildered when he said he was there
to see Dr Barnes. She continued to stare at him with guileless
blue eyes, neither saying nor doing anything. Had no one ever
asked to see Barnes before?

'He sent for me.' Ambler wished he'd kept the student
summoner with him to help explain his presence. He'd thought
it would be smooth sailing once he got to the door of the
building.

The receptionist's expression changed from bewilderment
to doubt, as if she were asking, 'What am I supposed to do
about that?'

'Might you let him know I'm here?'

'I guess,' she said dubiously. 'This is my first day. No one
told me what I was supposed to do if a stranger came in and
wanted to see him.'

'You might tell him Ray Ambler is here.'

'You're not a professor?' Her tone suggested this
development made her task even more confounding.

'If you would please tell him . . .' Ambler said mildly,
though he gritted his teeth.

When he got into Barnes's office a few minutes later, Barnes
came from behind his desk and offered his hand. The college
president was short but fit; his manner was a kind of in-your-
face friendliness that carried with it a challenge, so that with
his build and his manner, he reminded Ambler of a bulldog
that lived next door when he was growing up. After shaking
hands and beaming into Ambler's face, standing close enough
to him that Ambler wanted to take a step back, Barnes went
back to sit behind his desk.

The desk was of gleaming dark wood, its surface as large

as a ping-pong table, with absolutely nothing on it – no papers, no phone, no computer, no pen nor pencil. You'd wonder what he needed a desk for at all. Barnes watched Ambler for a moment before he spoke. 'I've been told you do detective work.'

Here we go again, Ambler told himself. I might as well wear a uniform.

Barnes beat around the bush for a minute, lamenting the disastrous effect a murder would have on the college's recruitment – the possibility, even if remote, people might think something about Trinity College prompted murder. When he got around to what he wanted, which was for Ambler to tell him how the police investigation of Olson's murder would proceed, Ambler was noncommittal.

'I know in general how a homicide investigation works. But I don't know anything about this one.'

Barnes's eyes popped open and then narrowed with suspicion, as if he'd caught Ambler in a lie. 'I'd read that you have a close friend, a homicide detective, with whom you work closely.'

'I have a friend, a homicide detective, but he won't have anything to do with this investigation.'

'I also understand you've been asked by Professor Abernathy's attorney to look into the circumstances surrounding George Olson's murder.'

Ambler was taken aback for a moment, but had no trouble figuring out how Barnes knew this. Doug Stuart, it appeared, kept Barnes abreast of campus happenings the president should know about. You had to wonder about a cozy relationship between the college president and the leader of the faculty. This was to say, you had to wonder whose side Stuart was on. Ambler's guess was his own.

Still, he was OK telling Barnes what he was doing. He'd already told Stuart. He wasn't working undercover. Though the idea of working undercover gave him an idea. 'Sam's lawyer asked me to keep my ears open, ask around, see if anyone on campus knew something no one else knew.'

He paused. 'I'd like to know your thoughts, Dr Barnes. A violent, tragic incident took place that you had no control over, no way to know such a thing would happen. No one could have expected you to prevent it, yet you have to respond, reassure the campus, explain to parents and alumni. I don't envy you your task. I imagine you're still in shock.'

Barnes nodded and smiled slightly; he seemed pleased Ambler acknowledged his awesome responsibilities. 'I can't overstate the importance of the safety of our students. Not only must they be safe; they must feel safe. Their sense of safety has been obliterated. It has to be restored. We have campus security. We have an increased police presence. We've brought in a public relations firm with expertise in this sort of thing. I'm leaving no stone unturned. Yet . . .'

While Barnes spoke, Ambler watched a strange phenomenon take place in his expression, as if he were doing one thing with his voice, talking, but something entirely different with his mind, calculating how to accomplish what he really wanted done, and his words were automatic, like a tape recording.

'I think you can help. That's why I asked you to stop by my office today.'

This was an interesting way to characterize his summoning. 'I expected to talk about the crime fiction collection. I'm sure dealing with the aftermath of Professor Olson's murder takes precedence over other things for you. But I doubt I'll be much help. Have you spoken with the police?'

Barnes made a gesture of distaste. 'I spoke with a captain of detectives or something like that. He was condescending, treated me like the village idiot, and told me nothing of consequence. Basically, he said to keep out of their way; they'd handle everything.' He looked searchingly at Ambler. 'Are the police always this circumspect about their investigations?'

'They do like to keep things close to the vest. I'd say universally they believe civilians get in the way.' Ambler weighed what he was going to say next. 'I have a couple of questions for you, too. This is a sensitive area, what with student privacy issues and such. But I'd like to ask about your security measures. For example, do you screen students when they enroll? Do you have a way to flag students – profile might be the term – who, for whatever reason, might be prone to violence, might have mental health issues?'

Barnes pursed his lips. 'We have a violence prevention center and we have programs to address sexual assault and domestic violence.' He paused for a moment. 'We don't screen for serial killers or mass murderers. I never heard of any institution that does. It's an impossible task.' He frowned. 'Are you suggesting a student shot Professor Olson? I thought the evidence pointed to Sam Abernathy.'

'I don't know of any evidence pointing to Sam.' Ambler's response was decisive. 'Do you know something I don't know?'

Barnes arched his eyebrows. 'Why does he have a lawyer if he's not a suspect?'

Ambler sighed. 'We're talking about evidence. You don't need much evidence to make someone a suspect. The law, though, does require quite a bit of evidence to convict someone of a crime. I'd like to ask you how Sam came to be a suspect . . . and of course, if you have evidence that points to him, I'd like to know about that, too.'

Barnes consulted with himself for longer than Ambler would have thought necessary to simply remember what he knew. It was more like the length of time it would take to sift through what you know and decide which part of it you'd divulge and which parts you'd keep to yourself.

'You know, I'm sure, the police suspect Sam—'

Ambler interrupted him. 'Why?'

Barnes was perplexed by the question. 'Because they think he did it, I would say.' He rattled off the points Doug Stuart had cited. Sam had an argument with Olson; someone saw Sam in the library.

Ambler interrupted him. 'That doesn't answer my question. Weren't other possibilities considered? I get the sense you're not being forthcoming. Are you worried about something? Are you protecting someone?'

Barnes's eyelids went up and down like he was signaling to someone with a window shade. 'Of course not. Why would you ask that? Who would I protect?'

Ambler was perplexed. He was engaging in a fencing match that there was no reason to have unless Barnes was hiding something. It wouldn't do any good to ask him what he was hiding because he'd swear he wasn't hiding anything. If Ambler were to guess, it would be that Barnes was part of a scheme of some sort to frame Sam Abernathy, or that Barnes took it upon himself to frame Sam and didn't want people considering other possibilities.

Ambler thought of two reasons this might be so. Barnes killed Olson and needed to frame someone. This wasn't probable but it was not impossible. The other possibility: Barnes and his conspirators, if he had any, took advantage of the murder to frame Sam and get him out of the way of the college's modernization plans.

Everything Barnes told him he already knew: Sam and Olson had an argument; someone allegedly saw Sam in the library around the time of the shooting; Sam had been a sniper in the army and owned a rifle that was now missing. Motive, opportunity and means: a pretty good basis for suspicion. In addition, no one so far had come up with a motive for anyone else to kill Olson. And when you came down to it, he didn't know for a fact that Sam didn't kill him.

For some, probably perverse reason, he decided to pursue the idea that maybe Barnes did kill Olson. 'Did it occur to you that you might be a suspect?' Ambler watched for Barnes's reaction . . . which was astonishment.

He took another shot while he had him on the ropes. 'Do you own a rifle?'

Barnes dropped his gaze like a guilty schoolboy before he answered. 'I grew up in Northern Michigan; I hunt. Of course I have guns . . . You're not suggesting I shot George? . . . That's preposterous. I have no reason on earth—'

Barnes's expression hardened into a glare of ruthlessness, the like of which Ambler had seen only once before . . . on the face of a man trying to kill him. Here, the ruthlessness in Barnes's expression spoke of unbridled ambition that was being threatened. Ambler saw in that unguarded moment a man who'd stop at nothing to get what he wanted.

Though ruthless ambition was clearly a central element of Barnes's character, he covered it with a veneer of civility. Once he realized he'd overreacted, given too much away, he swiveled his chair so he was no longer looking at Ambler and Ambler could no longer see his face. When he turned back, he'd gotten himself under control.

He smiled with his lips but not his eyes. 'I assume you made that accusation to provoke me, to show me that suspicions were easy to throw around and difficult to deflect. Your gambit was impressive; it suggests that, despite your modesty, you're as shrewd a thinker as I thought you were when I asked to see you today.'

Ambler had more questions about what he'd come to think of, at least for the moment, as a frame-up of Sam Abernathy. But Barnes made clear he was no longer interested in what Ambler thought they should talk about and intended to focus on what he wanted to talk about. When you were a college president, Ambler gathered, you got to be the one who decided the topic under discussion.

The college president was direct and straightforward. He wanted Ambler to keep him abreast of his investigation into Olson's murder. No one had ever made such a request of Ambler before, so he wasn't sure how to respond.

'I'm not really doing an investigation. The police do that. What I'm doing is looking around and asking some questions to see if I can find anything that casts doubt on the accusations against Sam.'

'I could make that difficult for you.' Barnes spoke matter-of-factly. 'The campus is private property.'

Ambler swallowed his response. He knew a threat when he heard one. Barnes could make it difficult for him. He could deny Ambler access to the campus. He could tell people not to talk to him. Ambler had both suspicions and misgivings about Barnes. But he needed him.

You had to wonder why Barnes wanted to know what his investigation turned up about the murder. If Barnes was the killer, he'd for sure want to know. On the other hand, he was the captain of the ship, so it was understandable he'd want to know what was happening on his watch.

After a moment, he asked, 'Do you mind telling me where you were at the time Olson was killed?'

Barnes didn't miss a beat. 'I was holding a cabinet meeting. The deans and the heads of the administrative departments can attest to that. We were together when we got the terrible news.'

He spread his arms out on his mammoth desk and turned his palms face up, as if he were making a presentation. 'To play your game, Mr Detective, I have an alibi, I don't have a motive, and what I didn't tell you was I'm a terrible shot. Ask any of my family. I couldn't hit a deer with a rifle shot if it were standing on the other side of the room.'

'You could have hired someone.'

Barnes grimaced. 'I could have but I didn't.' He glanced at his watch and then looked behind Ambler, as if something were happening beyond his office door that Ambler was keeping him from. 'You can investigate me. I'm fine with that. I'll give you free access to the campus, encourage everyone to cooperate with you. All I ask in return is that you keep me informed of your findings. The police obviously aren't going to be any help to me.'

He studied Ambler's face for a moment. 'There's nothing sinister in this. My position may not look to you like an embattled one. Yet I have adversaries – in the faculty, on the Board of Trustees, among the alumni – waiting for me to fail, watching for the tragic flaw, ready to jump at a chance to take me down at the slightest slip-up. I need to keep abreast of what happens on campus, especially now when everyone is on edge. More than a few college presidents have been forced out over less than a murder on campus.'

The explanation was convincing. That didn't mean he now trusted Barnes. But he didn't have any verifiable reason to doubt him either. 'Let's say I agree to keep you informed. Do I have a guarantee you won't interfere with what I'm doing?'

'I have no reason to. It appeared to me Sam Abernathy is the guilty party. You're telling me this might not be the case. I've read that your detective skills are formidable. You may not have the resources the police have, but your methods have produced results.'

He pulled his arms in and then spread them out in an arc in front of him like a preacher booming out a sermon. 'So there you have it: unfettered access to the campus in exchange for sharing information with me. No one needs to know about our arrangement. What do you say?'

'I need to think it over.' The idea of sharing information with anybody, with the possible exception of Mike Cosgrove, bothered him. He'd never done anything like that before. For that matter, he wasn't sure he wanted to be involved in this murder case at all. Sam was a friend, and friendship counted for something, counted for a lot.

Yet Sam so far hadn't been all that forthcoming, and against the advice of pretty much everyone he'd gone into hiding rather than face the charges that might be coming against him and proving them wrong. If Sam wasn't going to prove himself innocent, why was it up to Ambler to do so?

One possibility did nag at him. He wouldn't forgive himself if someone else was murdered, someone who might not die if Ambler stuck with this at least for a while. It wasn't for sure, and he had no evidence to support his thinking, but it was possible that a student – deranged, disgruntled, seeking revenge for a slight, a snub, an affront that Olson might not even have known took place – killed the professor. It might be this was the only murder the student would commit. But it was also possible the student had additional grudges he would act on.

Ambler had a lot to think about.

NINE

L ater that evening, after dinner and after Johnny had gone to bed, John went with Ambler when he took the dog for a walk. Lola had blossomed into a full-sized dog, growing to the dimensions her large puppy feet had predicted she would reach. Her saving graces were that she was easy-going, mild-mannered, had learned the basics of sit, go to bed, stay and (more or less) come, and was devoted to her pack. They walked without talking for a block, until John asked how the murder investigation was coming along.

'It's not really an investigation,' Ambler said. 'The police are doing that. I'm trying to find something that would help Sam. But it's not easy. I can talk to the faculty and the administrators maybe. The students are a problem. I stopped a group of them this afternoon to ask if they'd known Professor Olson. They stared at me like I'd asked for a handout. They don't like talking to someone as old as me, and I don't know how to talk to them. Then there's the cat-out-of-the-bag problem. Everyone at the college already knows I'm snooping around and why. The professorate as gossipers would put a knitting circle to shame.'

They watched Lola sniff a row of plastic garbage bags piled at the curb in front of an apartment building. 'And then there's the college president, who thinks I should be reporting to him. And if I don't, he threatened to bar me from the campus.' He told John about his meeting with Barnes.

They were quiet again until they got to the corner of Second Avenue, when John interrupted Ambler's thoughts. 'I have an idea. I'm not doing much these days. I could go up with you as a kind of assistant, hang out, get to know some of the students; they'd probably let me listen in.'

This was what the lawyer David Levinson had suggested and that Ambler had been hesitant to mention to John. Now he did. They talked it over on the walk back to the apartment,

Ambler warming to the idea as they talked. John was around
the age of the older students – the ones he'd seen when he
was talking to Doug Stuart and Walt and his pal at the incident
in the quad. John would fit in with them – it was a place to
start.

Students would talk more freely around him if he looked
as if he were part of a group rather than a loner. There was
also something about this guy Walt's sullenness and his cocki-
ness, both in his offhand manner with Doug Stuart and his
truculent manner with the kids on the quad that caused Ambler
to want to know more about him. He came across as a man
among boys, sharper – maybe it was more streetwise – than
those around him. This didn't connect him in any way with
George Olson's murder.

Ambler reacted to this 'Walt' the way McNulty sometimes
reacted to someone coming into his bar, knowing by a sixth
sense developed over the years that this guy was trouble. It
was the way Lola sometimes sensed that a dog walking toward
them or even across the street, who looked for all the world
to Ambler like every other dog, set her off, sent her on full
alert, sniffing the air for a better scent, her fur bristling, sinking
into a crouch not unlike Ambler's tai chi bow posture, ready
for trouble.

All John would have to do at the college was listen; there
was little chance he'd get into a situation that could lead to
his violating his probation. His background as an ex-con might
make him interesting and help his getting accepted by the
other students. At the same time, he could keep looking for a
music gig, something else that should help him fit in with the
other students also.

There were a couple of wrinkles. If he were associated with
Ambler, this would have a chilling effect on the conversations.
For John to become part of the student body, his role would
need to be kept secret. The idea would be to send him on to
the campus undercover, in the manner of confidential inform-
ants used by the police. For this he'd need Barnes.

Ambler would agree to let Barnes in on what he found out,
except when there was reason not to. In exchange, Barnes
would enroll John as a student through some kind of back-door

procedure. John would get an assumed name and false credentials. Ambler knew from experience that colleges had let undercover cops secretly enroll in order to spy on anti-war protestors and other radicals back in his college days, so he knew it could be done. But he'd need to approach this delicately. He needed Barnes's help. But he didn't fully trust the college president – and he'd bet Barnes didn't trust him either.

In the morning, he called the college and told Barnes he was willing to make an arrangement. Ambler would report on what he found out. 'Your end of the deal is to arrange for someone working with me to be on campus. You'd need to create a pathway for him to enroll in classes. But I don't want anyone to know his connection to me or his identity.'

This took some effort for Barnes to swallow, but eventually he agreed. John would get a student ID. No one in the faculty or administration would know his real identity. John bore a resemblance to Ambler but they would need to be standing beside each other for anyone to see it. They would keep their distance from one another on campus, and only talk when they were home.

Ambler suggested John ask a couple of professors, including Doug Stuart and Sarah Hastings, if he could sit in on one of their classes, telling them he was making up his mind on his major. The student population was small, but large enough for him to have been on campus without either of them having run across him.

For his part, Ambler could only afford an afternoon or two a week away from his crime fiction collection to spend with the Trinity collection, so he could drag the project out for a couple of weeks if he needed to. Dragging out the project might not be so easy because his student assistant, Rebecca Dawson, was as hardworking and efficient as Sarah had told him she was. In addition to helping him straighten out the collection's catalog, she was putting the finding aids for the dozen or so collections of writers' papers in order and adding new ones.

When she wasn't working with him, attending her classes, studying, and taking care of her kids, she was organizing a student protest to oppose the sale of the crime fiction collection.

'I hope you don't mind,' she said, her pretty face wrinkled with concern, when Ambler asked her about the picket line in front of the administration building.

He didn't mind at all. The students should be complaining. He was glad the protestors understood the importance of preserving the books and papers of even somewhat obscure authors, because what they did was part of the culture. Of course, the books and papers would be preserved, at least for now, at the 42nd Street Library.

But the collection, singular and unique at Trinity College, would be rolled into his larger collection and part of its identity would be lost. He had his own continuing battle to keep the crime fiction collection from being rolled into the larger Manuscripts and Archives collection and losing *its* identity.

He and Rebecca were sitting beside each other at a table behind the stacks and chatting, work forgotten for a few moments, when the reading room door opened and Rebecca froze, her face going rigid with either fear or rage or possibly both. Ambler followed her gaze and watched a young man enter the room without knocking. He was slight of build, wore a sport coat and a dress shirt with an open collar; he was one of those men whose vanity was immediately apparent, handsome, well-dressed, no wrinkles, well-groomed, not a hair out of place, appearing eager to please, except in this instance his face was twisted with rage.

'Norman, are you crazy? What are you doing here?' Rebecca's voice shook.

Surprisingly, Norman turned his rage on Ambler, who watched him in disbelief. 'You're Abernathy.' This was a statement of fact rather than a question, even though the statement was incorrect. Ambler chose to watch him rather than correct him.

'I told you to stay away from my wife.' He clenched his fists at his side and tightened his body menacingly, though the stance didn't fit his slight build and unsteady voice. He stopped a few feet from Ambler and stood there uncertainly. Ambler had stood and sunk into a bow posture when the man came toward him but relaxed out of it after a moment when Rebecca screamed at the intruder.

'This isn't Professor Abernathy, you jerk!' She was furious and stood so quickly she knocked over the chair she'd been sitting in. 'Get out!' Her voice rose like a siren. 'Get out of here, you fool!'

When she screamed, something snapped him into action. He moved swiftly toward her, grabbed her wrist, and wrenched it, bending her almost in half and forcing her back against the table, practically to her knees. She cried out in pain.

Ambler took a step toward Norman and touched his shoulder. 'Let her go.'

The enraged husband shook off Ambler's hand and pulled on Rebecca's arm harder, bending her further toward the ground. Ambler sunk, spun, and heel-kicked him behind the knee, at the same time grabbing his arm and giving it a gentle tug in the direction he'd bent from the kick, putting him on the floor. He looked up at Ambler from a prone position, his features twisted with pain and confusion.

Free of her husband's grip, Rebecca burst into tears, put her hands to her face and ran out of the room. Norman continued to stare at Ambler like a frightened animal in a trap. For his part, Ambler had no interest in continuing the fight, but he did have some interest in the man on the floor and what he'd said.

'Manhandling your wife won't solve whatever problem you think you have with her.' He didn't know why he thought he should give advice to this irrationally jealous husband. Not that it was advice anyway – it was a rebuke.

Norman panted, his lip curled in a snarl. 'Don't you tell me how to handle my wife. It's none of your business.' He spat out the words as he pulled himself to his feet. He glared at Ambler for a moment, his fists clenched at his side, as if challenging Ambler to another round. Despite his pose, the irate husband didn't come across as much of a fighter, and he probably could tell Ambler wasn't looking for a fight so the stance was to save face. He continued to glare in Ambler's direction until the sound of voices outside the door reached them, and he turned and walked toward the door.

Ambler went back to the bookshelves he'd been searching through earlier in the afternoon. When he glanced up again, everything was quiet and Norman was gone. He stopped what he was doing, sat down at the table again, and thought about what had happened and what it meant.

Rebecca's husband was a weak man crazed by jealousy and his own insecurity. He accused the person he thought was Sam of paying too much attention to his wife. That could mean different things. The most salacious one would be he'd discovered Rebecca and Sam were having an affair – a teacher–student romance, *eros* notwithstanding.

Sarah had said Sam was a ladies' man. Students adored him, especially the girls . . . young women. Rebecca was devoted to him . . . Could the enraged cuckolded husband have . . .? But Rebecca's husband shooting George Olson didn't make much sense. Yet he'd attacked Ambler because he mistook Ambler for Sam. He could have mistaken Olson for Sam. Or Rebecca might have been having an affair with Olson and Sam.

This was going too far. Despite Rebecca's outraged husband and the salacious possibilities that brought to mind, the 'jealous husband shoots his wife's lover' was a bridge too far . . . The scenario might make for a bodice-ripping romantic suspense story, but it didn't make much sense for the murder at hand. Still, an angry and violent husband meant something, as did the possibility of a straying wife. But what? Sarah had said Sam did nothing inappropriate with his students. Or did she say, 'nothing very inappropriate'?

A new wrinkle. More embarrassing secrets laid bare. What was it about Rebecca that made him think he needed to know more about her? Was it the way she talked about Sam, her dreamy expression and a kind of intimacy when she spoke his name?

Did she talk about Sam as she would a person she were intimate with and cared deeply about, or did she care about him as her professor, her mentor, caring about him – in the Platonic sense of *eros*, not in the way of romantic love – because he was in trouble. Jealous husbands more often than not have ill-founded suspicions and are known for making disastrously wrong judgments.

Ambler told himself he was making too much of this because

he didn't have anything else to hang his hat on. Sam was Rebecca's professor; she was his student assistant. They worked closely together. She admired him. He was her mentor. Of course they were close. Her crazy husband's accusations didn't mean her relationship with Sam was anything other than innocent. Everyone who knew Sam was worried about him. Why shouldn't she be?

Yet the tenderness in her tone, the dreaminess in her expression . . . the accusation of her husband.

He'd need to talk to Sarah Hastings. Here we go again, he told himself, uprooting people's private lives, uncovering secrets they have every right to keep to themselves, exactly what he'd told David Levinson would happen. He should do as his grandson would tell him when he asked the boy too many questions: 'What are you doing?' he'd ask. 'Minding my own business,' Johnny would answer.

He called Sarah's office from the phone at the reference desk and left a message asking her to stop by the library that afternoon if she had a chance, wondering as he did if anyone in this era of emails and texts still checked their office phones for messages.

The archaic approach to messaging notwithstanding, she did stop by the stacks as he was getting ready to leave, coming toward him with a briefcase hanging from one shoulder by a long strap and a pocketbook hanging from the other, with an armload of papers pressed against her chest.

'The message light on my phone was blinking. That hasn't happened in ages. I thought it must be an emergency.'

Ambler laughed, embarrassed that he might be thought archaic himself. 'I didn't know your cell-phone number to text.' He told her about his encounter with Rebecca's husband.

She didn't show any surprise. 'Yes,' she said. 'Rebecca has a troubled marriage. She's in an abusive relationship and is terrified of her husband, has no one to turn to, and doesn't know how to get out of it. Strangely to you or me, she feels safer staying with him. She believes if she leaves him, he'll track her down and kill her.' She paused, wrinkling her forehead, narrowing her eyes. 'I shouldn't really be talking about her. But since this happened . . .'

Sarah had learned of Rebecca's predicament because Rebecca wrote a short story about an abusive marriage for Sarah's creative writing course. 'The story was so authentically chilling I was afraid for her and asked about it.' Sarah put her stack of papers and the rest of her accoutrements on the table and sat down. 'In a way, I wish I hadn't. She made me promise not to tell anyone, and then told me the horror story that was her life.

'Her husband is the sales director for a local bank; he's a deacon in their church, on the Board of the PTA, and coaches their daughter's soccer team. Everyone in their neighborhood in Westchester admires him, a model husband and father, a pillar of the community, and behind blind doors he bullies and beats his wife and children. She's trying to get out but she has to do it her way. You don't just get on the next bus out of town with two kids and no money.'

Ambler was certainly sympathetic, but sometimes he got wound up looking for the answers he was after, and being single-minded meant he could come across as callous, as he did this time. 'Her husband thought something was going on between her and Sam Abernathy, something romantic. Is that possible?'

Sarah sat back and stared at him, as if he'd suddenly exceeded the bounds of propriety, made an obscene remark . . . or worse.

He caught himself but too late. The small reading room felt like it had been turned into a frigid meat locker. 'I'm sorry. I feel like a heel asking . . .' He wasn't going to be able to explain the thinking that brought about the question, so he didn't try.

'Because her insanely jealous and controlling husband thinks something illicit is going on, you assume he's correct?' She paused for a long moment, not exactly glaring at him but her gaze was piercing.

When she spoke again, her tone was subdued. 'Students – young women especially, but young men, too – who have troubled existences, or something essential missing from their lives, more often than you might think become infatuated with their professors. They see their professor as brilliant, successful, on an exalted level far above them, yet the professor takes an interest in them, considers what they think or say or write significant or important in a way no one else ever had.

'Sam is the best kind of teacher. He values students, and this enables the student to value herself. For someone who's not respected, not valued in their life, it's easy to fantasize that the professor sees them in the same special way they see the professor.

'I was being flip when I said a few days ago that students adore Sam. They do, but for the right reasons. Great teachers inspire students to find more in themselves than they thought possible. They teach students to think and make judgments for themselves. It's amazing what developing this confidence in oneself can do for a person.'

Sarah was so animated and spoke with such passion, Ambler suspected she was describing the effect a professor had on her; thinking this, he wondered if that professor might have been Doug Stuart.

'So Rebecca might be enamored of Sam.' She met his gaze for a long moment. 'But Sam wouldn't take advantage of her vulnerability.'

You had to think Sarah knew what she was talking about. Yet Rebecca was in a disastrous marriage, a situation that might make her reach out to a man who had some standing and who might help her get out of that mess. She was an attractive woman. Ambler didn't know anything about Sam's domestic life. He hadn't thought to ask about it. He hadn't thought there was any reason to. Now he wasn't so sure.

Yet despite Sarah's faith in Sam's sense of decorum, it was also true that something can happen between a man and a woman that neither of them planned or even wanted. And that thing that happens can have a force of its own, stronger than either of their wills. They fall in love when everything around them says they shouldn't. He thought about saying this but didn't.

Instead he said, 'A romantic relationship between a professor and a student isn't necessarily exploitive, is it?'

Sarah's expression darkened; once more he'd said the wrong thing. But she got control of her irritation and spoke quietly.

'The power dynamic between a professor and a student is out of balance, with all the power on the professor's side. That kind of exploitation happened a lot years ago, especially in programs in the arts like mine. Too many young women were left bewildered and broken-hearted, devastated, by super-sensitive, handsome, charming poetic-type dilettantes with hearts of stone.' Her expression was plaintive and forlorn. You couldn't help but know she spoke from experience.

Her tone sharpened. 'These days, if a faculty member were discovered having an affair with a student, he'd be fired.'

TEN

Instead of going right home, early that evening Ambler paid a visit to the widow of George Olson. The Olson residence – a three-story, brick, semi-attached house that resembled a row house but missing the rest of the row – was only a few blocks from the campus.

The street was tidy, modest single-family houses with an assortment of sidings, a few three- or four-story apartment buildings about as wide as they were tall, running perpendicular to Woodlawn's main drag, Katonah Avenue. The houses and the street had the down-to-earth feel of a well-tended, no-frills, longstanding working-class neighborhood.

Mrs Olson wore a widow's black dress of many layers. She met Ambler's gaze with red-rimmed, tired eyes. It appeared she'd been receiving visitors all day and had become inured to receiving condolences. Taking Ambler for one more mourner, she wasn't surprised he dropped by until he told her the nature of his visit.

He did offer his condolences as well, telling her he'd met George only briefly in Sam Abernathy's office. He got the impression from that encounter, he told her, that George and Sam were longtime friends, despite their disagreement of the moment.

He asked if she knew Sam was a suspect in her husband's murder?

She did but she didn't know why.

Ambler told her it was because of circumstantial evidence, and because the police had been told George and Sam had argued rather heatedly not long before the murder.

'I honestly don't know what to think about Sam. He came by soon after the news of the shooting, one of the first to do so, to tell me how sorry he was that we'd lost George. I would have expected him to be among the first to call . . . if I could have expected in my wildest dreams George would be murdered. I still can't believe it.'

They'd been speaking in the hallway, and after a moment she invited him in and they sat in a small sitting room off the living room that might actually have been a parlor. She offered him tea but he declined.

'There were tears in Sam's eyes as we talked.' She sighed and gazed past Ambler for a moment, her own dark eyes liquid. 'I'd no more expected George to be shot and killed and Sam to be suspected of his murder than I'd expect to see Martians walking along Katonah Avenue.'

Ambler didn't need to ask her if she knew who might have killed George. She'd pretty much answered that question. He did want to ask if she believed Sam had killed her husband. 'Sam and George were not only friends, they were good friends?' He said this in the form of a question.

They were good friends, she assured him, and the Olsons and the Abernathys, both childless couples, had socialized for years – concerts and plays in the city, dinner in the neighborhood every month or so, an Italian dinner on Arthur Avenue a few times a year.

She and Eleanor Abernathy were not friends in the way George and Sam were, she said. The two men hung out like teenagers, golfing in Van Cortland Park, taking in a ball game at Yankee Stadium a few times a year, watching football and baseball on television in George's den on weekends.

Ambler caught a kind of distaste in Mrs Olson's tone when she spoke of Eleanor Abernathy, as opposed to fondness when she talked about the men, so he told her he'd known Sam for quite a while but had never met his wife and wondered what she was like.

Mrs Olson – whose given name was Agnes and who'd grown up in Woodlawn and never left, living at home while she attended the college of Mount St Vincent on the other side of Van Cortland Park in Riverdale for her degree in social work – took her time answering and chose her words carefully, as if she might say something unseemly if she wasn't careful.

'Eleanor is a difficult woman. We've been friends – I guess you'd call it – for more than twenty years. But I couldn't tell you a thing about her – nothing about her job, her family, what she did when she wasn't with us. She's never said anything to me that was more than a pleasantry or the kind of banal comment you'd make to a stranger on an elevator.'

'That strikes me as strange,' Ambler said. 'Sam is such a gregarious guy.'

Mrs Olson nodded. 'They truly are the odd couple.' She hesitated. 'This may be a strange thing to say. But as far as I knew, over the years, she didn't have any more to say to Sam than she did to anyone else.

'George and I might not have been the most romantic couple in the world. But to see Sam and Eleanor together, you'd think they were strangers, with nothing in common, forced to spend time together. When we went out for dinner, she'd sit there like a child who'd been dragged along to an occasion she had no interest in and was bored and impatient for it to be over.'

Agnes's eyes opened wider in a way that suggested she'd right that moment made a discovery. 'You know. I'd never said that about Eleanor before, or even thought it, until you asked the question . . . I don't think theirs is a very happy marriage. It's not for me to say, and I shouldn't be saying it . . . but now that I'm a widow I don't have anyone's standards to live up to but my own.'

Her expression was stern. 'Isn't there a term for people who don't show normal feelings? Eleanor spoke to me about George's death. She tried to commiserate but she sounded as if I'd told her he was taking a nap. I didn't feel any sympathy from her at all . . . a supposed friend for more than twenty years.'

When Ambler got downtown after visiting Mrs Olson, he stopped by the Library Tavern. John and Johnny had gone to the movies and Adele was visiting a friend in Brooklyn, so he'd have dinner out. Since Adele's pregnancy, she'd begun spending time with a friend from her youth who was married with children and lived in Flatbush – that and reading a basketfull of books about motherhood. She also had a stack of books on fatherhood for Ambler.

After ordering a burger and a beer, he told McNulty what he'd been up to. 'I don't suppose you could find out if Sam Abernathy was having an affair with his student aide.'

McNulty finished wiping the bar in front of Ambler. 'My

guess is if you're a professor having an affair with a student, you'd want to keep it under your hat.'

'My guess, too. Yet you've told me often enough people sometimes let things slip after a couple of drinks. They rely on the discretion of the bartender not to bandy about what they've been told.'

McNulty's eyebrows spiked. 'You're suggesting I violate the bartender's hypocritical oath?'

'Hippocratic.'

'Hypocritical.' McNulty was emphatic.

'I'm asking—'

McNulty held up his hands. 'You can ask him yourself. He should be in any minute.'

'He's not supposed to . . .' Ambler started to complain, but realized McNulty wasn't to blame. Sam was the problem. Sure enough, before Ambler had finished his beer, he came through the door.

'What the hell are you doing here?' Ambler interrupted Sam's jovial greeting.

Sam's hail-fellow-well-met expression crumbled. 'What's the matter?'

'A number of things.' Ambler took a deep breath. 'First, when the police charge you, which should be soon, you'll be a fugitive from justice. If they ask me where you are, I'll have to tell them if I know. That's why I told you I didn't want to know.'

'I didn't expect you to be here,' he said morosely, and then acted so contrite Ambler felt sorry for him. He'd probably been spending his nights on McNulty's fold-out couch and had come to depend on the bartender like an adopted pup would.

Needing to take his annoyance out on someone, he said to Sam, loud enough for the bartender to hear, 'McNulty should know better.'

The bartender sauntered over. 'You can say you don't know. How does anyone know what you know? They can't see inside your head.'

'I'm not a good liar. Suppose Mike asks me . . . I'm supposed to lie to him?'

The argument went a few more rounds, and in the end Sam agreed to not be in any place – such as the Library Tavern – where Ambler might run into him. McNulty would make sure he didn't tell Ambler where Sam was hiding out. Agreement reached, Ambler went on to item two.

'Rebecca Dawson?'

Sam stiffened, tightening his grip on his beer mug; he met Ambler's gaze but couldn't hold it. 'What about her?'

'That's what I want to know.'

'She's my student, one of the best.' He sneaked a quick glance at Ambler from under his eyebrows. 'She has a work-study job as a student aide and helps with the collection. I'm glad you met her. She can help with anything you need to know.'

Ambler told him of the incident with her husband.

'The poor kid.' Sam stared at his beer. Ambler thought he would say more, but he didn't.

'Why would he tell you to stay away from his wife?' Ambler had assumed a prosecutorial tone.

Sam tried to sound offhanded. 'He's a nut job. Who knows what he was talking about? He's a bully. Last semester, he showed up outside one of her classes and punched a male student he thought was getting too close to her. He's been barred from the campus, so I don't know what he was doing there.'

Again Ambler thought Sam would say more. When he didn't, Ambler asked, 'Nothing going on between you and Rebecca? She gets starry-eyed when she talks about you. She's very concerned, more worried than I'd expect a student to be about a professor.'

Sam took a swallow of beer; his hand holding the glass was steady. 'I'm very fond of her. I saw potential in her she didn't see in herself. When she first took my class, she had no confidence. Now she's a top student.'

Sam shifted to his professorial voice. 'The young woman's had a difficult life, made mistakes – her husband being the biggest one. He doesn't want her in college. I encouraged her to keep on with her education, no matter what he said; not without reason, she's very bright. No telling what she might become if given a chance . . . if she can get her life in order, get out from under that asshole.'

Ambler repeated his question. 'Why does her husband want you to stay away from her?'

'First I've heard of it,' Sam muttered as if to himself. 'What should happen is she should stay away from him.'

He turned to face Ambler. 'I hope you don't think I've done anything inappropriate. I've taught college for close to thirty years. No one has ever suggested anything like that.' He was quiet for a moment. 'Perhaps I should call her and tell her I'm OK.'

'You absolutely shouldn't call her, or see her, unless you want to have her lying to the police about being in contact with you.'

'Perhaps you could tell—'

'I'm not going to tell her I saw you because I'm not supposed to know where you are.'

Sam mumbled some sort of agreement.

Ambler wasn't totally satisfied but he moved on. 'What was your angry argument with George Olson about?'

Sam looked puzzled. 'What argument? George and I have been friends since I started at Trinity back in the Dark Ages; we've had dozens of arguments over the years. You know we were at odds over the senate election about his siding with Doug Stuart.'

He paused, his expression downcast. 'I was disappointed George would stand by and do nothing when the college tried to sell the Mystery Writers collection. And disappointed he wasn't on my side in the senate race. I was sad – I felt betrayed – so those disagreements might have put a dent in our friendship; I was sad and disappointed, not angry. Who said there was an argument?'

'You did, for one. David Levinson said you told him George Olson tried to blackmail you. Barnes already knew about that argument, too.'

Sam's interest spiked. 'You talked to Barnes? What did he say?'

'Let's go back to the blackmail.'

Sam grimaced. 'That's not something I want to talk about.

I was being hyperbolic. I told you George and I sometimes argued. I might have called him a traitor, a betrayer, a flunky for Stuart.

'He knows things about me – minor indiscretions – that I wouldn't want bandied about. I know things about him, too. If I was going to kill him, I'd have done it years ago when I found him skinny-dipping with my wife.'

Ambler glanced away. Once again, he'd yanked a skeleton out of someone's closet, learned something he had no business knowing about. Sam's smirk didn't help. But now that he knew about it, he couldn't *not* know it, so he was curious because this didn't sound like the Mrs Abernathy that Agnes Olson had described.

Like other scholars Ambler knew, Sam spent his life with his head buried in a book or else rummaging around in his own full-of-ideas head. A true absent-minded professor, he was good natured and easygoing but oblivious. Lost in his own thoughts, he was more self-absorbed than other men might be, so could be a difficult man to be married to. Someone who might end up with a bored and restless wife.

Sam interrupted Ambler's reverie. 'I asked what Barnes had to say.'

'Nothing helpful.' Ambler decided he wouldn't tell Sam about his son's undercover operation, or his information-sharing agreement with Barnes. 'He'd heard that you were a suspect but he's willing to be convinced you aren't the killer. Mainly, I got that his biggest worries were the college's reputation and keeping himself in the good graces of the Board of Trustees, the alumni and the donors.'

'That would be Barnes, all right. He cares more about how things look than how things are.'

Ambler waited a moment before he said, 'I've been thinking one possibility is that an unstable, aggrieved student shot Olson.'

Sam spoke thoughtfully. 'It's possible. For years, the idea of a professor being killed by a student never entered my mind. Such things happened, I guess, but were so rare, you thought of them like you might think of being hit by lightning.

'These days, the possibility you might be shot and killed by some maniac can hit you anywhere – the grocery store, shopping mall or your classroom. College students feel more pressure, have more stress than the average person might think. The sciences in particular are stressful – the courses are difficult or, to be precise, rigid. You can't fake your way through them. George's "Intro to Biology" has a high failure rate. He was a caring teacher but a tough grader. A lot of students felt he was unfair.

'Most of our students come from working-class families. They've got loans and not much in the way of second chances if they flunk out. Pressure gets to people. What you suggest is not implausible. But I don't have anyone in mind.'

Ambler asked if he knew of any students who might fit the profile – stressed-out, failing, possibly deranged.

Sam didn't know of anyone.

'George never told you he was worried about a student, or a student threatened him?'

Sam shook his head.

'I ran across a couple of older students, maybe military veterans. One was named Walt. Does that mean anything to you?'

'No. What about him?'

'Nothing much. I watched him and a buddy bully some younger kids. That doesn't mean much. They don't fit the profile of the aggrieved, deranged loner. He and the guy he was with dressed and carried themselves like you'd imagine right-wing, anti-government, militia types would . . . That part is pure prejudice on my part. Stereotyping, I'd have to admit.'

Sam nodded. 'I'm amazed every semester by how often I initially misjudge some of my students by how they dress or sound. We're told to report unusual or threatening behavior to the counseling center, confidentially report any students we're worried about. You could ask someone in counseling, though they're not likely to tell you anything. Everything they do is hush-hush – student privacy. They keep secrets better than the CIA.'

ELEVEN

The next morning, Ambler called in to work and took the day off. His plan was to spend the day at Trinity, finish as much as he could of the assessment of the collection, and leave the investigation, such as it was, to John for a few days. He'd wait and see what John turned up while he did his own work back at the 42nd Street Library. If John came across anything interesting, they could talk about it in the evenings.

He spent the morning in the claustrophobic reading room, making sure the books listed in the database Rebecca Dawson had created existed on the shelves, and determining what condition they were in. A good few books were misplaced on the shelves, and a dozen or so were missing altogether; at least they weren't on any of the mystery fiction shelves. The fact that the missing books in each case were first editions – and could be quite valuable if they were in good condition and still had their dust jackets – gave him pause. He'd need to ask Sam about them.

Rebecca showed up on schedule in the early afternoon after her classes. Her expression was stoic and, after a perfunctory greeting, she buried her face in the computer. He didn't know what she was doing and didn't ask. She was clearly embarrassed by her husband's behavior the day before and didn't want to talk about it, or talk at all.

He wanted to say something to help her relax, but he didn't know how to begin. When he asked if she was doing OK, she looked at him vacant-eyed, nodded, and went back to her computer. He could easily break the ice if he told her he'd seen Sam, but he couldn't do that. It would be a bad idea to even mention Sam's name, given what happened, and it would be a bad idea for anyone to know he was in contact with Sam.

After the first few moments of chilly and uncomfortable

silence, he told her about the missing books and asked if they might be in the library's circulating collection.

She didn't know. 'Some of the professors come in and take books from the reading room. Sarah . . .' She corrected herself. 'Professor Hastings takes out books a lot. She says not to tell anyone she's reading mysteries, but I think she's joking when she says that. Scholarly professors aren't supposed to read mysteries, she told me.'

'These books are first editions and might be valuable. Did Professor Abernathy have a display case or locked bookcase where he kept valuable books?'

'Not that I know of. I remember he was worried about not finding some books that should have been on the shelves. We tried to track them down but we still haven't found them.'

Ambler decided one way to get Rebecca to relax was to pretend the incident with her husband never happened, ignore it completely. Reluctantly, he decided to talk about the work, forget about the husband – and Sam – for the time being.

The bright side of this approach was the work went faster and smoother. Things began to fall into place.

Rebecca told him one of the professors took it upon herself to re-shelve the series under Amanda Cross's real name, Carolyn Gold Heilbrun. She studied Ambler's face for a moment. 'I guess I can tell you; it was Professor Hastings. She told me Carolyn Heilbrun kept her real identity secret because she was trying to get tenure at an Ivy League college, and she wouldn't have gotten it if her male colleagues found out she wrote mysteries.'

'I remember that. She was the first woman to get tenure in the English department at Columbia,' Ambler said. 'This was in the Sixties. She earned tenure as a scholar, not as a mystery writer.' He held up the book. 'This was her second mystery.'

He examined more of the books shelved under 'Heilbrun'. 'I wonder if Sam has a copy of her first book. *In the Last Analysis* was nominated for an Edgar Award for first novel. She was afraid that if the book won, her identity would be revealed and she wouldn't get tenure. Then, in 1970, one of her readers discovered Amanda Cross was Carolyn Heilbrun, and her cover was blown. But she got tenure anyway in 1971.'

Rebecca nodded enthusiastically. 'Women like her had to fight so hard for everything. To get a place in a man's world. They made it easier for professors like Sarah . . . and I guess women like me.' Rebecca sounded wistful. 'But sometimes it doesn't feel so easy.'

Around three, Ambler decided to go to the student union for a late lunch. Deep in thought, he walked across the campus quad, the central common with intersecting walks connecting the buildings. The newer buildings were mostly three- or four-story brick, sterile, practical-looking structures used for classrooms and faculty offices. Through the gaps between the building, he could see taller dormitories and an oddly shaped monstrosity he took to be a gym.

Out of nowhere he felt a sharp, stinging pain in his left shoulder, as if someone had stabbed him with a hot poker – and knew immediately he'd been shot. Though he'd never been shot, never really had the pain of being shot described to him, he knew without doubt this was what happened. He spun around – partially because his body lurched toward the pain – his glance darting every which way, looking for he didn't know what.

What he saw was students wearing backpacks, walking singly, in couples, and groups of three or four, headed toward the various buildings, passing one another on the walks – swarms of them, like ants when their anthill had been kicked over.

Incredibly, no one stopped, no one noticed him. No one knew he'd been shot. As far as he could tell, no one else had been shot either. With a rising sense of panic, he realized he might be shot again, or that the bullet that hit him might kill him.

He hadn't heard the shot that hit him, and more shots could be coming at him now that he couldn't hear. He thought he should run, dodge, but he couldn't get himself moving. He thought the shooter might be coming for him. He thought he should shout, too. Warn the students about the shooter. He should yell for help. He should tell everyone he'd been shot.

He could think these things. But his mind couldn't get his body to act on them. Did he not want to bother people with his problems when they had their own business to take care of? Was he embarrassed because he'd gotten himself shot when no one else had? Was he afraid to cause a scene, make himself the center of attention? His heart beat loud enough he was surprised no one heard it. Now, he began to feel unstable, uncertain of his steps, light-headed. He was standing still, he realized, when everyone else was walking.

And then he heard a panicked voice: 'Hey mister, you're bleeding!' Another voice, or maybe it was the same one, a male voice, 'Sir, are you OK? . . . You're bleeding down your back?' After this, he heard a cacophony of voices. Another man's voice said distinctly, 'He's been shot!'

Someone else, this time, touched his uninjured arm, standing in front of him, a pretty, dark-skinned girl, her hair pulled tight against her forehead. 'Sir, I think you've been shot. You need to come over here and sit down.'

Talking to him like she was the kindergarten teacher and he was a shy kid, she led him toward the student union, talking nonsense as they walked— 'Right this way;' 'You'll feel better if you sit down;' 'We're going to get someone to help you;' 'You'll be fine in no time.'

An extremely self-possessed young woman, he thought to himself. A marvelous group of students; everyone so compassionate, no one panicking, except him. He tried to say something like this to the young woman, how remarkable all these young people were and how the older generation should stop criticizing them. But she'd already decided he was a half-wit and didn't pay any attention to him.

When he was seated on a bench, the fog in his brain began to clear, and he got her attention. 'I think it would be best to get everyone away from this area.' He met her wide-eyed gaze. 'I don't want anyone else shot. The shooter might not be finished. Has someone called the police?'

'Yes sir. We have. And an ambulance for you. You're bleeding a lot and none of us know what to do about that. I'm a nursing student, but I've only just started. I haven't even taken anyone's temperature yet.'

He smiled and wanted to kiss her on her forehead. 'My guess is if someone could find a towel or something like that and press it against the bullet hole, that might slow the bleeding a bit,' he said.

She cocked her head and looked at him with new respect. In a couple of minutes, a white towel appeared. She turned him around, bent him forward, and pressed the towel against his shoulder. 'Do you want to lie down? You could lean over on the bench.'

'I'm OK,' he said, though he did want to lie down. 'I still think everyone should get out of this area. Whoever shot me might start shooting again.'

'Security's clearing the quad now. They're pushing everyone inside the buildings.'

Ambler heard sirens faint in the distance, getting louder. Pretty soon, the college common was overrun with emergency vehicles. A team of EMS technicians gathered around Ambler, checking his vitals, hooking him up to an IV. No one asked him about the shooting. One of the EMTs, a young Black woman matter-of-factly going about her work, asked if he'd been hit anywhere but the shoulder and if he felt light-headed.

He told her he'd only been shot once and didn't know about light-headed but would try to stand to see how that worked.

'Let's use a stretcher,' she said.

He didn't argue.

When they had him up on the stretcher, she grasped his uninjured shoulder and held it for a moment. 'You're going to be fine.' She gave the shoulder a squeeze.

TWELVE

His son picked him up at the hospital that night, meeting him in the ER, pushing the wheelchair to the taxi he had waiting at the ER door of Jacobi Hospital.

John was sullen and angry, a mood Ambler had witnessed a few times on his prison visits. His son had never been a tough guy, not a gangbanger, not a criminal. He smoked pot and partied too much like too many musicians. His prison sentence was because of a senseless drunken fight, during which he wrestled for a gun his roommate pulled on him; the gun went off and killed the roommate.

During the prison visits, John had often been angry; more than once he'd alluded to happenings behind the blank grey walls and steel bars that he wouldn't tell his father about. Ambler knew prisons seethed with violence, that men John knew in prison had been killed there, that life was lived on the edge. Since his release, John had rarely spoken about his time behind bars, and Ambler hadn't asked about it.

'Chicken-shit bastard,' John said. 'He shot you because you were going to track him down. Hiding in the shadows and running away like a pussy.'

Ambler didn't like John's tough-guy talk; it made Ambler feel as if his son were a stranger. Then again, his son was almost a stranger, Ambler having left him to his mother's inept and negligent care when he was a boy.

'If I find the bastard, I'll show him how tough he is.' John went on like this for a while, working out his frustration and anger, his tone pugnacious and threatening, so much so that Ambler tried to rein him in.

'I know you're concerned about me.' He held his son's gaze. 'You don't know how happy that makes me that you care . . . and how undeserving I feel. I've got a lot to make up to you.' He smiled. 'And I can't do that if you're back in prison. And there's Johnny . . .' He didn't finish the thought when he saw the effect mentioning the boy's name had.

'David's paying you to gather information, not to take matters into your own hands. If we find out anything useful, it goes to him and, if he says so, to the police. No one wants you to fix this yourself.'

John's tone softened. 'How bad is it?' He'd noticed his father's grimace of pain.

'They said I was lucky.' Ambler tilted his head toward the wounded shoulder and arm now in a sling. 'The bullet that hit me wasn't very big – 150 grain. I don't know what that means but I guess it's a smaller caliber.'

John shrugged. 'A bullet doesn't have to be big to kill someone.'

His son should know. The bullet that killed his roommate was from a small-caliber handgun, yet big enough to send John to jail for many years.

Ambler was quiet, half-dozing for the rest of the ride, and startled when the cab pulled up in front of Adele's apartment. It took him a moment to register where he was. He bent to look out the cab window at the familiar building. 'What are we doing here?'

'Adele said she wanted you to stay at her apartment, so she could take care of you. I figured she knew best.'

John helped him into the building and rode up in the elevator with him, carrying a small suitcase. 'I brought some stuff and a change of clothes. She said you had toiletries and stuff here already.' He left the suitcase in the hallway and got back on the elevator when he saw Adele coming toward them.

She was scowling, coming at them rapidly, her eyes wide with worry and dismay. 'I knew this would happen someday,' she scolded before she reached them.

Ambler stared at her. He didn't think he should be faulted for getting shot but he kept quiet. She came into his arms, pressed herself against him and rubbed her tears into his chest.

'I'm OK,' he said after a moment, brushing her hair with his good hand.

'You're not OK,' she said.

A while later, after he'd eaten a bowl of spaghetti and

meatballs – he was lucky the wound was to his left shoulder – and drunk a glass of wine, she tried to prop him up in her bed. The process was awkward because his arm was in a sling and his shoulder hurt every time he moved and also because her protruding midsection got in the way, making her clumsy. When he was more or less splayed out across the sheets, she came to the other side of the bed and hoisted herself in beside him.

As they talked and he told her what he remembered of being shot, he realized, fully realized for the first time, that he'd missed dying by a matter of an inch or so. Adele didn't say anything more about her fear that he'd get himself killed trying to track down murderers. She'd hinted before that she worried about him, but this time he realized her fear wasn't new; she'd been afraid for some time.

She wouldn't lecture him. Fiercely independent herself, she wouldn't try to substitute her will for his, and she demanded the same respect from him. She could bring up his responsibility toward the soon-to-arrive baby, but she wouldn't do this either. It was her idea to get pregnant and for him to be the father of her baby. She told him at the time she'd raise the baby and expected no help from him.

Of course, he did feel responsible for the baby, and he had his grandson to think of, too, though this was less of a worry now that Johnny's father was out of jail – and stayed out of jail.

The police had finally gotten around to talking to Ambler after the shooting. A detective from the Bronx Homicide Squad interviewed him in the ER when the trauma team had finished their work.

The detective introduced himself as Detective Jenkins, a deeply dark-skinned man with broad shoulders and a massive chest; a formidable presence, though he spoke softly. He introduced himself formally and spoke formally, calling Ambler, 'sir', made no small talk, no jokes, no asides.

'What'd you see?' He met Ambler's gaze, as he did with each question.

'Nothing meaningful. Kids . . . Students walking to and from class, the grass starting to turn green, buds forming on the trees and shrubs, some crocuses blooming and daffodils popping up around the common.'

He didn't know why he'd described the landscape, which had no bearing on anything, and attributed his doing so to the pain meds and anesthetic the trauma team gave him when they dug out the bullet and cleaned and dressed his wound.

The detective asked again what he saw, what he heard, if he had any idea who shot him, if anyone had threatened him.

'I assume it's connected to the earlier shooting, the murder of George Olson,' Ambler said during a pause.

Detective Jenkins raised his eyebrows. 'Why would you say that?'

Ambler thought it was obvious, so he shrugged with his good shoulder.

'Were you a friend of the earlier victim?'

'Not really. I'd met him . . . I'm a friend of a friend of his, Sam Abernathy.'

The detective thought about this for a moment. His expression changed slightly, his eyes brighter, so maybe he'd gotten more interested. 'You and the victim and Abernathy had some dealings together? You want to tell me about that?'

'I could. But I don't think it has anything to do with my getting shot.'

Jenkins scrutinized his face. 'You said you didn't know who shot at you or why. Are you telling me now you do know?'

'I was thinking it might be a student or a former student with a grudge.' He felt himself losing ground in the conversation and again he thought he might not be thinking straight because of the medications. 'It's happened before.' Saying this wouldn't help, he knew, but he had to say something.

As he suspected, Detective Jenkins wasn't impressed. 'I'm looking for a connection, if that's what you're asking. What makes you think a student shot you? You're not a teacher, are you?'

'I'm guessing the aggrieved student or former student who shot Professor Olson shot me. I don't know why. He might have mixed me up with someone else. It's happened before.' Ambler knew his answer was lame. But he didn't want to tell Jenkins he'd been investigating Olson's murder and was most likely shot by the murderer who didn't want him investigating. Bringing this up would open a whole can of worms he didn't feel up to reckoning with at the moment. Jenkins didn't strike him as someone to discuss theories of investigation with.

'And that's why you think an angry student shot at you, because it's happened before?'

Ambler withered under the detective's penetrating stare. The stare wasn't angry or hostile; it was questioning, asking for clarity when Ambler didn't have any more answers to give.

After a moment of silence, Jenkins asked him again about Abernathy and George Olson. Ambler's explanation, which began with the phone call from the college president's office, rambled on long enough for Jenkins's eyes to glaze over. He put away his notebook before Ambler was anywhere near finished, looked at his watch, and began fidgeting with his cell phone.

When Ambler paused for a moment, Jenkins stood up abruptly and interrupted him. 'Do you by any chance know where this Abernathy is at the moment?'

Ambler said no.

'Talk to him lately?'

Ambler said no again, sure that the detective knew he was lying.

Jenkins gave him a final withering glance. 'If we need anything else, we'll call you. You can drop by the precinct tomorrow when you feel up to it and we'll have a stenographer take a statement.'

He handed Ambler his card. 'In the meanwhile, don't go walking around the college campus.' He paused for emphasis. 'You need to be alert wherever you are. Keep your doors locked. Stay out of dark alleys and off deserted streets. We have no reason to think the shooting was random. It's entirely possible someone meant to kill you, it was personal, and they'll try again.'

Ambler fell asleep before he'd finished telling Adele everything he'd meant to tell her. He'd gotten drowsy from the pain pill he'd taken, and for all he could remember might have fallen asleep in the middle of a sentence. He'd awakened a few times during the night when he moved the wrong way, which sent a shooting pain through his shoulder. He was aware of Adele in the bed with him; he was comforted by her being there but didn't reach for her.

When he next woke up, it was morning. He heard her in the kitchen and smelled something she was cooking that excited his senses; he felt more alive than he had.

After breakfast – oatmeal soufflé, a recipe she'd inherited from her mother – and despite Adele's protests, Ambler went to work. When he got there, Harry was waiting at the door to the crime fiction reading room, holding a copy of the *Daily News,* which he began waving like a semaphore flag as Ambler got closer.

'Have you seen this?' Harry hollered as soon as Ambler was in hailing distance, which was quite a way down the hallway.

Not wanting to take part in a shouting match, he didn't answer until he was closer. 'No,' he said when he was near enough to use a normal voice.

'Well, everyone else in the library has, including President Ledyard. I have a meeting in the director's office in an hour.'

The headline was something that would get Ledyard's attention: *42nd Street Library's Amateur Detective Wounded in Bronx Shooting.* The story, only a couple of column inches, was buried deep in the paper around page twelve, but not so deep the library's communications department couldn't ferret it out.

'It's not my fault. You and the greedy administration mucky-mucks sent me to Trinity College in the first place. I didn't even want the collection.'

'No one knew someone would be murdered. No one told you to get shot.' Harry hated controversy – his literary hero was Ferdinand the Bull – so when discord arose, he panicked. That Ambler was the source of more discord than the rest of his staff put together was not lost on Harry.

'Calm down, Harry. If I shot someone, the rulers of the library would have something to complain about. I'm the victim here. I should be lying in a hospital bed . . . Instead – a loyal employee, knowing the library is underfunded and understaffed, I come into work. I should get a commendation not a rebuke.'

'Try telling that to the director . . . or the president—'

'No, Harry, *you* tell them that at your meeting this morning.'

Harry's eyes widened. 'I can't tell them that . . .'

Ambler chuckled. 'I'm kidding . . . You don't have to tell them I deserve a medal.'

Harry thought this over. 'I guess I can tell them it wasn't your fault.' His tone was beseeching. 'It wasn't, was it?' And then, plaintively, 'And it won't happen again, will it?'

'I certainly hope not.'

For all he accomplished that day, he might as well have stayed at home. The Antiquarian Booksellers' conference was coming up at the end of the month, so he registered for that. Something to look forward to. And with luck, the murder of George Olson would be solved by then, with Sam Abernathy exonerated and no one else injured or killed in the process of solving the crime.

He spent the rest of the day digging – awkwardly, with one good arm – through boxes of papers from a literary agent who represented dozens of mystery writers. His clients published mostly in paperback, and the papers consisted mainly of letters from the agent, to and from his authors, and to and from editors at Dell, Pocket Books, Ace, Bantam, and such. The work was pretty tedious, but it kept his mind off the pain in his shoulder and kept him from thinking too much about who might have shot him.

Adele met him at the end of the workday, and he persuaded her to go to the Library Tavern for the hamburger special instead of making him dinner. McNulty noticed his injury but didn't say anything about it until they'd finished eating and the after-work crowd had thinned out enough for him to stop and chat.

'I was shot once, a long time ago, in the leg,' McNulty told them. 'Then it got infected because I didn't change the bandage when I was supposed to.' He turned to Adele. 'Make sure he changes the bandages.'

'How'd you get shot?' Adele asked.

McNulty waved off the question. 'It's a long story.'[1] He nodded toward Ambler. 'How'd he get shot?'

---

[1] The long story is *What Goes Around Comes Around: a Bartender Brian McNulty Mystery* (St Martin's Minotaur, 2005).

Ambler told him what happened. 'Do you know where Sam was yesterday afternoon?' He didn't really suspect Sam, but you have to be sure.

'I'm not supposed to tell you where he is or was, but he was nowhere near Woodlawn. I wouldn't be surprised if he never went back. He doesn't like it there.'

'Why wouldn't he like it there? He's a tenured professor at a liberal arts college. It's a great job. About to become obsolete but still . . .'

'I think it's his wife . . . He's mentioned her a few times in what you'd call unflattering ways. You'd think she was his jailer . . . or what's that bird gets hung around somebody's neck?'

'An albatross?' Adele ventured. 'Did he say that? . . . That's no way for a man to speak of his wife.'

'You don't know the wife. Some wives aren't so nice. I could tell you about my ex-wife but that would be an even longer story.'

Ambler thought about warning McNulty about the pitfalls of getting Adele started on the mistreatment of women. He didn't, because the bartender would ignore the warning. He made up his own mind about how to deal with any given situation.

He'd gone round and round with Adele before. Most women liked McNulty and, as he would say, he liked women both individually and collectively. This didn't change the fact that by his lights some women were less admirable than others. When Adele talked about the importance of electing a woman president, McNulty brought up Margaret Thatcher.

'The point is,' he told Adele this time around, 'some marriages are a trap that neither the husband nor the wife can figure how to get out of, so they drive each other nuts.'

Adele was in high dudgeon. 'If you were up on your Marx, you'd know marriage was devised so men could dominate women. When I was a child, my mother couldn't get a credit card without her husband's permission.'

'*The Origin of the Family, Private Property and the State*,' McNulty said. 'By Engels, after Marx died. Women were property handed over in a transaction between their father and their husband.' He winked at Ambler. 'When the state withers away, so will marriage. Sam just wants his marriage to wither away a bit sooner.'

'I wonder what Mrs Abernathy has to say about the marriage.'

Ambler had been thoughtful as he listened. 'I think I'm going to have to find out,' he said to no one in particular.

The following evening, John found Ambler in the crime fiction reading room. The library was open until 8:00, so he'd stayed to catch up on some work and to wait for Adele who was working the reference desk.

'That guy you told me about? Walt. It's Walt Nichols. I found out a few things about him. He's done time, for one thing. Trinity College has a reentry program for former offenders. A lot of colleges do. Nichols did his bid long enough ago that he's off parole, so he can do what he wants.

'Guys like him you gotta be careful with. He's smart; he's been around; he's come across snitches before. So you can't ask too many questions. Just sit around and listen. I get the feeling he's still in the life.'

Ambler listened in a kind of amazement. John sounded like a hybrid of McNulty, with his street smarts, and Mike Cosgrove, with his sixth sense of whom to ask what and when.

'He's got this group of wannabes around him – wannabe gangsters who don't have any idea what the life is like. This guy Walt, he's for real. I haven't seen a hard stare like that since I left the joint.'

Nichols was interesting but didn't fit the profile of someone who'd be up on a roof taking potshots at people. The person who did that would be a loner, someone with a grudge, not someone who wanted to make a living outside the law or, as John put it, was in 'the life'.

The ex-con might be someone the police would want to keep an eye on, and might be a threat to the college in some way if he was working a grift, but he wasn't likely to be the Trinity College of the Bronx sniper – and getting on his bad side might put John in danger.

Ambler told John this. 'The most likely person is a loner with some strange obsessions, maybe a fascination with guns, certainly a grievance. If you do it carefully you might ask about the murdered professor. It's possible someone in that group held a grudge against Professor Olson and fits the description – doesn't fit in, has a grievance, likes guns. If you come across someone like that, I can check with the administration to see if he took a class with George Olson.

'It's possible our pal Walt had a grudge against Olson. I doubt it. But I'll check. When you find out the names of his hangers-on, I can check those, too, especially if someone has a grudge. It doesn't have to be against Olson. Someone who thinks the world has done him wrong – an incel, maybe.'

John listened, nodding every now and again, neither agreeing nor disagreeing, absorbing. After a moment, he said, 'I could still find out about Nichols, what he's up to. Why not? I know a guy from the Bronx, an old head who I was tight with in the joint. He ran a crew in stir and he ran a crew when he was on the street.

'He got out a year or so before me and told me he was through with the life. His uncle owns a bodega in the South Bronx. When his bid was up, he was going to work for his uncle and maybe take over running the business so his uncle could retire. This guy made his chops when the gangbangers out there now were babies. He was a legend in that part of New York. Everybody in the Bronx knows him. If he wants to be left alone, they'll leave him alone. But he'll know what's going down. He's like a Puerto Rican godfather.'

After John left, Ambler wondered if he might not have made a mistake getting John involved in crime-solving so soon after getting released from prison. John needed to prove something to the world and to himself, an attitude that could easily get him in trouble.

THIRTEEN

McNulty didn't mind all that much having Sam around. The guy didn't make demands. The only problem was he talked too much. When they were in a room together – McNulty's living room, or dining room if it happened to be lunch or dinner time, which was also Abernathy's bedroom – Sam felt conversation was in order.

McNulty didn't see a need to talk, unless there was something to talk about, which wasn't usually the case. In particular, McNulty didn't want to talk in the morning, and morning was whenever McNulty woke up. He preferred silence until long after he ate breakfast, either at his dining-room table or at Tom's up the street, and read the newspaper. He had no interest in talking to anyone about what he read in the paper – and especially no interest in hearing about what someone else read in the newspaper. This was how Sam got on his nerves.

The guy maybe should have been a radio news announcer instead of a college professor, because he'd read something in the newspaper and then tell McNulty about it, something McNulty either didn't care about or had already read himself. That McNulty never responded, not even with a grunt, didn't bother Sam at all. This was why McNulty began getting up a little earlier than he preferred, telling Sam he was going for the paper, and sneaking off to Tom's, and when Sam caught on to that, hoofing it down to the greasy spoon at 100th Street, where Sam couldn't find him.

One afternoon on his day off, as McNulty was having a late lunch at one of his haunts at 108th and Broadway, he spied Sam hotfooting it down the street, taking a look over his shoulder every now and again, as a man does when he's up to no good. After Ray's visit to the bar the other night, McNulty wondered if his chatty roommate might be doing some sneaking out on his own. So he popped out of the saloon, leaving his Reuben half-eaten and his cup of Joe half-drunk, and followed him.

It was a long walk, more than McNulty had bargained for. But McNulty was a stubborn man. By the time Sam turned east on 79th Street, he'd given up looking over his shoulder, so McNulty picked up his pace and stayed close to him. Sam did take another quick glance before he opened the door of the Lucerne Hotel, but McNulty had guessed he might do that and took evasive action. After a moment, he watched through the window on the hotel's front door as the elevator door closed on Sam and went in and called Ray at the library.

Less than an hour later, Ray – broken wing and all – was sitting beside him in the lobby watching the elevator doors.

'Well,' said the bartender after another hour had passed. 'It's not what you'd call a quickie.'

Ray was nervous – and he was the guy who'd started this cloak-and-dagger stuff. 'I'm not sure I want to be seen,' Ray said.

'Maybe we could ask the clerk for a couple of potted palms,' McNulty chuckled. 'You're going to tell him you know what he's up to, so what difference does it make if you catch him *in flagrante delicto*? You won't have to beat around the bush and he won't embarrass himself getting caught in a lie.'

'It's the girl I'm worried about . . .'

'You wanna dance, you gotta pay the fiddler.'

Ray shot him a disapproving glance. 'Jesus, McNulty. She's young enough to be his daughter.'

'It's not the years, it's the miles,' McNulty continued in his philosophical vein.

Ray gave him another look.

McNulty brushed it off. 'Well, my work here is done. I left a half-eaten sandwich on a bar thirty blocks uptown. If I leave it there much longer, the bartender will eat it.'

'Take a cab,' Ray said, and handed him a ten.

McNulty looked at the bill disdainfully. 'I did you a favor. If you wanna start payin' me, it'll cost you more than that – a hundred a day plus expenses, I think is the going rate. Or maybe that was an old movie. In this case that's a Reuben sandwich and a cup of coffee.' He chuckled and cuffed Ray on his good shoulder. 'Keep your money. You'll need it. You got a baby coming.'

FOURTEEN

Not long after McNulty left, Sam – accompanied by Rebecca Dawson – stepped out of the elevator into the lobby. She had hooked her arm through his and was leaning against him, dreamily watching the world in front of her, a gentle smile on her lips, when her roving gaze met Ambler's. It took her a moment to react. When she did, she stopped dead and yanked her arm away from Sam's.

He turned toward her in surprise and then followed her dead stare to Ambler. His gaze locked on Ambler's. He whispered something to Rebecca, who stood with her head bowed like a prisoner in the dock. He then took her elbow and ushered her toward the door. When she left without looking back, he came toward Ambler, spitting fire.

'You son-of-a-bitch! What are you doing?' Sam came upon him so fast and came so close and shouted so loudly, Ambler thought he'd get bowled over. 'This is how you prove I'm innocent!?' His gaze fixed on Ambler's sling, as if he wanted to give the injured arm a good yank.

For some reason, probably because he knew Sam well enough, Ambler didn't feel threatened. 'If you'd been honest with me, told me what was going on, this scene wouldn't have happened. I don't want to get mixed up in your private life. I didn't want to embarrass Rebecca like this.'

Sam huffed and puffed for a moment longer, and then deflated as if Ambler had pulled a plug and let out the air puffing him up. 'You feel terrible? How do you think I feel? If her husband finds out, he'll beat the daylights out of her, if he doesn't kill her.' He sat down heavily in the chair McNulty had recently left and leaned his head into his hands.

Watching Sam in his misery, Ambler thought about how little we know of other people, even those we think we know well. He and Sam became friends because of their shared interest in crime fiction, more specifically and more importantly their shared interest in collecting crime fiction and doing their collecting for a library.

Many book collectors – if not most – collected in order to have something no one else had. They didn't collect to share – they might show their collection to a friend or to another collector, but they did this to provoke appreciation, if not envy. Collecting for a library was different. A library curator collected papers, memorabilia and books in order to make the stuff available to anybody who wanted to see it, or for researchers or writers to use it.

While Ambler had been waiting for Sam to emerge from what he fully expected was a tryst in the hotel, he'd concocted a scenario. Since Sam lied to him about Rebecca, he might well have lied about other things, including whether or not he killed George Olson.

To flesh out the scenario, Ambler created an explanation for the first editions missing from the New York Mystery Writers collection: they weren't misplaced or overdue. Sam had taken them and sold them to finance his illicit affair with Rebecca.

Taken as a whole, Ambler figured he'd developed an arguably plausible line of thinking that provided a motive for Sam to have killed George Olson and taken a potshot at Ambler himself. He wasn't convinced he was right, that the scenario could hold water. But he wasn't convinced he was wrong either.

So he'd try it out on Sam. Maybe it would lead Sam to admit he was a murderer. Stranger things had happened (but not any spontaneous confessions Ambler could think of at the moment, except perhaps on a TV show). If nothing else, hearing Ambler's perhaps far-fetched chronicle of events might convince Sam to stop making up stories and holding back information. If Sam would just be straightforward, they might come up with a way to get him out of the mess he was in.

Here goes, he told himself. He tried to put on the hard-assed, seen-it-all, no-quarter-given expression he'd seen Mike Cosgrove use a few times with a suspect, but figured he'd probably come up short. Looking at Sam huddled in his chair, his face buried in his hands, Ambler felt like he was kicking the man when he was down.

'George Olson threatened to expose your affair. That's what your argument – the blackmail you mentioned to Levinson – was about. The shame of exposure, the near certainty of losing your tenured sinecure might not have been enough reason for you to kill him. But exposing Rebecca to the rage of her deranged husband would be.'

Sam came halfway out of his chair, fire in his eyes. 'What are you talking about? You've lost your mind!' He stopped halfway between standing and sitting, staring at Ambler in amazement.

He didn't know if Sam was shocked because the accusation was so far-fetched, or stunned because Ambler had figured him out. He went ahead anyway. Play 'em like you got 'em.

'You got yourself into a situation there was no way out of. You could fool a lot of people. But you weren't sure you could fool me. So you put me in a pickle by coming to me for help, relying on our friendship to suck me in.

'But I got too close to everyone involved, including Rebecca. And when Rebecca's husband came around throwing out wild accusations that you knew I'd figure out weren't so wild after all, I became a threat to you but also to Rebecca . . .

'And then there's part two. Sooner or later I'd figure out that a few very valuable first editions were missing from the collection. I know my way around the book collecting world well enough to track the sales and possibly track down the buyer. If I did that, I'd find out who'd taken and sold the books.

'I'd also figure out why you needed to steal and sell the books. Once your affair was discovered, or better yet before it was discovered, you and Rebecca and her children would disappear. That might have been what you were talking about this afternoon, why she took a chance on meeting you.

'Your affair discovered, your academic career would be finished. Maybe you could get a job in a bookstore or a library one day. But you'd need a pretty hefty stake to get you out of the Bronx and set you up in your new life with Rebecca . . .'

Sam plopped back on to the chair. His face ran through a half-dozen expressions, from boiling rage to crumpling with unshed tears. He spoke resignedly, no fight left, but with the composure a lifetime of lecturing gave him.

'You have some of that right – about ten percent . . . I didn't take the missing books but someone did. And I didn't report the theft when I discovered it because I wasn't sure what had happened – and then I was sure. I thought at first: so what? I found the books, spending years searching through yard sales, used bookstores, auctions. No one else cared a damn about the collection or what was in it – until someone tipped Barnes off that some of the books might be valuable, quite valuable.

'Then, I realized that was the point. Now that the collection was up for sale, the theft would be discovered and I'd be blamed. My reputation would be ruined. So who would benefit from doing that? . . . Barnes, or one of his flunkies, would be my guess. Once the theft was discovered, he could argue that was why I'd fought the sale; I didn't want my crime discovered. Far from not wanting you involved, I was glad you were the first buyer on the scene. I knew you wouldn't throw accusations around without checking with me first.'

Ambler weighed what Sam said. The explanation was plausible, but plausible wasn't enough. 'You don't know for sure Barnes was responsible, do you?'

Sam shook his head. 'No. That's a guess . . . It's also true I wanted to do something for Rebecca. I wanted to get her away from the danger she's in before something terrible happened to her. But I wasn't going to go away with her. You're wrong about that.'

His expression was belligerent where Ambler expected it might be contrite. 'You don't need to know my personal life . . . Enough to tell you I have a difficult marriage. My difficulties aren't like Rebecca's. I'm not in danger.

'I care about her very much.' His tone softened. 'You might say I'm in love with her . . . Right now, she clings to me like a drowning person and perhaps she thinks she's in love with me.' He drifted away for a moment into his own thoughts, his composure slipping, his expression now made sad, perhaps hopeless, by memories that must be painful.

'She's drowning. In time, if she gets away from the ogre

she's married to, she won't be drowning. She's young and smart; given a new start, she'll make a better life for herself. By then, if I were with her, I'd hold her back.'

His eyes lit up; a new vision wiped away the painful memories and smoothed out the lines those memories had etched into his face. Ambler watched a transformation, a man come to grips with himself. 'If I stayed with her, I'd become a weight on her, an obligation she needed to fulfill that would keep her from happiness.' He met Ambler's gaze for the first time since he began speaking and smiled grimly. 'I'd be to her what my wife is to me, a debt to be paid for with her happiness.'

Ambler didn't have much to say. He was inclined to believe what Sam had told him, yet the confession didn't clear up anything. 'So George Olson knew you were having an affair.'

Sam straightened up ready for battle, and waved an arm as if he was going to argue, but caught himself and instead waved off what Ambler had said, as if the term 'affair' used so casually made sordid a connection between him and Rebecca that was good and pure and not to be sullied by a term suggesting it was otherwise. His expression said Ambler should understand this.

Whether Ambler understood the nature of Sam and Rebecca's relationship wasn't important. What was important was no one would care about the subtle distinctions. Sam had violated the policy of the college because, not to put too fine a point upon it, he was, like the term or not, having an affair, committing adultery with a student, both of them married. Whatever else it meant, trying to keep an affair secret didn't add up to a ringing defense on a murder charge, even if he was willing to admit to it, which he wasn't. Sam's confession, as difficult and embarrassing as it was, had no exculpatory effect on his being the prime suspect in a murder investigation. Ambler told him this as non-judgmentally as he could.

'Not even for you? After all I've told you, humiliating myself, you're not convinced I'm innocent? You think I may have murdered a dear friend and tried to kill you, another friend.' He tried out a pathetic expression. 'You mustn't think much of me.'

Ambler kept his tone even. 'I think enough of you to tell

you the truth. Whether I think you guilty or innocent won't make a damn bit of difference. Maybe there isn't enough evidence to convict you. The prosecution needs to prove you guilty beyond a reasonable doubt. In theory, you don't need to prove your innocence. In reality, sometimes you do.'

Given Sam's hangdog expression, you'd think he'd already been convicted. 'There's one more thing,' he said. His eyes glittered with the crazed certainty of a revivalist preacher. 'You can't reveal any of what I've told you or what you've seen. No one can know I was with Rebecca when George was shot. You'll sign her death warrant, if you reveal that.'

Ambler now understood Sam's false alibi and his reason for going into hiding. His first reaction was to say he couldn't promise to keep what he knew to himself. Yet a memory of a death not so long ago that might not have happened if he'd kept what he knew to himself gave him pause.

'For the moment, I can keep quiet about what you told me. I'm taking a chance doing that. You might be lying to me, and someone else might get hurt or killed because I kept quiet.'

'Not by me.'

'If you're telling the truth, you need to do some things to help yourself. You said you were in your office when George Olson was shot. That's a lie. Someone very much on your side went to your office at that time looking for you and you weren't there. This person hasn't told anyone this. But there will come a time . . .'

'I know who it is.' Sam shook his head. 'I've known all along I made a mistake saying I was in my office. I had a meeting scheduled with Sarah . . . She never misses a meeting. She's never late. I'm so sorry I put her in a position where she might have to lie for me.'

'You can't ask her to lie . . . If push comes to shove, I won't let her lie for you.'

Sam nodded laboriously, as if it caused him pain. 'A hell of a mess, isn't it? Sarah's not going to tell anyone.' His tone was too confident, and this bothered Ambler.

'She might have to. That's not your only problem about where you were. Someone said they saw you in the library at the time of the murder.'

'Whoever it is would be lying. I wasn't even on campus at the time George was killed. That's been my problem all along. I can't prove I wasn't on the campus without implicating . . . someone, and I won't do that. I can't do that.'

'How do I know you're not lying about being with Rebecca? She'll do anything for you . . . perhaps even come forward at the last moment and testify you were with her . . . Is this what you're preparing me for?'

'I'll never tell anyone I was with her . . . not even you. You're guessing I was with her. I didn't say I was.'

Sam was talking in circles and making it impossible for Ambler to figure out what was true and what wasn't. A minute ago he'd said he was with Rebecca. 'If you're going to keep playing cat and mouse with me, I'm not going to believe anything you tell me . . . Let me guess. You can't say you were in your office at the time of the murder. No one saw you because you weren't there, and Sarah knows you weren't there.'

'You don't know that.' Sam's caginess didn't fit who he was and he wasn't any good at being deceitful.

'Why can't you tell me the truth? You're all tangled up in lies and fabrications and before long you'll hang yourself.'

Sam hung his head. He looked woebegone. He'd spent his adult life as a scholar. To be a scholar was to search for the truth, to be honest about where it led, especially to yourself. Most of Sam's fight was internal. Telling lies brought him to a quagmire precisely because of his strong inclination to tell the truth. Ambler sympathized with him but couldn't trust him.

'Most of what I've told you is the truth. I've kept back only those things that would hurt someone else.'

'Is Sarah Hastings part of your conspiracy to set Rebecca Dawson free?'

As was his wont, Sam weighed his words before he spoke. 'To an extent. She knows Rebecca's situation. Rebecca confides in her, though I've asked Rebecca not to say anything about us.'

'That you're sleeping together.'

Sam winced.

'George Olson figured out you were having an affair with Rebecca? He tried to blackmail you?'

Sam winced again, like a boxer staggered by damaging blow after damaging blow. Ambler – as the boxer's relentless opponent – needed to keep him on his feet until he was sure of the knockout.

'Olson wanted you to drop your campaign for senate president or he'd expose your affair? He and Doug Stuart were afraid you might actually win.'

Sam latched on to this, showing some life. 'I would've won.'

'That isn't what I asked.'

Sam paused longer than he usually did. Ambler pictured him rummaging through his mind, cluttered with lies and half-truths, in search of a satisfactory answer. He spoke quietly. 'It wasn't what you think. George did know, or suspected, something out of the ordinary in how I treated Rebecca. I suppose she and I didn't hide our affection for each other.' He smiled, a dreamy, lopsided smile, beaming like a teenager.

'You might say we were sure of our innocence. We didn't need to hide; we weren't guilty of any wrong. We did need to keep our *affair*, if that's what you call it, from her husband for obvious reasons, from my wife out of kindness, and from the campus because of a rule that disallowed romance between faculty and students, a policy that didn't account for our situation.'

Sam deluded himself that the college rules didn't apply to him and Rebecca. But what else would you expect from someone in love? Sam wasn't finished. Ambler didn't interrupt him.

'Another thing you're wrong about . . . that George was pressuring me to support Doug. Quite the opposite. We argued because, in his way, he was trying to help me. He said if I became embroiled in a scandal, I'd not only *not* become senate president, but my entire academic career would go down the drain as well.

'His concern was me, not Stuart. He was coming around to support my candidacy; something happened that soured him on Doug Stuart. He wouldn't tell me what it was. But he clearly wanted me to end what he thought was an inappropriately close relationship with a student, with Rebecca.

'Things got heated when he said some demeaning things

about her, implying she was a . . .' He glanced at Ambler
helplessly, unable to repeat what Olson had called her. 'He
basically said what went on between us was sordid, that I was
in it for a sexual romp.' Sam smiled sheepishly. 'The conversation deteriorated from there.'

Ambler found himself nodding sadly, like a wise old uncle,
except Sam was as old as he was. 'Everything you tell me
tightens the noose around your neck . . . not to be morbid.
How does what you just told me exonerate you of anything?'

'What reason would I have to kill George? He was my
friend.'

'He was going to tell the world about you and Rebecca.'

'No, he wasn't . . . And why would I shoot at you?'

'To keep me from finding out you killed George.' Ambler
realized his argument was going around in circles, too. The
case against Sam wasn't as strong as everyone thought, or as
he originally thought, or – for that matter – as Sam himself
must have thought, or he wouldn't have gone into hiding.

'Your "taking it on the lam", as it were, made you look
guilty. Why did you run if you aren't guilty?'

'So I wouldn't have to tell anyone about Rebecca.'

'So you were with Rebecca at the time of the murder?'
Ambler said this as a pronouncement.

'I didn't say that.'

Ambler was exasperated. 'You did say that.'

Sam's hands were folded between his legs and he bent
forward, wringing them. Sweat beaded on his forehead. 'I
thought, since I didn't shoot George, if I stepped out of the
way for a while the police would find out who did kill him.
When they did, I'd return and that would be that.'

Ambler was flummoxed, ready to throw up his hands in
defeat. 'Let's say for sake of argument I believe what you're
telling me – which I don't. Who took the books?'

Sam opened his hands in a kind of gesture of surrender.
'The books? I said Barnes because he had a reason. But it
could be anyone. The library's pretty loose about letting the
faculty borrow books. No late fees. Often, a faculty member
won't bother to check the books out. It was the same with the
crime fiction collection. Anyone on the faculty who wanted

to borrow a book could. It was an honor system. It's not a large faculty. I know all the mystery readers – more of them than you'd think among the intelligentsia.

'When I found the books were missing, it hit me over the head. All of them were first editions, some signed, most of them with book jackets, all of them collectible. A reader would need to have amazingly eclectic tastes – Rex Stout, Vera Caspary, Chester Himes, Mickey Spillane, P. D. James – to take that array of books. So I realized it was something else.'

'And the suspects?'

'I told you. Barnes.'

'How long was this going on?'

Sam looked crestfallen. 'I don't know that either. I caught on soon after Barnes announced he would try to sell the collection.' Sam glanced at Ambler like a turtle from under its shell. 'When I learned of his plan, I did a quick inventory and realized which books were missing.'

'So the books were taken after the news of the potential sale got out?'

'It's possible it happened before that. But, as I said, my thinking is it was done so it would appear I was trying to stop the sale of the Mystery Writers collection because if the sale took place and the collection was appraised, my book-stealing scheme would be exposed.

'My book-stealing! . . .' he exploded. His face reddened and his cheeks bulged. 'I built the collection for the library, for the college, for posterity.' He snuck a glance at Ambler. 'Why would anyone believe I'd steal books from the library?'

At that moment, Ambler noticed a man and a woman waiting for the elevator watching them intently, and realized why. Sam was in a state of high anxiety, frowning one minute, grimacing the next, leaning forward like he might lunge at Ambler before collapsing back in his chair as if overcome by despair. To them it must have looked like Ambler was browbeating the poor man into submission.

He sighed heavily and tried to soften his tone. In fact, he did feel a surge of sympathy for Sam, but not enough to stop. 'Some of your colleagues believe you're a murderer. Why wouldn't they believe you were a thief?'

Sam sank into his own thoughts again. 'What do you believe?' He spoke so softly Ambler could barely hear him.

'What I believe isn't important. Did George Olson know about the pilfered books?'

'Oh my God . . . you think I killed him!'

Ambler felt like a Judas but he went on. 'As I said, what I believe isn't important. Please . . .'

'As a matter of fact, he did.' Sam spit out the words. 'I told him . . . I asked him to help me think through who might have taken the books and why. He didn't believe it was Barnes or was intended to put the blame on me. He thought it was more likely professional thieves'

'Did you tell anyone else?'

Sam's tone was more subdued. 'Rebecca knew. She helped me track the missing books . . . And Sarah, because she's such an avid mystery reader, I thought, hoped, she might have taken them to read and hadn't gotten around to returning them.'

'And?'

Sam acted as if he was confused by the question. 'She didn't know anything about the books . . . What are you suggesting? Don't you trust anyone?'

FIFTEEN

That evening, when Ambler got to Adele's apartment, she told him his son had called and was stopping over later. He was still in the Bronx. Adele ordered from the Chinese restaurant on Ninth Avenue.

'I thought it might be easier if we ate in,' she told him, 'because of your arm in the sling. I know you don't like takeout, so I ordered dishes that aren't terrible as takeout, nothing with breading.'

While they ate – twice-cooked pork, Szechuan cold noodles, chicken with peanuts and dried chilis – and drank Tsingtao beers, he told her about his talk with Sam Abernathy.

'Every time he opened his mouth, he incriminated himself. I meant to ask him about students who might have had a grudge against George Olson, but I didn't get a chance. I was too busy trying to comprehend everything else he was telling me. I hope John has some news . . .'

Adele wanted to say something and was hesitant to speak. He could tell because her attention wasn't fully focused on him; she was preoccupied. This usually meant she was going to tell him something he didn't want to hear.

After a few moments of silence, he'd had enough. 'What is it?'

'What?'

'What do you want to tell me?'

They knew each other well enough so she didn't pretend he'd guessed wrong. 'I've been thinking about what you asked John to do and what it might be like for him to be among the men you told me about . . . the former prisoners.

'I came across a study of PTSD leading to violence and aggression in vets of Afghanistan and Iraq while I was looking up something else.' She paused and, when she met Ambler's gaze, he thought she might cry. 'Don't get mad, but I also came across some things about PTSD and maximum-security prisons. I wondered if John's moodiness and temper might be a form of PTSD.'

Ambler's heart sank. He'd worried about the same sort of thing – that John's time in prison had damaged him in ways that would be difficult to overcome. Putting him back among ex-felons in a potentially violent situation, Ambler worried he might have set his son up for trouble he wasn't yet ready to handle.

When he didn't say anything, Adele said, 'John and the ex-prisoners he's trying to find out about might have too much in common. In prison, John was in danger of a violent outburst from someone at any moment; just as the soldiers in a war are always in danger. Given John's trauma, it feels like something bad could happen.'

Ambler pushed his hands against his face to try and erase the tragic scenes he was imagining. 'I should have known better.'

'I'm not criticizing you.' Adele's tone was comforting but it didn't help. 'Getting John to help you made perfect sense, and he's excited that he's doing something important. That's good for him, too.

'I didn't think about the possible problems until the other night. An aggressive panhandler came up to us. I thought John was going to punch him. The poor homeless man was cowering; he was no danger to anyone. John became an entirely different person, a mean person, a bully. Johnny was terrified. I think John scared himself too when he came to his senses and realized what he'd almost done.'

'I'll talk to him . . . I'm a little worried, too. Adjusting to life after time in prison is hellish. It's not only the way other people see you, it's how you see yourself, also. You think you're not like everyone else, that something went wrong with you. There should be more counseling for ex-cons. But I don't want to suggest counseling. That would sound like I don't have confidence in him.'

They were quiet for some time, each in their own thoughts. They'd come to be like that with one another. Like an old married couple, Adele said a couple of weeks before all this started. He'd thought then she might have meant they should get married.

'That's the last thing I'd want,' she'd said – and laughed. 'Then we *would* be an old married couple.'

Nonetheless, they'd fallen into a pattern where they might as well be married. He wanted to be with her whenever he could. Some of the reason he spent so much time at her apartment, even before she took him in to nurse him back to health after he was shot, might have been to escape from his own apartment, overcrowded with John and Johnny, who talked about things he didn't always understand, and their world of hip-hop music and video games. But another reason was he felt at loose ends when he wasn't with her and like he was where he was supposed to be when he was with her.

When John arrived later that evening, he was excited. 'I caught up with my old road dog. And I was right about Walt Nichols. Oscar says he's a knock-around guy, picking up small-time jobs here and there. He laughed when I told him the guy was in college.'

'Do you know why he's going to college?'

'I heard him talking to a couple of other guys about it. He took courses when he was in the joint. He did good in them, all As. He liked it, so when they told him about a program for ex-felons, he figured he'd finish up his courses at Trinity and graduate.'

John glanced from Ambler to Adele. 'I don't know if I believe him . . . He told me he was getting As at Trinity also. He's majoring in computer science and figures there's an angle in there where he can get rich.'

John also told them more about his prison friend, Oscar Diaz, who'd gone straight after his time in prison. He liked running a bodega, despite the long hours. His reputation was such – he'd been a gang leader in his younger days and served more than one prison term, the last one for manslaughter – that, despite his store being in a high-crime area, no one bothered it.

John didn't have much more to say about Walt Nichols, and Ambler began to believe Walt, despite his outlaw ways, was an unlikely suspect. Still, he couldn't be ruled out.

He asked Adele if she'd do a background check on Nichols, find as much as she could on him in the library databases.

'I won't find much,' she said. 'You'd have better luck asking some of the professors who've had him in class.'

'I could do that,' John said.

Ambler thought that might not be a bad idea. The best person to talk to would be Doug Stuart. He'd know most of the faculty. And he knew Walt Nichols. Stuart didn't have much reason to help get Sam out from under suspicion. For that matter, he'd probably have more interest in helping Walt Nichols than he would in helping Sam. Still, it would be worth a shot for John to talk to him, but he shouldn't expect much to come of it.

He told John he should tell Stuart he was working for David Levinson and not mention Ambler. Also, he should ask about five or six students and not put extra emphasis on Walt Nichols.

'There's an English professor, a creative writing teacher, Sarah Hastings, you should talk to,' he told him. 'In fact, you should start with her. I'll let her know. She can tell you about Doug Stuart and suggest other faculty who might be helpful. She might even suggest students you haven't come across yet. We don't want anyone to know we're focusing on Nichols.'

When John left, Ambler called Mike Cosgrove and asked if he'd run a records check on Walt Nichols. Mike would have access to the FBI's national database, which the library didn't; only law enforcement could get to it.

'I'm told you finally got yourself shot,' Mike said when he answered. 'Welcome to the club. I take it you have a suspect by now the cops up there don't know about.'

'I don't know what the homicide cops in the Bronx are up to. The guy I talked to wasn't very friendly.'

Mike snorted. 'There's no percentage in being a friendly cop in the Bronx. Tell me about your suspect.'

'Not really a suspect. A student my son says is an ex-con who may still be an outlaw.'

'Why would he shoot you?'

'To keep me from finding out he shot George Olson.'

'Why would he shoot him?'

'I don't know.'

'A stab in the dark. You were shot from a distance like the earlier victim?'

'I didn't see anyone with a gun anywhere near me.'

'Did they tell you what kind of weapon the bullet they took out of you came from?'

'No. I assume it was a rifle, too.'

Mike was quiet for a moment. 'You know . . . I thought of this after the first shooting. We're talking about a college campus, right? Not many people walking around carrying rifles. You'd think someone would notice if someone was.'

'Back doors? Alleys. A car parked nearby.'

'Still, the shooter would be taking a helluva chance.'

'Could he have hidden it on the roof?'

'The uniforms would do a thorough search. They could miss something, but it's doubtful; they've got a lot of experience looking for hidden guns.'

'So?'

'I had a guy once was carrying his rifle in a pool cue case. If it were me, I'd have your son take a look around that roof – inside exhaust pipes, chimney if there is one, vents, air conditioner, electrical boxes; he'll figure it out. If he doesn't find anything, and he probably won't . . . The college has a pool room, right? Every college has pool tables somewhere.'

Ambler wasn't sure.

'Take my word. He should ask around the building the shots came from if anyone saw someone carrying a pool cue case on the days of the shootings.'

Ambler was skeptical but he said he'd do it. In the morning, he called John and told him what Mike suggested.

'I'm gonna be asking a lot of people a lot of questions.' John's tone was jocular. 'This investigation stuff isn't like in the movies. I feel like a door-to-door salesman.'

'That's what it is. Lots of knocking on doors, asking questions and not getting answers, lots of failures and dead ends, few successes, and most of those not all that satisfying. Not much in the way of triumphs.'

'Well, it beats doin' time.' John laughed in a way that surprised Ambler, a light-hearted, easy laugh he hadn't heard from his son very often; a laugh you might hear from someone comfortable with himself.

After the call, Ambler called President Barnes at Trinity, who said he'd arrange for lists of students in George Olson's classes over the past couple of years, but not their grades because of privacy concerns.

He didn't really need grades for Nichols; John had already told him the guy was getting good grades. Thinking that, he wondered again where his fixation on Walt Nichols came from. Nichols did his time. Shouldn't he have a chance to turn his life around also, despite his larcenous tendencies? It wasn't right for Ambler to complain about the injustice of people making assumptions about John because he'd been in prison, and then to go and make those same kind of assumptions himself about Nichols.

That afternoon also, Ambler had a follow-up appointment at the surgical clinic at Bronx Municipal, so he stopped by Harry's office shortly after he got to work to tell him.

'I'm glad you stopped by,' Harry said as soon as he opened the door. 'I was going to call you.' Harry's expression was somber if not mournful.

Ambler felt a lump in his chest; another uh-oh moment. His first thought was the crime fiction room had been dropped from the library's budget. The mayor was proposing to cut $50 million from the NYPL budget overall. The axe had to fall somewhere.

He was partially right. Close but no cigar.

'The donation earmarked for enhancing the crime fiction collection has fallen through. The library won't have the funds to acquire the New York Mystery Writers collection after all . . . I'm sorry we put you through all of this trouble . . .' Harry was truly dismayed, his lips pressed tightly together, his wrinkles begetting wrinkles. 'Perhaps none of this would have happened . . .' He seemed to be addressing Ambler's damaged shoulder. '. . . if we hadn't been so eager – leaping before we looked – to grab that collection. I'm sorry.'

OK, so he wasn't going to get Sam's collection, which he hadn't wanted in the first place. So much had happened in the interim. So much was going through his mind. He knew from the beginning something wasn't right about this anonymous donation for the specific purpose of acquiring the Trinity College Mystery Writers collection. Harry was right. He should have been wary of a strange coincidence. What was the saying? 'Never look a gift horse in the mouth.' Well, this was one gift horse whose mouth he should've looked into.

'You're taking this better than I thought you would. It must be a crushing disappointment. All that work evaluating the collection for nothing. Not to mention getting shot in the process.'

He'd stopped by Harry's office in the first place to tell him he needed to take the afternoon off for his appointment at the hospital in the Bronx.

'You didn't have to come in at all,' Harry said. 'A gunshot wound is a serious thing. Maybe you're ready now to give up being a gumshoe.'

Ambler laughed. 'Gumshoe? . . . Where'd you get that? You've picked up on the lingo. Maybe you have a future as a gumshoe yourself.'

'Not likely . . . and I'm looking forward to your retirement from the field.' His tone became what Ambler guessed might be his sin-forgiving, absolution-dispensing, confessional voice. 'You might be surprised to learn that Adele agrees with me. She wants you to be around to see . . .' Harry's eyes opened wider and his cheeks turned red. 'Well, never mind.'

Ambler returned to the crime fiction reading room deep in thought. The suspicious donation to the crime fiction collection that sent him back to the Trinity College campus didn't fall out of the sky. The mythical $200,000 donation had a purpose. Mythical because the donation itself never existed. So why? Better yet, who? You also had to wonder where the $200,000 figure came from . . . precisely $200,000.

He learned of the existence of the donation after his first visit to the campus and shortly before he was told of George Olson's murder and learned that Sam was a suspect. The mythical donation provided Ambler a reason to revisit the campus. So who wanted him back on campus?

The surgical clinic at Jacobi Hospital reminded him of what a remarkable endeavor New York City was: the Bronx

Municipal Hospital Center, of which Jacobi was a part, was only one of the Health and Hospital Corporation's eleven acute care hospitals. The city also had 217 public library branches in its three library systems, in addition to four research libraries including the 42nd Street Library; more than 1,800 public schools, hundreds of parks and playgrounds, plus dozens of museums and art galleries, the City University of New York with its twenty-five separate colleges, and a police force larger than the armies of half the countries in the world. How could anybody run such a beast?

The Jacobi clinic waiting room could give the UN general assembly a run for its money in terms of diversity, but was far out front in terms of the misery it held. Ambler felt he took up valuable space and time that was needed by patients with far more sickness and pain than he had. He waited his turn patiently, though the wait was a lot longer than he would have hoped.

The surgical resident who saw him had been part of the trauma team that patched him up right after the shooting. His name tag read Dr Armando Lopez and he said he was from Guatemala when Ambler asked. He was efficient and brisk, not to say brusque; not interested in talking about where he was from or any other sort of small talk. He did get interested when Ambler asked about gunshot wounds in general and his in particular, answering Ambler's questions in detail, using medical terms Ambler wasn't familiar with.

'You were lucky the bullet missed the subclavian artery. I've seen patients who bled out from a bullet to the shoulder. The bullet you got was a fairly small caliber, so the damage was contained; a bullet from an assault rifle would've ripped your shoulder open, taken out the artery and most likely the brachial plexus with it.'

Ambler was curious about what might have happened to him, and the doctor didn't mind telling him. 'If the bullet tore up the brachial plexus, you wouldn't have walked out of here the night of the shooting. You'd have been in surgery with an orthopedist and a neurosurgeon. Even after that, you could have lost the use of your arm, or the arm itself – or not to be overly dramatic, you could have bled to death.'

Ambler left the clinic with prescription refills for an anti-biotic to take for ten days, and one for pain medication which would last only a couple of days, instructions for caring for the wound, and an appointment in two weeks to remove the stitches. He'd also learned that the small caliber bullet had most likely come from a rifle. He walked the six or seven blocks to the train along streets lined with trees wearing reddish buds like a fringe, and small lawns trying to turn green, thinking that he was happy to be alive.

SIXTEEN

That evening, after Ambler and Adele had finished dinner, John called and then came over to report. His mood was buoyant. 'Quite a day,' he said. 'I wouldn't mind a glass of that wine.'

John seldom drank since his release. Avoiding alcohol wasn't a condition of his probation; he just wasn't interested. So Ambler was surprised, but didn't mind pouring him a glass.

John wasn't exaggerating that it had been quite a day. He took a long sip from his glass and glanced from Ambler to Adele with a satisfied smile. 'Walt Nichols found me on the roof of the library.' He waited for their reaction, still smiling. 'He had to have followed me. Even though I was pretty careful, I'm not an expert at this second-story stuff. I realize now he was suspicious of me from the beginning. A con can spot a snitch like a dog can smell a rat.

'He went off on me. Didn't even ask what I was doing. He knew.' John laughed, a kind of snort. 'I hadn't thought up a good reason why I was snooping around on the roof of the library because I never thought anyone would ask.' He chuckled again. 'I told him I came up for the view and the tranquility. He caught me with my head stuck in an air-duct vent, so he wasn't falling for that.

'He went on about me being a snitch . . . and before I could think of a comeback, he guessed I was an undercover cop. So I went along with that; it was better than anything I could think up.

'He was menacing but careful, too smart to kill a cop unless he had no choice. He asked me what I thought I was going to get out of nosing around him and his friends. He thought I was after drugs.

'So I blew some smoke up his ass.' He turned to Adele and apologized. 'I've been away from nice people for too long. You get treated like scum long enough, you start to act like it.'

He took a sip of wine and drifted off in a kind of dreamy way for a moment.

Puzzled, Ambler said, 'What happened?'

'I told him it wasn't drugs, it was the shooting. I figured he and his pals had the smarts to know what went down. They might know some dirt on Sam Abernathy that would help us lock him up. You could tell he wanted to believe me but wasn't sure. He asked if I knew about you. I said I didn't. He said you were a cop posing as a librarian, trying to prove Abernathy didn't kill the guy.

'"Cops wouldn't do that," I told him. "The guy must be a private eye. We got our suspect," I said. "I'm looking for somethin' that'll hang him."'

'Did he believe you?'

'Cons who've been in the life as long as he has don't believe anybody. If he's the killer, he thinks everybody's out to get him. He can't be sure he didn't slip up somewhere; maybe someone saw him, maybe someone talked. He knows he's guilty, so he can't help thinking someone else knows, too.

'He'll be careful around me now. He'll tell the other guys to clam up. But I think he believed I was after Abernathy and not him.'

Ambler found himself smiling while he listened to his son. He felt like a doctor or a tradesman like a carpenter or a plumber, discovering in your son the traits you had that made you what you were. Maybe John could take over from him, perhaps become an actual private investigator, and he could retire. John interrupted his thoughts.

'I'm glad you told me about Sarah Hastings.' He was beaming, his smile as wide as a gate. 'I've never met anyone like her. We talked for a long time.'

Sarah was pretty. She was smart. She was unaffectedly and perhaps unconsciously charming. And she seemed to have turned John's head, sidetracked him. Perhaps he wasn't cut out for detective work after all. Ambler prodded him. 'Did she tell you anything useful?'

'She's really smart,' John said, oblivious to the question. 'And sensitive. She's the only person I've ever talked to about being in prison who understood what I was talking about.'

Great, Ambler said to himself, he's smitten. 'She's very nice and pretty and charming. What did she say about Walt Nichols? Did she suggest any other faculty members you should talk to?'

'She told me not to trust Doug Stuart.' He let this sink in. 'Did you know she was once married to him?'

'I did.'

Adele perked up and turned on him. 'How do you know so much about this Professor Pretty and Charming?'

'Jesus,' Ambler said to himself. To Adele, he said, 'It's a long story.'

'I bet it is.' Her eyes narrowed.

John was in his own world. 'Marrying him was a mistake, she told me. "See," she said. "We all make mistakes and we all deserve another chance."' He glanced at the ceiling, or maybe through the ceiling to the heavens. 'She invited me to dinner.'

After John left, Ambler and Adele made love for the first time since he'd been shot. Making love wasn't a frequent occasion for them, so it was unexpected and a surprise when it happened, intense and passionate, though this time – because of his shoulder – cautious and a bit awkward.

Afterward, when she lay beside him, her head resting on his chest, he said, 'I liked that you were jealous.'

'I wasn't jealous. I was feeling amorous and I wanted you to feel like that, too, so I fooled you . . . Your son is besotted with the college professor.' She leaned on her arm on his chest. 'Is she really pretty?'

'Pretty like the farmer's daughter; not glamorous, but fresh as the proverbial daisy. He's right about her sensitivity; she's a poet.' He thought about that for a moment. 'She's a poet; he's a musician. Maybe there's something there.'

In the morning, while they ate breakfast, Adele's homemade granola, she told him she hadn't found anything about Walt Nichols. 'He doesn't come up anywhere – not even news accounts of his arrests. I bet if you checked income taxes he wouldn't be there either, one of those people who live off the grid. He probably has a family – there are a number of Nichols in the Bronx – he sponges off. You could go knock on doors. I think you'd do better to see what John finds out.'

She was right. But John needed to be careful now that Walt
Nichols was on to him. Whether he thought John was an
undercover cop or not, if Nichols thought he was about to be
exposed, John would be in real danger.

That afternoon, Ambler received a call from Edward Barnes
and didn't know who it was. He didn't remember the first
name of the president of Trinity College.

'You've been remiss in reporting on your activities. Getting
yourself shot hasn't done anything to improve the public face
of Trinity College of the Bronx.' He paused. 'That was a poor
attempt at humor. I was shocked it happened and worried
about your condition. Doug Stuart told me he'd spoken to a
colleague of yours and was told you're recovering well.'

Ambler was intrigued once more by how much academics
liked to listen to themselves talk, and how little use they had
for what anyone else might have to say. 'I'm coming along.
Sorry to tarnish the college's image.'

Barnes chuckled, an awkward and strained sound, and then
invited – summoned might be a better word – Ambler to tea
that afternoon.

Ambler arrived at 4:00 and was ushered into a small dining
room adjacent to the president's opulent office. His desk was
still unencumbered. The tea service was silver and the cups
china. There were also finger sandwiches and scones with
pats of butter and little jars of jelly. Ambler couldn't remember
the last time he'd felt so civilized.

Barnes wore a charcoal grey two-button suit. Male
members of the professoriate wore sport coats, often tweed,
and slacks, often corduroy, and often mismatched. Ambler
was curious as to why Barnes wanted to distinguish himself
from the faculty, to dress more like a banker or a Madison
Avenue executive than his colleagues. What his dress and
manner made clear, whether intentional or not, was the
separation.

In the old days, scholars were the decision-makers in
colleges and universities. A scholar might ascend to dean or
provost or even president, but he – and in the old days it was
invariably a he – remembered where he came from, the relationship with the faculty was collegial, and the dean or provost,

and sometimes the president, was not reluctant to return to the professoriate and give someone else a turn.

Relationships had changed over the prior fifty years. The power and authority as well as the numbers of full-time faculty had diminished. In its place, higher education had developed a managerial class that saw itself as the decision-makers and the faculty as more or less the hired help. The trappings of shared governance were still honored but the substance was gone. Ambler knew these things because he'd once planned on a career as a scholar and teacher, but the plan, like the plans of many, got waylaid.

He didn't so much dislike Barnes as he disliked what Barnes stood for, a symbol of the disregard for scholarship, except in areas where it could make money. Knowledge for the sake of knowledge had no standing with the new owners.

'To get right to the point . . . because I have a meeting in a half-hour . . .' Barnes scoffed down a couple of the tea sandwiches like he was gobbling down hot dogs at Gray's Papaya. 'Lunch,' he said, by way of explanation. 'Do you have any thoughts on who shot you or why? Has your son come up with anything?'

Ambler decided to take a chance. 'Can you get me whatever files you have on a student, Walter Nichols?'

'Student records are confidential. You'd need a court order for them to be released.'

'You can request them . . . Suppose I'm with you when you're looking at them.'

Barnes took a moment to weigh the pros and cons. 'Is he a suspect?'

'Everyone's a suspect. Suspicion is not accusation.'

'There must be something about him—'

'That's what I'm trying to find out . . . if there's something about him.' Ambler drilled the antsy college president with a hard stare. 'It should go without saying, but I'll say it anyway. This is between you and me. No one else should know that I asked you for these records. A suspicion doesn't rise to the level of an accusation, and sullying this man's name without proof he did anything wrong would be a travesty.'

Ambler was about to say he was trusting Barnes. He didn't

because he realized he *didn't* trust Barnes. Instead, he wanted
to tell him he'd wring his neck if word got out that Walt
Nichols was under suspicion, but he didn't say this either.

'It would be out of the ordinary for me to request the records
of one student.' Barnes glanced at Ambler suspiciously, an
expression you might see from a poker player unsure of his
hand. '. . . I'd need a plausible reason.'

He was stalling, and Ambler didn't buy it. 'I'm sure you
could come up with something. He's part of the program that
sends ex-offenders to college. You could request all of their
records to see how they were doing, so you could decide
whether to keep the program going.'

Barnes rubbed his chin, reminding Ambler of a movie villain
about to swindle the fair damsel. This lasted only a few seconds
before he made a decision. 'That might work. I'd want to
see if the program is progressing.' He hesitated. 'It would be
better if you weren't here when I requested the records. Come
back tomorrow late in the morning.'

Ambler agreed. 'Is there anything else you want from me?'

'Find the maniac who's shooting up the campus.' Barnes
banged the small table to the tune of clattering teacups. 'The
last time I spoke to the police, the lieutenant said, "Nearly
fifty percent of murders never get solved."

'I asked if he was going to arrest Sam Abernathy. He said
they'd like to talk to him. This is what we pay taxes for?'

Ambler didn't know what to make of Barnes. He was a
snake-oil salesman with an advanced degree. Yet some alli-
ances you make based on mutual interest. Barnes had no
interest in him beyond his being useful in helping gain something Barnes wanted. Yet, he had to admit, the same could be
said of his interest in Barnes. That their interests were allied
momentarily had thrown them together. Once those interests
no longer coincided, they'd have nothing to say to one another.

His connection with Sam was different. They both cared
about libraries and they cared about collecting crime fiction
and preserving the papers and whatever of mystery writers for
posterity. But their interest in one another went beyond that,
to a shared view of what was important in life, what kinds of
pursuits were worthwhile, which kinds of actions were right

and which were wrong. He might question the rightness or certainly the wisdom of Sam's involvement with Rebecca. And he didn't like that Sam had been telling more lies than Pinocchio. But he didn't question that Sam did what he did because he believed it was the right thing to do. Not for expediency. Not to take advantage of a troubled young woman in a desperate situation.

Thinking about Sam and Rebecca, he thought about her aggrieved, angry and violent husband and considered that he might have dismissed the bullying and abusive young man too easily. Could he be sly and devious enough to have killed George Olson and framed Sam for the murder?

Ambler was devious enough to plan it for him. If Sam was murdered, Rebecca's husband – Ambler didn't remember his name – would be an obvious suspect once it came to light, as it would, that Sam was sleeping with his wife.

Killing George Olson was collateral damage, and framing Sam got him out of the way – serving a long prison term – and left the cuckolded husband in the clear. The possibility it happened this way was far-fetched but everything else he thought of was far-fetched too. The best thing to do would be to talk to Rebecca. It was unlikely she'd cover for her husband, also unlikely she'd know about the plan if he'd had one. Her husband suspected she was having an affair; the question was whether he *knew* she was.

He hadn't seen or heard from Rebecca since he'd seen her with Sam in the hotel. And probably, if she had her way, he wouldn't see or hear from her ever again. Understandably she'd be embarrassed after their encounter. But he would've thought she'd have checked with him when she learned he was shot.

He took a walk over to the library. He hadn't been there since the shooting. It was possible she'd been toiling away on her database, putting things together for him to finish the appraisal. And sure enough, she was there, sitting at the computer in the reading room that housed the crime fiction collection staring into space.

'Hi Rebecca,' he said, and she jumped as if he'd caught her with her hand in the till. She turned on him and stared, her eyes unblinking, as if he held her life in his hands.

'I didn't mean to startle you. Is everything OK?'

'Sorry,' she said, brushing at her hair, then smoothing the front of her T-shirt which read, 'Women's Rights Are Human Rights'. She began to stand and then sat back down. 'I'm on edge these days.' She gazed into his eyes; hers were pools of sadness. 'I'm so sorry you got shot. I hope you're OK. I don't—'

Ambler pulled a chair from a nearby carrel and sat facing her. 'I want to ask you about your husband.'

Her face went rigid, as if he were hurting her. 'Are you going to tell him? . . . You can't. He'll kill me.'

Ambler spoke softly. 'I'm not planning to tell him anything. I'd like you to tell me about him.'

She sighed. 'You must think I'm awful. I'm so embarrassed talking to a stranger about cheating on my husband. I never in a million years thought I'd be that kind of woman.'

He didn't want her to justify her infidelity. But he didn't know how to say that without getting tangled up in talking about it himself. 'I'm sure you have good reasons for what you do—'

'Then why were you spying on us?' The tables turned quickly. 'I could have died right on the spot.' Her voice rose. 'And it was none of your business. You don't know what my life is like. You don't know what Sam's life is like. Who are you to judge?'

She realized she was shouting, so she lowered her voice. 'I don't think I can work with you any longer. I feel humiliated every time you look at me.' Tears trickled down her cheeks.

He was making a mess of things, so he tried to calm her. 'I'm not interested in judging you and Sam. I have enough to worry about in my own life. I want to know if your husband is a murderer.'

The tears stopped. Her eyes popped open. Her jaw dropped. 'Norman?' She took a moment to absorb this, taking long enough that he feared she wouldn't say anything. When she did speak, her tone was bitter. 'Norman's a coward. He terrorizes women and children. He might murder me. He'd be afraid to try it with anyone else.'

Wives weren't always the best judges of what their husbands

were capable of. He didn't want her assessment of her husband so much as some facts about him. He didn't want to set her off again, so he chose his words carefully. He didn't want to argue with her. 'Does he own a gun?'

She shook her head. 'I wouldn't let a gun in the house with the kids.'

'Was he in the military?'

She shook her head again. 'Norman's all for the military. All for war against anyone: Russia, China, Korea, Iraq, Iran. But he'll let someone else do the fighting.'

This was delicate, bringing up the affair again, but he tried anyway. 'Norman came after me when he thought I was Sam. Could he have mistaken George Olson for Sam and shot him?'

She took the question seriously and didn't get sidetracked. 'I suppose it's possible. I don't think he knows how to shoot a gun. But he might have learned. He's obsessive like that.

'At one time, he thought he was going to build a business buying clothes made in Asia somewhere – by slave labor if he could get away with it – and selling them to stores in the US. He'd be the clothing manufacturer with labels and all this.

'But none of it actually existed. The factory that did the manufacturing was in Asia. The stores were in the US. All he had was a name. He didn't do anything but take orders and send them to the plant in Asia, pay the plant in Asia a pittance, and then bill the stores ten times what he paid the plant.

'It sounded to me like it should be illegal, like a pyramid scheme. But it was perfectly legal. Still, it didn't work and he lost all our money. But he learned how to do whatever it was he did, worked at it night and day until it fell apart. So if he wanted to learn to shoot a gun, he would.'

'Could he have shot George Olson in order to frame Sam?' Ambler explained his convoluted rationale which she had a difficult time following.

'He'd shoot Professor Olson and blame it on Sam? How would he do that?' She didn't wait for an answer. 'And why would he do that? Why wouldn't he just shoot Sam and get it over with?'

Ambler went over his thinking again. This time he had trouble believing it himself. 'I've probably read too many detective novels,' he mumbled. 'He'd need to have thought ahead, put together a diabolical plan. If he out-and-out killed Sam, he'd be a logical suspect and undoubtedly get caught. This way, Sam would be charged with the murder and be put out of the way for a long time. Your husband would have you to himself . . .'

Rebecca blushed and squeezed her eyes closed. He regretted what he'd said, or rather how he'd said it. It sounded crass, as if he thought of her as a sex toy, to be handed back and forth from man to man. He waited in the heavy silence; he'd said too much already.

Rebecca turned from him and busied herself at the computer. After a moment, she spoke without turning toward him. 'That doesn't sound like Norman.' When she did turn to look at him, her gaze was steady. 'That's not how he thinks. Once he knew I'd been with another man, he wouldn't want me anymore. I'd be damaged, a fallen woman. He wouldn't touch me . . . except maybe to strangle me.'

Her voice caught. She gasped. 'My God, I sound like I'm a piece of trash . . . If it weren't for the kids, I'd wish he did strangle me. Or I'd do it for him. Hang myself.' She wasn't talking to Ambler any longer; battling her own demons took precedence. After another few moments, she said she had a class and left. He wondered if she'd ever be back.

SEVENTEEN

That evening, John called him. It was difficult to hear what he was saying because of a poor connection, a cacophony of babbling voices and loud salsa music in the background.

'Where are you?' Ambler was worried.

'I'm calling from a payphone in a bodega in the South Bronx. It's loud in here. That's OK. I don't have to hear you. You need to hear me . . . Brace yourself. Walt Nichols is trying to sell a gun. A long gun that's hot. He wants to trade it for a Glock . . . I set up a meet with him through Oscar. He thinks I have a Glock to trade.'

'Wait!' Ambler shouted into the phone. Adele and Johnny, who were working a jigsaw puzzle together, both jumped up and dashed to stand beside him. 'You can't do that . . . You'll get yourself killed . . . John! John! Listen to me! Are you there? Can you hear me? Don't go to that meeting. Call the police. I'll call them . . .'

'I can't hear you . . . I think you said, "Don't go." I'm not meeting him. I'll be with a couple of guys chillin' on the street. I want to see if he shows up and if he has that Remington 700.'

'This is going too far.' Ambler squeezed his cell phone; his mind and his heart were racing. He tried to keep his fear out of his voice. 'John, listen to me. What you're doing is too dangerous. If he's the killer, he has nothing to lose killing you. He knows what you look like. What you've done so far is great. Take a step back now.'

John's tone was steady, excited but controlled. 'I didn't get all of that . . . I want to see if he shows up and if he does where he goes from there. The guys with me are Oscar's pals. Old heads; they know the territory and won't do anything stupid or let me . . . I'll call you later tonight.'

That was it. He was gone. Ambler stared at his blank phone

for a moment and wondered if he'd signed his son's death warrant by sending him out into the Bronx to find a murderer. Then, he shifted his gaze to his wide-eyed grandson. Johnny stood in front of Adele, who had both her arms around his chest, pulling him against her.

'He hung up,' Ambler said stupidly, as if everybody didn't know.

'What was that about?' Adele pulled Johnny tighter against her.

'Where's my dad?' Johnny's voice shook.

'It's OK.' Ambler kept his voice calm; he tried to be reassuring but he knew he didn't pull it off. He was as scared as Johnny was. 'Your dad is following up a couple of leads. He's in the Bronx. I told him to be careful. But he knows that. He'll be careful.'

Johnny was a fan of his grandfather's murder investigations, and exaggerating – as kids do – had already envisioned that Ambler, his father, and Johnny himself would become a private eye operation when his dad got out of prison. Now reality set in for the boy. His dad was in danger.

The next few hours were the most tension-filled Ambler could remember. He and Adele tried to send Johnny to bed in her room, but he was having none of it. For the first hour or so he asked unanswerable questions about what his dad might be doing and when he might call again. He told Adele and Ambler a half-dozen times that his dad could handle any bad guy. And asked them two or three more times if he was right that his dad could handle any bad guy.

An hour passed and then another. The television was on, tuned to a baseball game. All three of them faced the TV but none of them could tell you the score or even who was playing. Johnny nodded off leaning against Adele's shoulder. Every few seconds, Ambler looked at his phone on the coffee table in front of them. Every minute or so he picked it up and looked at it more closely, checked his texts and even his emails, checked the ringer selector to make sure it was on.

At some point, Adele fell asleep leaning against his shoulder as Johnny slept against her shoulder. Sometime, during the night's darkest moments, he fell asleep himself. A sliver of sunlight reached the couch from the narrow kitchen window, flashed across his eyelids, and awakened him. It took a moment to realize where he was and remember what he waited for. He grabbed for his phone. Nothing had changed. No phone call. No text. No email from John.

He tried to slip out from under Adele. But his movement caused a reaction like a cascade of falling dominoes. Everyone blinked at everyone else. 'You've got to get to school,' he said to Johnny.

'Where's my dad?'

What could Ambler say? 'You need to get ready for school.'

Adele kept changes of clothing for Johnny because he'd stayed with her often before his father got out of prison, so he went off to take a shower and change while insisting that if they sent him to school, he'd leave as soon as he got there to go look for his father. Ambler was very much afraid he'd do what he said.

While Johnny got dressed, Ambler talked with Adele about what to do and if she should stay home with the boy.

'And what are you going to do?' She sounded angry at him as he'd sounded angry at her. Neither of them was angry; they were worried about John.

Ambler's cell phone rang. He snatched it off the coffee table and it slipped out of his hand and flew across the room. Adele picked it up and handed it to him, her hand shaking, her face pale.

'Hi Pop!'

'John! Are you OK?'

'I'm fine. I got home real late and figured everyone was asleep at Adele's. It was too late to pick up Johnny, so I crashed here and figured I'd come by and pick him up and take him to school in the morning.

'What happened last night was Oscar's pals met up with Walt. He had a Remington 700 to swap. He wanted five hundred bucks plus the Glock for the 700. They told him no. None of us had that kind of dough anyway. I was kicking myself because I hadn't prepared for that. We could have had the murder weapon. But we're not done. I followed him and we know where he lives.'

John came to get Johnny – who cried and clung to his father for a half-hour after he arrived. Because they'd all gotten up so early, they had time to pull themselves together and eat breakfast before Johnny and his dad left for school. Johnny swore an oath of honor he'd not tell any of the other kids what his father was up to.

Later, John called Ambler at the library and asked him for five hundred dollars. 'I think we should buy the gun. If we don't do it fast, he could sell it to someone else or panic and get rid of it.'

Ambler had some savings and could come up with the five hundred; yet it was money he might never get back. In addition to that, he thought John's idea was too risky. 'Let me think about it. Call me back in an hour.' Ambler wasn't exactly stalling; he really didn't know what to do. The smart thing would be to tell the police. But John's telling them Walt Nichols probably had a murder weapon in his possession might not be enough for them to do anything about it.

He called Mike Cosgrove.

'I don't know what they'd do,' Mike said. 'Who was the detective who interviewed you? I'll call him, tell him what you told me, and see what he says.'

A half-hour later Mike called back. 'No go. They'd want to talk to your son and his two pals. My guess is the pals – the stellar citizens arranging to swap an unregistered Glock for a stolen rifle used in a murder – won't be eager to talk with the police about it.'

Ambler went back and forth with Mike for a few minutes about whether John should take the chance of buying the gun from Nichols and then turning it over to the police.

'Dealing with a suspected murderer is always going to be dangerous. If we're going in with a warrant to get a weapon from a murder suspect, we'd go in with a SWAT team or tactical unit. I wouldn't just knock on his door. Then again, sometimes subterfuge works. We send UC guys into more dangerous situations than the one you're talking about.'

'What would you do?'

'I'd follow procedure; that's what I'd do. You might tell your son to consider letting the cops in the Bronx handle the investigation their way.' He paused. 'But if he's anything like you, he won't.'

'I'll tell him.'

'Give me a call if I can help . . . before you're ass-deep in the Big Muddy again, if possible.'

When John called a little while later, Ambler told him what Mike said and suggested he tell the police what he knew and let them take it from there.

'Fat chance they'd believe me . . . and donkeys will fly before Wilmer and Freddy volunteer for a chat with the cops. I know what I'm doing. Wilmer and Freddy will make the deal, not me. All I gotta do is come up with the dough.'

Ambler was still out of sorts when late in the afternoon he went to get Walt Nichols's student records from the Trinity College president's office.

'You can examine the files,' Barnes said. 'But you can't take any of the files or copy them.'

Ambler didn't find anything of interest, except for some FAFSA financial aid forms showing Nichols had been a work-study student assistant to Doug Stuart for the two prior semesters. This was enough for Ambler to want to pay a visit to the faculty senate president again.

'I've already spoken to Doug about the young man,' Barnes said when he noticed Ambler's interest in the FAFSA forms.

'What did he say?'

'He was shocked anyone considered Walter Nichols a suspect in a murder.'

Ambler fought back a surge of anger. 'I thought you agreed you wouldn't tell anyone about my interest in Nichols.' For the second or third time – just about every time he'd seen him – he wanted to throttle Barnes.

He hadn't had the urge to smack anyone because of their smug expression since he was in grade school. But Barnes had that same kind of brattiness – the supercilious expression, upturned nose, and lips parted into something that was part-sneer and part-smile and at the same time neither one – as his nemesis in fifth grade, whom he did smack across the face one afternoon and ended up in detention for a month.

'I take Doug into my confidence, and he does the same for

me. I don't keep things from the representative of the faculty, as I don't keep secrets from the president of the Board of Trustees. I wouldn't last long as a college president if I didn't have the trust of those two institutions.'

Ambler wasn't impressed. 'My guess is you pick and choose what you tell them. And you should have chosen not to tell Stuart about my interest in Nichols, especially given their close connection. He's liable to tell Nichols and all hell could break loose.' Ambler remembered Nichols's run-in with John on the roof, not to mention the whole deal with the gun sale. Barnes, because he cared only what he thought and disregarded what anyone else thought, had done exactly the worst possible thing he could do.

He certainly wasn't going to tell him about John discovering Walt with what very likely could be the murder weapon. But maybe he could use him for something, too.

'I want one more thing from you,' Ambler said. 'You have petty cash or discretionary funds, right?'

Barnes's antenna went up. 'What are you getting at?'

'I need five hundred dollars. You might get it back. But you might not.'

He eyed Ambler like he was trying to hold him up. 'I didn't know you got paid for what you did.'

'Consider it expenses.'

'For what?'

Ambler couldn't resist baiting his new nemesis. It was almost as good as smacking him.

'I need it to buy a gun.'

Barnes's shocked expression was real. It was as if his hair stood up straight. 'Wait . . . I can't be a party to violence. I never agree to any kind of activity that requires a gun. That's for the police.'

'The money is to buy what might be the rifle that killed George Olson.'

'From whom?'

'Most likely the killer.'

'Who?'

'Loose lips sink ships,' Ambler said in a hushed tone. 'I'll tell you when we know for sure.'

Barnes hemmed and hawed, argued and prevaricated but finally came around. 'We send 1099s to all of our vendors; this will be noted as a security consultation. You'll be listed as the vendor.'

Ambler surprised himself by asking for the money; he hadn't known until he did it that he was going to go along with John's plan to buy the rifle from Nichols.

EIGHTEEN

The gun exchange took place that night and went off smoothly enough. Wilmer and Freddy, seasoned negotiators obviously, talked Nichols down to $250 plus the Glock for the rifle. The wrinkle Ambler hadn't figured on was the cost of the Glock, which was $500, so even with the money from the college's discretionary funds and the discount the retired gangbangers negotiated, he was still going to be out $250.

Money well spent, Ambler told himself later that evening, after John and David Levinson delivered the rifle to the 53rd Precinct, telling the detectives who it belonged to and what it might have been used for.

Ballistics checked the bullets that killed George Olson and the one taken from Ambler's shoulder against the rifle and made a match. The police also discovered that Walt Nichols held a weapons expert qualification badge when he was in the army. The following evening, a squad from the Bronx special operations unit and the detectives from Bronx homicide set out to arrest Walt Nichols. That should have been the end of the story.

Yet, as sometimes happens, it wasn't the main event but the aftermath that became the unmitigated disaster.

When the Bronx violent felony squad and detectives from the 53rd Precinct broke down the door and entered Walt Nichols's apartment in the Mott Haven section of the Bronx, they found his body in a doorway, half in the kitchen and half in the living room. He'd been shot twice in the torso and once in the head. The murder weapon was later determined to have been his newly acquired Glock.

No fingerprints on the gun. No sign of forced entry. Detectives from the Bronx Homicide Squad determined Nichols was shot during and after a struggle over the Glock. They based this on their finding bullet holes in the ceiling and in one wall, as well as where the bullets were in Nichols.

Three days after the police found Nichols's body, on a Wednesday morning shortly before 8:00, they arrested John Ambler as he left his father's apartment to take his son to school. Ambler, following behind John and Johnny on his way to work, grabbed his terrified grandson, who was trying to wrestle his father away from a burly uniformed cop three times his size.

'This is ridiculous,' Ambler told the uniformed sergeant who was the only one who paid any attention to him. Two plainclothes detectives with their gold shields hanging from their breast pockets did their best to ignore him and Johnny, but they pretty much failed. The boy's screams and sobs were impossible for anyone to ignore.

Ambler told the sergeant he wanted to see the warrant.

'He'll see the warrant when we get him uptown.' The sergeant nodded toward John. 'You don't get to see the warrant. I don't even know who the hell you are.'

'I'm his father.'

'He's grown up now,' the unfazed sergeant said. 'You had your chance. He'll have to do this on his own.'

It took all morning to calm Johnny down. No chance the boy could go to school. No chance for Ambler to go to work. Back upstairs in the apartment, working like a one-armed paper hanger, he made Johnny a second breakfast of sausage and pancakes, called Adele and David Levinson and told them what happened.

It also took most of the morning for David to track John down. The lawyer finally called shortly after noon. Adele had come over to Ambler's apartment on her lunch break, and leaned against him with her arms around Johnny, listening while Ambler took the call.

Levinson was his usual blustery self. 'He's in the House of Detention in the Bronx, waiting for arraignment. I'm on my way up there now. I went to Central Booking in Manhattan first. I hoped I could catch up with him before they took him to that hellhole in the Bronx. They're supposed to arraign him within twenty-four hours – I worked on that suit when I was at Legal Aid – but the Bronx is another country. They can lose prisoners for days, if not weeks.'

His tone changed, turned serious. 'They don't always grant bail, and if they do, it's gonna be high.'

'Why?' Ambler tried to keep the panic out of his voice. 'What's John charged with?' He'd assumed it was a gun charge because John had arranged the exchange of the Glock for the Remington rifle. Now he feared worse. And the truth was worse than that.

'Murder Two.' The lawyer's tone was flat. 'I'll know more after the arraignment. With luck, late this afternoon or tonight. I'll try for no bail. But he has a prior, so that one's dead in the water.' Levinson paused and then went on in an unfamiliar formal tone. 'Do you own your apartment?'

'No.' He knew right away why Levinson asked.

'I do.' Adele pulled Ambler's arm and the phone closer to her. She understood also. 'I have equity because real-estate prices went up so much.'

Ambler started to say no but couldn't bring himself to say the word.

'I'll draw up a property bond agreement.' Levinson told her the documents she'd need to bring to his office in the morning.

Adele rushed off to gather the materials she needed to prove she owned the apartment and an assessment of the apartment's value. Ambler was still in shock. To try to pull himself together, he and Johnny took Lola for a long walk along the East River Greenway all the way to Battery Park and back. It was the only thing he could think of doing. Johnny couldn't sit still and he couldn't concentrate on anything. He couldn't imagine what the boy felt. It must be what he felt when his mother died. Ambler couldn't himself imagine it.

What ran through his mind as they walked were memories from a decade before, when the son he loved more deeply than anyone else in his life was locked away in a prison, steel bars and concrete walls separating him from John and nothing he could do about it. The dread he felt that it could be happening again kept tears brimming in his eyes for the hours-long walk.

As he did a few nights ago, Johnny asked questions over and over, different questions but the same compulsive questioning. Ambler gave versions of the same answer. Everything would be all right. The police would realize they'd made a mistake. His dad hadn't killed anyone. It wasn't so unusual for the police to find out they'd arrested the wrong man. The court would set the bond and his dad would be out of jail by tomorrow. It might even happen that David the lawyer would show the judge how the police didn't have any evidence to hold John and he'd be out of jail later tonight. Everything would be all right, Ambler assured his grandson again, and wished to all the gods in heaven that it were true.

Levinson called after the arraignment. He was pleased with himself because he'd talked the ADA into a manslaughter charge rather than the Murder Two the police had originally come up with. The lower charge meant lower bail. 'Murder Two the judge could have ordered him held without bail,' the lawyer said. 'Lucky for us, the attorney assigned the case was new enough on the job not to have become a hater yet. We'll need a hundred grand. I can try to get it lowered but your friend's equity in her apartment is enough to cover it if I can't.'

'What the hell happened? Why are they charging John with anything?'

'He was handy. They didn't have a suspect. Someone remembered John handled the gun sale—'

Ambler interrupted. 'But he didn't. A friend of his from prison got two local guys—'

This time, Levinson interrupted. 'If you remember, I turned the murder weapon over to the police. There was no mention of two guys handling things or of anyone else. As far as I knew, and what I told the police, John arranged to get the rifle from Walter Nichols.'

He paused for emphasis. 'In my business, you learn pretty quick there are numerous versions of what happened. It's hard to know which one is true. Sometimes, you never know what really happened. The jury or the judge believes someone and they don't believe someone else. That's how justice gets done.'

Ambler didn't care what Levinson thought about different versions of truth. He knew what the truth was here. And John had told the truth. 'What did John say?'

'The prosecutor told the judge what the charges were and why they'd charged John. John pleaded not guilty and wisely said nothing else. I didn't spend a long time talking to him.

He asked how they could charge him; he wasn't anywhere near Nichols's apartment.

'I said that was good. Did he have someone who could verify that he was someplace else. He started to say yes and then he said no. He didn't mention two local guys or his friend from prison. I didn't ask about them, of course, since I didn't know about them.'

David got on the phone with Adele. She'd gathered up all of the papers she needed and arranged to meet him at his office in the morning to go to the Bronx and post the bond to get John out of jail.

'Your dad should be home tomorrow,' Ambler told his grandson.

'Are they letting him go?'

'Not exactly. But everything will be OK,' he said for the gazillionth time.

Ambler spent the night at his apartment with Johnny. John arrived late the next morning. Bags under his eyes. The eyes themselves as red as rust. He'd developed a twitch at the corner of his mouth he'd not had before. He was fidgety and on-edge in a way he hadn't been since he'd been released from prison. He was reluctant to talk about what had happened, returning to the shell he'd been in while in prison.

Johnny didn't care; the only thing he wanted was to be with his father. When John sat down, the boy sat next to him. When John went to the kitchen, Johnny followed. John seemed both not to notice him and to make no move to separate himself.

It wasn't until late in the evening when Johnny finally went to bed and Ambler made ready to take Lola for her nightly walk, that he got the sense John was ready to talk. Without saying anything, John put on his jacket and followed him and Lola out the door.

'The weirdest thing,' John said after they'd walked a couple of blocks in silence, 'was the way they said it happened. It was like a nightmare I had for years after Colin was killed. I was wrestling a big guy for his gun – like what happened with Colin but it wasn't Colin. After the gun went off and the guy fell, I had the gun in my hand and shot him again. That's what happened to Walt. The guy who killed him shot him in the head after it was over, after Walt was already shot.'

Ambler hadn't known the details of Nichols's death. He did know that in John's battle for the gun with his roommate Colin, the gun fired only once and it was never clear whose hand was holding it when it went off. He waited for John to say something about the charges against him and why there was confusion when there shouldn't be.

After a few moments of silence, he said, 'I don't understand why the police arrested you. What about the guys who did the transaction? Your friend Oscar's pals. Can't they vouch for you? Weren't you with them around the time Walt Nichols was murdered?

'The police think because you delivered the rifle to them you were the one who did the gun exchange. Oscar and his pals could tell the police what really happened; that you weren't involved in the actual exchange and that you were with them at the time Nichols was killed.'

John's tone was harsh, a rebuke. 'Wilmer and Freddy have nothing to do with this. Neither does Oscar. As far as Walt's murder goes, they don't exist. I didn't tell the lawyer about them. Now I'm telling you to forget you ever heard of them.'

For a moment, Ambler didn't understand. And then he did and got really mad. John was mouthing a gangster code. Omertà. You don't sing to the cops. You don't rat on your partners. He should know better than that. A prison term was at stake. He had a child. He wasn't part of the underworld. Ambler calmed himself and spoke quietly.

'It's not like they're guilty of anything. You're facing a murder charge. You need someone to back you up. None of you killed anyone. I'm sure your friends would understand you need to clarify things—'

John cut him off. 'I wish it was that easy. Those guys helped me out; they don't deserve trouble for doing that. Oscar's on parole. All of them have records. If I talk about Wilmer and Freddy, Oscar's going to come up. He has anything to do with handling, selling, facilitating the sale of a gun, he goes back to prison. I can't do that to him.'

He stopped and met Ambler's gaze. His eyes glistened. 'Oscar protected me in the joint. You don't know what that means; you couldn't understand. I was an innocent. Prison would have ruined me if it didn't kill me. You think you know what evil is? You don't. Punks in there are crazy, drooling at the mouth crazy, out in general population. Nothing to hold them back.

'Oscar was a rock. He was the man. No one messed with him. So no one messed with me. He's paid his dues. He's an old man, older than you. He does another bid, he dies in prison. He's running a mom-and-pop store, enjoying his family. I'll go back myself before I send him back.' He turned away, not before Ambler saw tears glistening on his cheeks. 'You don't think I've thought about going back . . . about Johnny?'

He walked away . . . and then slowed down until Ambler and Lola caught up. He was calm. 'Sorry for the drama.' He chuckled. 'It's worse than that.' He threw up his arms like Moses on the mountain and spoke to darkness around them. 'It's fucking amazing how you can get into a mess like this without doing anything wrong.'

Ambler felt a pang of guilt that nearly brought him to his knees. John was in this mess because Ambler involved him in a risky investigation too soon after he got out of prison. He started to say this, but John waved him off.

'How can it be your fault? How can it be anyone's fault?'

Part two of the mess was John wouldn't say where he went that night after he left Oscar and his pals. Ambler was so frustrated by this that tears came to his eyes. But John wouldn't budge.

'Maybe something will happen to change things. But right now, I can't say.'

Ambler was sure it was another stupid 'code of honor among thieves' thing and he hoped his son would come to his senses. He spent a mostly sleepless night at Adele's, fighting off despair and getting straight in his head what he needed to do next. Arguing with John wouldn't change anything. He needed to figure out what happened, find out who killed Walt Nichols and why.

In the morning, he went over his plan with Adele – who had left him floundering in the bed in the middle of the night and gone and slept on the couch – while they ate a hasty breakfast of coffee and toast. He told her he was baffled.

'Have you thought of the possibility,' Adele asked calmly, 'that someone hired this Walt person to kill the murdered professor for whatever reason. And then, when it looked like the Walt guy would get caught, hired someone else to kill him or did it himself.'

Ambler bought into the idea that someone paid Nichols to kill George Olson. The possibility had been in the back of his mind since he'd begun to suspect Walt Nichols of the murder. He didn't know this for sure; he couldn't prove it.

Yet it made sense – more sense than anything else he could think of – so he was going to act as if it were true until life and events told him something else was true. He could create a list of a few – a very few – people he knew of who 'might possibly' have hired Walt to kill Olson. But there 'might' be any number of potential conspirators he didn't know about.

If he was going to get anywhere, he had to consider plausibility. People were usually killed by someone they know. What was most plausible was someone on the Trinity College campus had George Olson killed. One likely culprit was Sam. If not Sam, who?

By late that morning, sleep-deprived Ambler had come up with a place to begin. At work, he made a series of phone calls, beginning with Sarah Hastings. By noon he'd arranged a gathering at her house, inviting Sam, Rebecca and John. He wanted to get them together in one room and see if their stories matched. If the stories did match and they weren't lying and he could rule them out as murder conspirators, maybe they could help him figure out who next on the list of possible murderers to rule out, until he got to someone he couldn't rule out.

After Walt Nichols's murder, despite his being their prime suspect, the police hadn't closed the case on George Olson's murder. Ambler wasn't sure why, but this meant they still wanted to talk to Sam. And, by the look of things, Sam still didn't want to talk to them.

So Sam Abernathy was still 'a person of interest' in the case. Because of this, McNulty – the erstwhile actor – had fitted him out with a costume/disguise. He came to the door wearing a Yankee cap, biker shades and a false mustache, so everyone thought he was the pizza delivery man.

The group Ambler assembled, gathered in Sarah's small living room, resembled nothing so much as the suspects in the final scene of a Charlie Chan movie. Ambler felt foolish and wondered if anyone else made the connection; probably Sam did. Well, he didn't really suspect any of them of murder. But of course, he might be wrong. They could all be part of an elaborate conspiracy against him and John.

Though the way Sarah and John looked at each other and the fact they'd managed to sit beside each other, scrunched together on the couch, suggested another sort of conspiracy, as did Sam and Rebecca, the other two love birds huddled at the other end of the couch. He half expected the lights to dim and the two couples to start making out like teenagers at a birthday party.

He tried hard not to begin by saying 'The reason I asked you all here tonight . . .' But what he did say was almost the same thing. 'I wanted to talk to all of you at the same time because I'm hoping if we tackle this together, something will click, and you'll come up with information and ideas you wouldn't come up with separately. The sum will be more than its parts.'

He did believe what he said, although the idea came to him as he said it and not before. 'Sam, you and Sarah must have some idea of why George Olson was murdered. Let's say for the sake of argument Walt Nichols was hired to kill Olson – he didn't, as far as we know, have a motive for the murder on his own. So who might have hired him to do the job?

'Who would want to kill Olson? In the farthest reaches of your imagination, who do you see hiring Nichols to kill him? Did George have strange habits, gamble, do drugs, visit prostitutes? Could he have had a secret life? Sam, you knew him best . . .'

Sam glanced at everyone – who continued to regard him suspiciously, as if given his disguise they still weren't sure it was really him – and then turned his gaze on Ambler. 'George didn't do any of those things. He was an open book – a good man, a dedicated teacher who loved science. He was happy

with who he was. He didn't need anything else; he had his
students and his work . . . What I think is he knew something
that made him a threat to the person who marked him for
death . . . someone greedy, ambitious and ruthless.'

'Who?' Ambler asked, while everyone else watched Sam
like he was a conjurer.

The conjurer took a moment, extending the drama, before
he said, 'I don't know. I can't imagine anyone on the faculty
who'd want to kill George. Sometimes there are bitter disagreements when the senate committee doles out the conference
and travel grants. George takes the heat for that. But everyone
knows it's Doug Stuart who makes the decisions. Still, I don't
see anyone murdering a colleague over a travel grant.'

'What about Barnes?' Ambler expected a reaction from Sam
or Sarah. Doesn't everyone hate their boss? It was worth noting
that he hadn't heard anything from Barnes since the latest
murder. You'd think he'd want to know what Ambler knew
about the murder of one of his students, someone they'd been
talking about.

Sarah had been deep in thought while Sam was speaking,
and he wasn't sure she'd heard his question. When she did
speak up, her voice had a faraway sound, as if she hoped to
distance herself from what she said. 'Doug,' she said. 'Doug
is greedy and ambitious.'

The assembled, including Ambler, turned to her in surprised
silence. Was she suggesting her ex-husband was a murderer?

NINETEEN

She cleared up that confusion as soon as she noticed everyone watching her in varying states of amazement. 'I'm not saying he's a murderer. I meant he's ambitious, and he cares excessively about money, more than anyone I've ever known. He'd do anything for money.' Realizing the implication of what she'd said, she put her hand to her mouth. 'I don't mean he'd kill for it. I meant he likes money – or more accurately he likes what money can buy.'

Ambler was curious. He hadn't thought more than passingly of Stuart as a suspect. But Stuart did have a close connection to Walt Nichols that might or might not mean something.

'We all like things money can buy, don't we?' he asked Sarah. 'But avaricious men don't become college professors or defenders of the environment, do they? You'd think the opposite, that he'd be an enemy of the greedy capitalists destroying the natural world in pursuit of profit.'

Sam spoke before she did, addressing Ambler. 'Have you seen the car he drives?'

Ambler hadn't.

'He buys a new one every couple of years, one of those high-end electric deals that probably set him back fifty thousand dollars or more.'

Ambler turned to Sarah, who nodded.

'His house is net zero,' she said. 'He had it built after our divorce in a posh area in Mount Vernon.'

'How does he afford all that on a professor's salary?' Sam glared at Sarah and then at Ambler.

Ambler thought about his own paltry librarian's pay. Some professors were rich to start with, family wealth. Others got rich at Harvard or Stanford or places like that, in fields that allowed them to start businesses alongside their academic work. Liberal arts college professors were unlikely to have the kind of labs or equipment that would lead to creating money-making enterprises out of their academic work.

'Doug was always secretive about money,' Sarah continued without prompting. 'I didn't care enough to pry. He created a business of some sort he did on the side. Consulting. He might have had shares in a start-up venture around environmental building or design. I don't know, except that I know he spent a lot of time making sure he had money.'

'I hope you don't mind my asking.' This time, Ambler realized he was asking an impertinent question before he blurted it out. 'Does he pay you alimony?'

'No. I didn't ask for any.' She was thoughtful again. 'I never knew how much money he had. As I said, he was secretive about it. And I don't know anything about money. I don't care about it. He made fun of me for that – he used to call me "Blondie", an airhead poet who didn't understand what was important in life.

'He admired wealthy people – wealthy men – and tried to ingratiate himself with any of the alumni or Board members he knew were rich. He wanted me to play up to them, too.'

She reddened. 'We fought over that. One night, after a reception, he was furious because I embarrassed a donor who was obnoxiously coming on to me.' Her voice rose. 'He said I should humor the jerk.'

She glanced at John and something passed between them. 'You'd think it would be the other way around, wouldn't you . . .?' She spoke so quietly Ambler could barely hear her. 'A husband would be angry at his wife for paying attention to another man . . . Not Doug. It would never occur to him I might find another man more attractive than him.'

Everyone was quiet for a moment until Rebecca said, 'My husband slapped me more than once because he said I flirted with some man. Each time, it was the man bothering me.' She stared at her hands after she said this, embarrassed and not looking at anyone, but she went on. 'It was safer for him to slap me around than to stand up to a man.'

She looked up then, this time at Sarah as if speaking directly to her. 'He's greedy, too. But too much of a coward to be ruthless.' She turned to Ambler. 'Does that count?'

Ambler tried to put this delicately, speaking quietly. 'Could your husband have mistakenly thought something was going on between you and George Olson?'

She didn't seem to care any longer about discussing her infidelity. 'He would've taken it out on me. He doesn't hurt anyone else, only me.'

Again, there was silence.

'Let's go back to Barnes,' Ambler tried. 'He knew almost everything I knew. I, unwisely I think now, agreed to tell him what I found out about George Olson's murder. I did that so he'd help me when I needed information about someone at the college. He knew I was zeroing in on Walt Nichols as a suspect. He might have had him killed to keep him from talking.'

'Or he might have told someone else what you told him,' John said. 'From what you said about him, I doubt he'd care about keeping an agreement.'

Sam jumped in. 'You can be damn sure if Barnes knew something, he told Doug Stuart, too – and vice versa. They're as thick as thieves.'

'Can anyone think of a reason Barnes would have George Olson killed?' It was a silly question, but Ambler was grasping at straws.

Sam jumped in again. 'George was changing sides; Doug probably told Barnes that. I'm sure George was going to support me for faculty senate president. If that happened, if George turned against Doug and supported me, I'd become faculty senate president and put the kibosh on selling the crime fiction collection, and a lot of other plans Barnes had.'

'Why wouldn't he just kill you?' John asked.

The question stumped Sam.

After a moment, Sarah said, 'Faculty disputes can be bitter and vicious. But we're not the Mafia; we don't settle differences with guns and bodies buried in vacant lots.'

'You'd be surprised who turns out to be killers,' Sam said.

For a moment, everyone froze. Ambler wondered if, like him, they were thinking about John. 'From what I've learned,' Ambler said, 'Walt Nichols was a good student. Did either of you have him in class?' Neither did, so he asked, 'Do you know anyone who did have him in class?'

'He was a protégé of Doug's,' Sarah said. 'Doug was a mentor for most of the students in that ex-offender entry program. They were a special project for him. He has a kind of messiah complex; he likes having disciples, along with his stable of groupies.'

She probably sounded more bitter than she meant to. But what she said gave Ambler pause. He hadn't thought about talking to Walt's friends. John would know them. But they weren't likely to want to talk to either him or John, not now, after Walt's murder. Stuart was another story. No reason he wouldn't talk to Ambler again, and he might intercede with his disciples and encourage them to talk. On the other hand, given Stuart's unholy alliance with Barnes, he could have something to hide also. George Olson might have gotten wind of something nefarious Barnes and Stuart were up to. He asked Sam.

'I wouldn't put anything past them.' Sam spoke with conviction, but he didn't know what they might have been up to. 'George cared about his research and he cared about his students.' Sam's tone was solemn, as if he might be giving a eulogy. 'He was also protective of the traditions of the academy, especially as concerned the faculty role in shared governance.

'Like many of us, he didn't like the changes Barnes was trying to push through. Barnes doesn't give a hoot about the traditions of the academy. He wants to turn the college into an amalgam of a day-care center, an amusement park, and an employment office, pampering the students and catering to corporate America.'

Ambler sympathized with Sam. He didn't like how higher education had changed and continued to change. It came down to money, of course. No room these days for liberal education and the life of the mind. The sciences did a little better, as did technology; they were marketable. But the humanities were a relic of the horse-and-buggy days. The college education of the future: 'Get your degree online in thirty days without opening a book.'

When you came right down to it, what made more sense would be for a group of the faculty to get together and murder

Barnes, the progenitor of the soulless education of the future that they couldn't abide. The possibility of blackmail occurred to Ambler, too.

Might Olson have discovered Barnes took shortcuts in bringing in one of his new programs, perhaps received a financial incentive, a piece of the action? If the faculty found out they'd be up in arms. And suppose Barnes went around the Board, too, did a shady deal in secret. He could be forced to resign.

Ambler could speculate all he wanted to. It meant nothing. He needed facts. 'Could Olson have caught on to Barnes doing something unethical?' he asked Sam.

'Barnes is slick.' Sam had a way of clearing his throat before he spoke and saying 'um' now and again, which gave more gravity to his pronouncements than they might deserve. 'He doesn't do anything until he's lined up the Board, the faculty, and the student government behind him. And, as I said, George wasn't interested in what went on outside the classroom and the lab. Despite his position in the senate, he didn't pay much attention to the administration. Doug would be more likely to have something on Barnes, if anyone did.'

Ambler was reminded of something Sam had told him. 'You said George might have had a falling-out with Doug Stuart. You don't have any idea why?'

Sam shook his head. 'I wish I knew. The election is in two weeks. Unless this is cleared up, I don't stand a chance. The police haven't said conclusively that Walt Nichols killed George, so some people still think I did it.'

An alarming thought flashed through Ambler's mind. The police could conclude Walt Nichols killed George Olson and in revenge John killed Nichols. The cases solved, Nichols dead, John back in prison, Sam would be in the clear. Sam undoubtedly had the same thought but wouldn't of course mention it.

'Who are the other officers of the faculty senate?' he asked.

'Florence Randolph is the secretary-treasurer; that's the only other officer,' Sarah said. She reminded Ambler he'd met Florence the first day he came to the campus. 'Our librarians are faculty at Trinity. She's a full professor and we put her up

during the last election as a counterweight to Doug. She's
sincere and conscientious but no match for Doug as a
politician.'

'That was a waste of time,' John said as he and Ambler rode
home on the Metro North train to Grand Central. 'I thought
we'd find out more. Walt didn't kill that professor on his own.
He had no reason to. Don't cops look for a motive?'

Ambler didn't know what the police were looking for, or
if they were looking for anything. If Mike Cosgrove was
working the case, he could point out to him the probable
connection between Nichols and someone on the Trinity
campus who hired him to kill George Olson.

But Mike would already know to look into that possibility.
As far as Ambler knew of what the Bronx cops were thinking,
they could be looking into that connection. They charged John
but Levinson wouldn't have persuaded the ADA to reduce the
charge and let John out on bail if the cops were sure of their
case. At least, he hoped they weren't sure of their case.

He told this to John. The evening's get-together hadn't been
all he might have wished for. Yet, as he sometimes felt when
poking around in a murder investigation, he was hopeful.
What the little group talked about tonight could have
produced nothing, and like many interviews and conversations could have led to a dead end. But it didn't.

'Tonight wasn't as bad as it might have been,' he said, and
then watched the lights from the Bronx apartment building
streak by, interrupting the darkness outside the train window.
Once in a while, he saw his own reflection, and realized
he looked as somber as John did.

'The good thing – and this won't mean much to you – the
good thing out of what we talked about tonight is I have three
conversations I want to have – actually, four; I have something
I want to talk to Sam about, too. When an investigation goes
really bad, you don't have anything to do next. You've turned
over all of the stones and found nothing that tells you where
to look next. As long as there's someplace to go next, you
have hope.'

'Who are you going to talk to?' No light of hope shone in

John's eyes; instead Ambler looked into dark pools of despair. 'The president, Barnes, is one. Who are the others?'

'Professor Randolph, the librarian, who might know something I don't know about Barnes and Doug Stuart. And Professor Stuart himself.'

For a moment, John was quiet and watched out the window past Ambler. Ambler watched too, the lights flashing through the darkness, the occasional reflection of two somber faces.

'I never did get to see Stuart,' John said. 'I remember Sarah told me not to trust him.'

Ambler wasn't sure he trusted Stuart either, or Barnes, or anyone else including Sam. He had no special reason not to trust Stuart, nor did he have much reason to dislike the man, other than he'd hurt and divorced Sarah and he was helping Barnes sell off Sam's crime fiction collection.

On the positive side, Stuart had a lot going for him. By all accounts, he was a wildly popular teacher, a recognized scholar in his field, an environmental activist; he championed a program helping former felons attain a college education, a program John might be eligible for one day. Ambler told himself that if he were wise, he'd withhold judgment on Stuart until he saw how much help he might be.

When they got home, he called Adele to ask her to go back to her databases to see if she could find anything of note about Barnes or Stuart. He should have thought of that before. She was more likely to find information about them than about Walt Nichols.

'Nice of you to think of me.' Her tone of voice could cut glass.

'I'm sorry.' And he was. He'd told her he wanted to be with her; she needed company during her pregnancy; she was nervous and a little bit scared. He'd virtually ignored her for weeks, except for the few days when she was taking care of him.

'I know you're worried about John. So am I. I'm sorry I'm so snappy. Don't pay any attention to me. My moods are all over the place. Tonight I felt like I was the last person on earth. No one cared if I had a baby or not. No one cared if I lived or died.'

'Are you feeling OK otherwise? Is everything OK with . . .'
He hesitated to say 'the baby'. He didn't know why.

'Yes. I'm feeling better the last few days. It's the in-between
stage. I don't feel sick. The opposite, I'm hungry all the time.
And I haven't reached the bloating stage when I'll feel like
I'm carrying a watermelon under my shirt. Why'd you call?
. . . And don't tell me it was because you missed me.'

'Do you want me to come over? . . . When I take Lola out,
we could just walk over to your place.'

He listened to the silence for a moment. 'I'd like that,' she
said shyly, and he felt a little flutter in his chest. She was still
shy when he and Lola arrived at her apartment. He held her
tightly for a long time in the hallway, feeling the warmth of
her body from beneath her robe until, after a few moments,
she began to move her lower body slowly, rolling her hips in
a blatantly erotic way that sucked his breath out of him. They
talked hardly at all and made love as a man and woman might
who'd been longing for each other.

In the morning she was as chipper as he'd ever seen her.
She kissed him lightly a half-dozen times as she made coffee
and poured them bowls of granola. He told her about the
gathering the night before and what he planned to do that
day and asked her about finding out what she could about
Barnes and Stuart.

'You'll find out who the killer is. We'll fix this,' she said.
'It's not possible that John will go back to prison for something
he didn't do. How can the police be so stupid?'

Ambler tried to latch on to Adele's cheerfulness and borrow
her determination. He was tired, physically tired. Last night
with her had rejuvenated him. He'd awoken into what felt like
an invincible springtime. But remembering what lay in front
of him tried to take his strength away. He wanted to stay where
he was; drink another cup of coffee, read the paper, go back
to bed with Adele, and then read a book.

He wasn't defeated, not discouraged; he was weary. He
wanted someone else to take on the task of finding the murderer
of Walt Nichols and George Olson. Someone else to question
Barnes and Stuart, poke holes in their stories, someone else
to discover tidbits of information no one else recognized as

important, which would lead him to the next piece of information and the next, until the unraveling of those tidbits led him to the truth, or enough truth to free his son from suspicion.

He'd been discouraged before, run into brick walls and walked down blind alleys, but he'd bounced back. This feeling was different, not something he could explain to Adele, not something he could explain to himself very well. It might be because it was John's life at stake this time and he couldn't face the possibility that he'd fail.

'You look so tired,' Adele said, and came behind him to gently touch his injured shoulder. 'You should be convalescing in a bucolic rest home and not chasing after murderers. This will end. We'll find some time for you to rest and heal.'

Again, she was looking out for him when he should be looking out for her. He told her this. 'I felt tired for a moment,' he said, 'like I might if I were running a race. At some point, you think you aren't going to make it; you can't get to the finish line. And then you get a second wind. That's all I need – a second wind. I'm going to kiss you now for a long time, and that will give me a second wind.'

'And a boner,' Adele said.

TWENTY

He had to cool his heels in Barnes's waiting area for a half-hour. He should have called ahead. At least he did call to find out that Stuart's office hours were later that afternoon. He sat in the uncomfortable fake leather chair and watched the cute work-study receptionist chew gum while she spoke Spanish into her cell phone and an approximation of proper English into the desk phone the two or three times it rang – her redeeming feature was she smiled prettily at him each time she glanced in his direction. Waiting, if nothing else, gave him time to think about what Barnes might tell him that would be useful.

'I have a meeting in ten minutes.' Barnes made a show of looking at his watch, trying not to let on that he was nervous.

Ambler stood in front of the desk. 'Who did you tell, besides Stuart and the Board of Trustees person, that I asked for information about Walt Nichols?'

Barnes took his smart phone out of his suit pocket and consulted it, his frown suggesting Ambler's question kept him from dealing with important matters. After a moment, he looked up, a deeper frown suggesting he was sorry Ambler was still there. 'I don't recall telling anyone. Why would you think I did?'

Ambler kept bearing down. 'Because he was murdered, and I want to know who killed him. Someone you told might be that person.'

For someone who'd reached the exalted level of a college presidency, Barnes did a poor job of hiding both his agitation and guilt. 'That's highly unlikely.' His phone clattered on to the top of his desk, which this time held only a laptop computer and now the cell phone, not a single piece of paper. Barnes couldn't make up his mind whether to pick up the phone or take another look at his watch.

Ambler put his hands on the desk and leaned closer to

Barnes. 'You told the head of the Board of Trustees. Who's that?'

'You can't be serious. You suspect Graham Williamson? He's president of . . .' Barnes caught himself. 'I'm sorry about your son. I'm sure you believe he's innocent . . . but that doesn't excuse . . .' He froze and backed away from Ambler, even though the desk was between them, as if Ambler might attack him.

'I know you told him . . . and your partner in crime, Doug Stuart. Who else?'

Because of whatever battles Barnes was fighting with himself, he lost his air of superiority. Like a dog who submits to the attack of a fiercer dog, he rolled over, belly up, and gave up the fight.

'That's all. I gave Doug a heads-up because Nichols was one of his mentees. And I gave Graham only a bare outline of what was afoot, so he wouldn't be blindsided by anything that came out in the newspapers.

'Believe me, what I told him was cursory, and he had little interest in it anyway.' Barnes regained his footing. 'We pretend Graham has his finger on the pulse of the campus. In reality, if something noteworthy or scandalous comes up, he wants to be able to say he was aware of it. Otherwise, he couldn't care less.'

'And Doug Stuart,' Ambler said. 'You can't keep secrets from him because he keeps the faculty in line. Even if I believe those are the only two people you told, it doesn't make a difference because you have no idea whom they might have told, including Walt Nichols and any accomplices he might have had.'

Barnes dug in his heels. 'I don't suppose anyone told you anything that would be helpful to me. You said Sam Abernathy didn't kill George Olson. You implied the last time you were here that the student who was murdered, Walter Nichols, killed him. Do you still think that?'

'Yes.'

'What do the police say?'

'I don't know.'

'They think Sam Abernathy killed George. Why don't they think he killed Walter Nichols?'

Ambler's reply wasn't entirely truthful. 'They're still investigating. The police don't make announcements until they have their ducks lined up. But it's pretty clear Walt Nichols shot and killed George Olson. The question is why?'

Barnes's questions irritated him. Not so much because they weren't reasonable enough questions, but because of what they forced him to admit, if only to himself. He needed to find whoever hired Nichols to kill Olson and, when he did, he'd find the person who killed Nichols.

As was his habit, Ambler glanced at the bookshelf alongside the office door as he was leaving and was surprised by something he saw. He picked up one of the books and turned to Barnes. 'I wouldn't have thought you a mystery reader.'

'I'm not really.' His manner softened, as if he was pleased Ambler had shifted the conversation to something more personal and friendly. 'Not much time for pleasure reading in this job. I ask my staff to purchase any books written by faculty members. Sometimes colleagues drop off a book they think I'll enjoy.' He had a friendly conspiratorial smile on his face. 'To be honest, I rarely read them.'

'Do you know where this one came from?'

Barnes shook his head. 'Would you like to borrow it?'

Ambler put the book back on the shelf. 'No. Thanks. I've read it.'

As he walked across the college green to the humanities building and Doug Stuart's office, he wondered if he'd made a mistake not taking Barnes up on his offer to borrow the book. The book was Rex Stout's *The Hand in the Glove*, one of the very few first editions of the only Dol Bonner mystery Stout published. Ambler was pretty sure it was one of the missing first editions from Sam Abernathy's New York Mystery Writers collection.

Doug Stuart was holding a conference with a student, and two more waited in the hallway to see him. His office door was open, so he saw Ambler take a peek in and waved, but then went right back to talking with the student, a young woman. Both were engrossed in a paper on the desk in front of them. The two students in the hallway were women and quite young also, so little chance any of them were friends of the murder victim.

He took a walk while he waited for Stuart to finish his conferences, thought of checking on the crime fiction collection in the library, thought about going back to Barnes's office to get the book. In the end, he sat on a bench and watched the students walking to and from classes, singly, in couples, in small groups, almost all of them wearing jeans with backpacks hanging from their shoulders, sometimes with books and notebooks pressed against their chests, not so different than students looked when he trod the hallowed halls of ivy.

Of course, there would be differences. Forty-some years ago most of the students on these cement walks would have been white. Colleges had been working on increasing diversity since the late Sixties. Today, even at this somewhat selective city liberal arts college, Asian, Black, and Latin students taken together outnumbered the whites; also different, a significant majority were young women, where in his day the majority would have been men.

When Ambler got back to Stuart's office, the professor was alone; the door was open.

'Come in.' He waved good-naturedly. 'Leave the door open. If a student shows up, we'll need to take a break. But short. My conferences only last ten or fifteen minutes.'

Stuart was as relaxed and sure of himself as Ambler remembered him. He locked his affable and inquisitive gaze on Ambler and didn't let go until Ambler was seated. Alert, smiling, jaunty, dressed more like an outdoorsman (one who took hikes along nature trails or paddled a canoe, rather than a hunter or fisherman) than a college professor, he treated Ambler like Ambler expected he treated his students: offering an engaging welcome, willing to meet the student on their level, letting them know their concerns were his concerns, while subtly establishing that he was the superior, the student the underling.

Once again, Stuart assumed he was in charge of the conversation. 'I assume you're here about Walt's death. A tragedy. I'm heartbroken. Walt had had a troubled life, but I truly believe he was turning it around. A brilliant student, tremendous potential . . . And your son? I was so sorry to learn of his arrest too. You must be beside yourself with worry.'

Stuart's smugness angered Ambler; he had to choke back his rage and an urge this time to throttle Stuart whose veneer of sympathy failed to disguise a clear accusation: 'I'm so sorry your son is a murderer.'

Everything about Stuart irritated Ambler, and at the same time threw him off track. He couldn't pin him down. Given the facts that were known about Nichols's death, either Stuart didn't know Nichols was at least a suspect in George Olson's killing, or he was pretending he didn't know.

Since Ambler had no clue which was true, he didn't know how to begin. He remembered what John said via Sarah Hastings: not to trust Stuart. This meant, for one thing, he didn't have to play fair. 'Murder reverberates,' he began. 'More lives are changed than only those of the victim and the killer.

'I'm sorry Walt Nichols was murdered. I understand you were his mentor, so I imagine you're shocked and saddened by his death. But my son didn't kill him.'

'Oh?' Stuart's reaction was a poorly performed theatrical gesture of surprise. 'I understand there was a struggle. Walt was a hardened criminal. He was changing, reforming, but a violent streak remained. I'm sure what happened was unintentional—'

Ambler interrupted him. 'John didn't kill him intentionally or unintentionally. The police will figure that out sooner or later, and we'll be left with finding out who did kill him. What my son did do was discover your mentee was almost certainly a murderer.'

Stuart sat back and rubbed his chin, mimicking the pose intellectuals had developed over the years for the physical manifestation of a thinker.

'I'm surprised to hear you say that. Why did the police arrest your son if that was the case? Of course, I don't know what happened when Walt was killed and I don't know who killed George; I wasn't privy to either happening . . . Should I accept what you say is your conjecture or known fact?'

'You can call it conjecture. I didn't come here to argue with you. I came to ask for your help to get to the truth.'

Stuart ignored what Ambler said and stayed on his own wavelength. They engaged in an unacknowledged skirmish to decide who controlled the conversation. 'Your son did know Walt. Isn't that right? He spent some time on campus, I've learned.' His eyebrows went up. 'Helping you in your investigation, wasn't it?'

It was interesting Stuart admitted to knowing John had been on campus. He wasn't supposed to know that and could only have learned it 'in confidence' from Barnes.

Ambler wanted to keep Stuart talking. If he did so, the cagey professor might unintentionally tell Ambler something he didn't know was important but was useful to Ambler. He might also contradict something he'd said earlier or reveal something by accident that he didn't mean to reveal. To keep Stuart talking and perhaps make a mistake, Ambler needed to stay calm and not react to anything irritating, insulting, or provocative Stuart might say.

'I don't expect you to accept that John is innocent solely on my say so,' he said. 'Or to accept that your mentee is a murderer. I don't have proof that would persuade you so I'm not going to try. But you might reserve judgment and answer a couple of questions that could help me find proof of what I say, even if you don't believe I will.'

Stuart glanced at his watch. 'I don't have a lot of time, right now.' He wasn't trying to be dismissive as Barnes had been; he might even have been conciliatory. But it was clear he wanted Ambler to leave. 'My office hours are over at three and I have a class after that.'

Ambler didn't take the hint. 'We have a few minutes.' He settled into his chair to let Stuart know he wasn't going anywhere just yet. 'Do you know if Walt Nichols was continuing his life of crime while he was attending college?'

Stuart's eyes narrowed, and he took longer to answer than his answer would have suggested. 'I'd be surprised if that were true. As I said, I felt the young man was turning his life around. He was a good student. He wanted to do something meaningful with his life. He cared about the world around us, the environment. No one gave him a chance to do something useful with his life when he was growing up. He was grateful for the opportunity we gave him now.'

Stuart sounded as convincing as the late-night TV commercial barker touting a miracle weight-loss program, but Ambler didn't challenge him. Instead, when Stuart's commercial was over, he asked about the other men in the program who might have been friends with Nichols.

Stuart's response was surprising. He went to his computer and printed out the names of the men in the program – all of whom, if you asked Stuart, were turning their lives around and planning to give back to the community.

Stuart didn't know them as well as he knew Walt, he said, but in truth he didn't know Walt that well. 'It might be I only saw the side of him he wanted to show me. It wouldn't be the first time a student in the program put something over on me. A few years ago, one of our best students, well-liked by everyone, was arrested for armed robbery as he was about to begin his senior year.'

He smiled sadly but after a moment brightened, becoming his affable self once more. 'Yet we have many more success stories.' He became thoughtful again. 'In a way, it's surprising we have any success at all. The odds are stacked against the formerly incarcerated.

'They call them correctional facilities not prisons. But that's only a name. At one time, I think society intended the goal of those institutions really should be to help the incarcerated turn their lives around, as the purpose of reform schools once might have been to help their inmates reform. Whenever that time of belief in redemption was, it's long gone. We're a much meaner and more selfish society today.'

Positive energy flowed out of Stuart, the kind that made you feel he was glad to see you, thought well of you, was eager to be friends. While his speech about Walt Nichols sounded canned, now he came across as sincere, saddened by how society treated 'the least of us'.

You might think of him as a beaten but undaunted idealist. After all, his academic field of environmental studies was an attempt to save the world from those bent on destroying it in

their careless, if not conscienceless and irresponsible, pursuit
of profit.

Nonetheless, Ambler was sure everything Stuart said was
calculated, his words weighed carefully before he uttered them.
He was as bright as everyone said he was and, Ambler had to
admit, so far had been two or three jumps ahead of him, as
aware as Ambler was that they were in a battle, each determined to outlast the other.

It felt like the learned professor had been up since before
dawn putting his plan together, while Ambler had only recently
finished a leisurely breakfast. Stuart, because of his alliance
with Barnes, knew a good deal of what Ambler knew – for
one thing, he knew Ambler was all but certain Walt Nichols
shot to death George Olson, at the behest of, on the orders of,
hired by someone else. Ambler's problem was he didn't know
what Stuart knew.

What he'd have to do now was assume he was right that
Nichols killed George Olson and that Stuart knew that as well
as he did, even though he pretended otherwise. If this move
produced anything useful, the next move would be to act as
though he knew who killed Nichols and see what that produced.

Stuart made a show of consulting his watch again. This
time, Ambler looked at it, too.

'Is that a Rolex?'

For the first time, Stuart was flustered, embarrassed. 'As a
matter of fact, it is . . . a gift.'

'Nice present.'

'It belonged to my grandfather . . . a family heirloom.'

Ambler nodded as if to approve. But he remembered Sarah
telling him her ex-husband grew up poor. The reason one wore
a Rolex, as Ambler understood it, was to show off, to let others
know you made more money than they did.

'You remember I have a class . . .'

On an impulse, Ambler said, 'Would you mind if I sat in
on it?'

Stuart did a double take. Ambler was pleased; he'd finally
done something his adversary hadn't expected.

'Sure,' Stuart said after hesitating, his uncertain, questioning, but eager expression asking if Ambler was putting him on, at the same time showing a shy hope he wasn't.

The classroom was full, everyone seated when they arrived; no one came in late. A hum of excited expectation made the classroom feel alive. Eager faces watched Stuart's every move. Stuart didn't disappoint them. His lecture was electrifying, coming in short bursts, assisted by a PowerPoint slideshow and interrupted by sharp, rapid-fire questions that challenged the students. He called on them by name – and it was a good-sized class, not a lecture hall, but forty or fifty students.

He'd ask them to comment on or evaluate what he'd said, often asking them to take a side in competing aspects of an argument he'd presented. This particular lecture was about population growth. The question was whether it was imperative for governments to limit the numbers of children a family could produce. At one point, he asked if the family should continue to be the basic form of social organization. By the end of the lecture, the classroom was buzzing like a dancehall on Saturday night.

Ambler felt like he'd been through a pep rally, except everyone was arguing different sides of different issues. The fascinating thing was how everyone was arguing with passion but without rancor. Before the students left, Stuart reminded them of a reading assignment in the syllabus, and a 500-word think piece on the topic they'd discussed due next class. Ambler half expected applause when Stuart folded his laptop and sent the class on its way.

After the class, Stuart was as relaxed and confident as he usually was – another day at the office – when Ambler complimented him on the class. He tried to hide it but clearly was pleased.

'Of all the things I do, that's what I like best, engaging a class of students, opening them up to their own possibilities, their potential to use their own intelligence and imagination to address the world's problems.'

For a moment, facing him at an intersection of sidewalks on the college common, where in a moment each would go his own way, Ambler felt a wave of sadness over what he vaguely suspected and hoped wasn't true. Strangely, he felt sure he saw a flicker of sadness push aside the self-assured cheerfulness in Stuart's eyes, leaving in its wake a glimpse of deep and dark sadness and pain, and wondered where it came from.

'It was good talking to you,' Stuart said, holding out his hand. 'I hope things work out with your son.'

Ambler shook hands and stopped himself from saying he'd be seeing him again.

TWENTY-ONE

'What I didn't do and should have done,' Ambler said to McNulty after his second beer at the Library Tavern that night, 'was try to find out what George Olson knew that got him killed. Instead, I fixated on this idea that a disgruntled student was the killer. Thinking that way I got John involved, and look at the mess that created.'

McNulty asked if he wanted another beer but he didn't.

'I also spent too much time thinking I needed to find out why Sam Abernathy had so many secrets.'

McNulty nodded and poured himself a beer from the tap into his coffee cup. 'I put my foot in my mouth on that one. I've been around you too much, so when I see something suspicious, I think I gotta look into it. So, we caught old Sam with his pants down.

'But you were right in a way. The killer was a student – maybe a hitman type rather than a disgruntled type – and you wouldn't know that if it weren't for John.'

'It's not worth the price of his going back to prison.' Ambler was quiet for a moment. 'What I think now is the unraveling of all this begins with finding out what George Olson knew or did that got him killed.'

'Sex or money.' McNulty opined.

'Two possibilities I've come up with are Rebecca's husband hired Nichols to kill Olson because he thought Olson was the professor having an affair with his wife. This is unlikely for a host of reasons.

'The other possibility is Olson discovered some chicanery going on with Barnes. But nothing points to Barnes – except for his being ruthlessly ambitious.' Ambler was quiet again for a few moments. 'Olson was turning against Stuart, Sam told me. Why did he turn against Stuart?'

'That's easy,' McNulty said. 'He found out something that

made him think the guy shouldn't be the faculty boss, or whatever you call it.'

They went back and forth for a few more minutes. Ambler liked to bounce ideas off his bartender friend because McNulty saw the world differently than most people. He knew gangsters as well as corporate big shots, local politicians and numbers runners, high-priced lawyers and dope dealers; he didn't distinguish between them but judged them by how they dealt with him and those around them when they were drinking at his bar – and how they tipped.

Having been raised by an unreconstructed Communist father, McNulty had his own ideas on what he termed bourgeois morality, which meant he was on occasion willing to bend the law to accomplish his aims, a characteristic that had helped Ambler out on occasion. He was also a card-carrying – Equity and SAG – actor, which talent he'd also used to help Ambler in the past. On this evening, Ambler having decided against his better judgment to have that third beer after all, the two men hatched a plan.

'Of course, I can do it,' McNulty said, having refilled his coffee cup from the beer tap a few times.

Ambler wanted to find out what Olson might have discovered about Barnes and Stuart that might have gotten him killed. Barnes said he didn't remember how he came to be in possession of a Rex Stout first edition that might be worth a couple of thousand dollars and appeared to not be aware of its value or not to know it had been part of the New York Mystery Writers collection. But that might have been a ruse by Barnes who knew very well where the book came from.

The plan was for McNulty to use his acting talent and call on Barnes playing the role of a competing antiquarian bookseller who'd learned the college's New York Mystery Writers collection was for sale and wanted to see the collection himself, as he might purchase all or part of it. Ambler gave him a quick course in book collecting and appraisal.

Since Barnes wasn't an expert in book collecting either, McNulty didn't have to become expert; he just needed to know a little more about it than Barnes did, like the professor one chapter ahead of his students in the textbook. McNulty would make an appointment with Barnes when he woke up the following morning, which for McNulty was early afternoon.

While the bartender attended to Barnes, Ambler made a stop on the Upper West Side on his way to the Bronx and Trinity College. He wanted a private word with Sam Abernathy, so he paid a surprise visit at McNulty's apartment. Sam was indeed surprised.

'What are you doing here?' Sam made an instinctive move to close the apartment door he'd just opened but caught himself. He laughed nervously. 'I'm surprised to see you. What's up?' he asked, his tone filled with misgiving, as if Ambler might actually be the repo man.

Ambler brushed past him and went into the apartment. 'I want to clear something up.' He raised his eyebrows. 'Why are you so nervous?'

Sam sighed. 'I've been jumpy like this since this whole escapade began. I'm not cut out for the outlaw life. Even before all this began, I was a nervous wreck . . . because of my affair with Rebecca.' He met Ambler's gaze with puppy eyes. 'I'd never done anything like that in my life. And then the proposal to sell the collection, the stolen books, poor George's murder, my being accused of the murder . . . I'm surprised I'm still sane.'

Ambler didn't think he was dropping a bomb. Sam knew what was coming. 'At what point did you make your anonymous donation to the New York Public Library, and how did you get them to believe you?'

Sam tried for an expression of disbelief and then indignation. Neither worked, so he gave up. He smiled shyly. 'I knew you'd catch on sooner or later. It was a harmless enough ploy—'

'And its purpose?'

'I wanted to give you a reason to spend time on campus that everyone, including you, would recognize as legitimate. First, I came up with the plan because of the books. I wanted you to discover they were missing before anyone else did. I knew your reputation. You might find out what happened to them. Then, when I was accused of killing poor, poor George, I thought if anyone could save me it would be you.'

'You could have asked.'

'You might have said no. As it was, you ended up not believing what I say anyway.'

'You kept lying to me. That's not a way to build trust.'

'Do you believe me now?'

'Almost. I doubt you'd have come up with your sham donation to get me snooping around if you were guilty.'

'I guess I disappointed the library when I withdrew the donation. I'm sorry for that.' His tone was abjectly apologetic. 'I'm sorry to have tricked you and now to have disappointed you about the donation.'

'You didn't disappoint me,' Ambler said brightly. 'I wanted you to keep your collection, as long as you weren't willing to murder people to do so.'

He told Sam about his discovery of the rare Rex Stout book on Barnes's bookshelf – Sam confirmed that it was from his collection – and the plan he and McNulty had devised to find out where it came from.

The librarian, Professor Florence Randolph, was next. Ambler hadn't seen her since his first day on campus. It was a mistake not to have talked with her before now, since she would be up on whatever intrigue was going on with the faculty senate.

He found her in the library the next afternoon. She was expecting him and remembered him right away. They met in the small conference room he'd arrived at on his first day on campus. She greeted his first question with an anemic smile that quickly became a scowl, which he believed was more or less perpetual.

'You want to know what I think of Doug Stuart? He's a disgrace to the professoriate. The students love him because he acts like such a free spirit, forever youthful, a crushed idealist. He's manipulative, smiling to your face, belittling you behind your back.

'He keeps his position on the faculty senate by doling out favors to some, making thinly disguised threats to others. He controls the tenure and promotion committee with his toadies. He controls funds for travel and conferences and college research grants. The only faculty not beholden to him are the very few who have their own sources of research money, mostly faculty in the hard sciences and they don't care what happens to the rest of us.'

He asked her about George Olson.

'A toady.' She paused and admonished herself. 'That's not fair. George tried to make peace, find middle ground. I was disappointed in him because he appeased Doug when he could have stood up to him. At one time, he might have had the backing to defeat Stuart if he ran against him. He didn't have the backbone.'

This gave Ambler pause. 'Was Stuart holding something over him?'

A sad smile replaced her scowl for a moment. 'George loved to teach. He cared about his scientific projects, too. But no one else did. He worked with fungi . . . His NSF grants ran out years ago. He hasn't gotten new ones because a college like this doesn't have the money to build the kind of lab you need, so he mostly puttered around. He was an associate professor and would have needed Doug to get full professor because he hadn't published anything of note in years. But I don't think he cared that much about full professor.'

'Sam told me something happened between Olson and Stuart, or Olson discovered something about him. Because of whatever came between them, Sam believed George would support him in the senate president election.'

This struck a nerve. Florence Randolph's eyes opened wider, her brow wrinkled, her voice took on a hushed, conspiratorial tone. 'Sam's right. George must have told him what he'd discovered—'

Ambler interrupted her. 'Sam doesn't know. Do you?'

Her voice lost its edge, the excited pitch becoming flat with disappointment. 'No. I know something happened because for a few days before George was killed, everything changed between him and Doug. They hardly spoke. In the past, you'd often find one of them in the other's office chatting about something. That ended. The three of us meet weekly. The week before George was killed the meeting was cancelled.' She paused as if trying to catch up with a thought or a memory.

'One afternoon a day or two before his death, George came

to my office. He asked if I had a few minutes. That wasn't so strange. We chatted often. He'd stop by when I was working in the faculty senate office. We, the officers, have tiny, make-shift offices. George and I kept our doors open – not Doug, who kept his door closed.

'George came by that day, stood in my doorway for a moment. He was anxious, jittery as a cat. Usually he was good humored, kind of jovial. He seldom had any real reason to stop by; he did so because he felt that part of his duty as a person was to bring a little sunshine into everyone's life. This day was different. His face said he was bringing bad news.

'Doug came down the hall as George was standing there. When George saw him, he looked that way, looked at me as if to say we were in big trouble, and hightailed it down the hallway back to his little office. The next thing I knew he was dead . . .'

Ambler hoped for more, for her to say something like, 'George did tell me Stuart and Barnes had a secret plan to sell the college to the Saudis. When the deal closed, they'd take the proceeds and hide out in South America.'

But this was not to be. It would have been too easy. Fate required Ambler to spend more time beating his head against a few more walls before he'd find out what he needed to find out. Or he might never find out . . . and his son would go back to prison and rot there for a couple more decades.

'If you were to guess what George Olson wanted to tell you, what would it be?'

She pounced on him like she must pounce on one of her students who asked for an extension on a paper. 'What good would that do? If you're any sort of investigator, I'd expect you to rely on facts.'

Ambler wanted to complain, 'But I don't have any facts . . .' He didn't because it would be whining. Instead, he pushed his luck. 'What would you guess if it were to have been something about Doug Stuart that George intended to tell you that day?'

She frowned. 'That Doug stole children, cooked them and ate them . . . or else he and Barnes had a plan to swindle widows and orphans.'

She sighed and took on a businesslike tone. 'I don't think this idle speculation gets us anywhere. Are you thinking Doug murdered George? That would be a lot easier to believe than Sam having done it.' No pause for him to answer. 'Unfortunately, I have to tell you you'd be wrong. I was with Doug when we got the terrible news.'

'I'm not accusing him of the actual shooting.' Ambler told her that he believed without being sure that someone had paid Walt Nichols to kill Olson and then that someone killed Nichols. 'I don't have much reason to suspect Doug Stuart. I'm grasping at straws. If I knew what George Olson appears to have known, I'd have a better idea whether to suspect Stuart or not . . . Out of curiosity, why were you with Stuart at the time of the murder?'

'We were supposed to be arranging to transfer the senate bookkeeping from him to me. I'm the secretary-treasurer after all, and taking care of the bookkeeping and financial accounting should be my job. Doug has done it for years. The secretary-treasurers before me – all toadies – were figureheads. They didn't do anything, except now and again transcribe the notes of the faculty meetings.

'When I tried to put those notes in order, I needed to scour the campus for colleagues who attended the meetings and kept their own notes to fill in the gaps from meetings my predecessors didn't attend, or that they attended but didn't take notes on – which believe me were many.'

'Was there anything from the meeting notes that suggested impropriety? Were there controversies?'

She was dismissive. 'Controversies? Practically every meeting there were controversies, especially after Barnes arrived. Most of the time, Doug had the votes to squash any controversy that came up. Other times, George worked out a compromise.'

Controversy was a polite word for quarreling, Ambler told himself. Squabbling, fighting is conflict. Conflict could be a word for battle. Battle suggests violence. 'Were there any recent controversies that were heated, acrimonious?'

Once more he'd hit a nerve. Professor Randolph perked up. 'Actually, there was. The junior faculty were up in arms because

of a reduction in senate funding for travel and conferences for
the second or third year in a row. Doug has dictatorial power
over how senate funds are allocated, and he's never faced
much in the way of challenges until recently.'

She was quiet for a moment. 'So if we were to make a
movie version of this, you might say a few of the junior faculty
were angry enough to lynch Doug.'

'What about Olson?'

'They'd hang him, too. He stepped in to calm things down
and promised to do an audit of how the funding priority
decisions have been made for the past few years and provide
it to the faculty. The fact is he didn't do it or, if he did, he
didn't tell anyone about it.'

'Maybe he wasn't finished. Do you have the financial
records?'

She shook her head. 'Doug ran the faculty senate as his
own fiefdom. George had access to some things. But they iced
me out. Neither of them helped me with compiling the histor-
ical notes of senate meetings. I've been secretary-treasurer for
over a year and still haven't seen any of the financial records.
I'm responsible for a quarterly financial report. Doug gives it
to me and tells me to present it.'

The more she talked, the angrier she got. 'I did that twice.
I told him and George I wasn't going to do it again until I've
seen the financial records. He told me George needed them
to do the audit he was working on and I could have them after
that . . .' She paused. The anger went out of her voice and her
eyes clouded with sadness. 'And then poor George . . .' She
glanced away.

Ambler respected her sadness and waited a few minutes
before asking, 'Aren't there oversight committees and finance
committees? Stuart can't run everything himself.'

'Sure we have committees, way too many . . . committees
for everything. From the department's point of view, from the
administration's point of view, nothing can get done without
a committee discussing it first. Everyone grumbles and tries
to avoid them because they take up too much time. No one
rocks the boat because if someone asks too many questions
– they'll form a committee.

'Most of the older faculty have spent their careers in their own cocoons. They want to do their scholarly pursuits and not be bothered. Until recently, they were able to conduct their classes with little or no oversight; they were the experts in their subjects. Faculty want to be left alone and they're willing to leave others alone. If someone's willing to do the college service work, let them go to it with our thanks.

'The administration has become more powerful in recent years, slowly but inexorably usurping powers that once belonged to the faculty.' She laughed. 'In the far distant past, the faculty had oversight over the administration. To put it bluntly, the faculty told the administration what to do; now, it's the other way around. Half our classes are taught by adjuncts, higher education's migrant workers.'

The good professor was gearing up to go on for the rest of the afternoon about the injustices done to faculty if Ambler didn't get her back to the issue at hand – the faculty senate's financial records. Wasn't the love of money the root of all evil? She hadn't said she suspected anything was amiss with the finances. Nonetheless, Ambler wondered if this might be the case.

The challenge here was to encourage Professor Randolph to track down those financial records without her catching on as to why he wanted them. If she caught on that she was helping him investigate Doug Stuart, she might act differently around him and tip him off that that was what she was up to.

It took him some time to persuade her that it was extremely important to get her hands on those records. He did this by coming up with a well-known trope of the mystery novel, a red herring at the expense of George Olson's memory, hoping that George would have approved. He asked Randolph for the names of the younger faculty who were the angriest and were most likely to have it in for Stuart or George Olson or both.

'It's possible George did do that audit and took his preliminary findings to one of the Angry Young Men. They disagreed about what his findings meant. One particularly angry junior professor wanted, say, George to publicize the audit, and George didn't want to. Or this young faculty member felt the report meant the younger faculty had been swindled and wanted

George to do something about it, and George – trying to keep things calm – dragged his feet.

'One thing led to another, and the young professor determined George Olson stood in the way of the underpaid junior faculty getting money they needed and deserved. So, this particular professor, being a marksman like Sam, decided to take George out of the way.'

Randolph, being a person of some intelligence, pointed out a number of holes in Ambler's theory, which he didn't deny. Instead, he told her it was necessary to 'rule out' even the most improbable possibilities in order to get to the truth.

'We could rule this out if you find the financial records and any audit or report George was working on at the time of his murder.' He let that sink in before saying, 'You'd want to keep under your hat why you were doing this.'

She caught on to this also. 'You mean not let Doug find out.'

Ambler did a little soft-shoe here. 'Not only Stuart. It's important not to let anyone know they're under suspicion. It's not right to cast suspicion on someone when you're simply trying to find information.'

This one she bought. She said she'd try and find the records without raising suspicion. 'I've been bugging Doug for them for months anyway.'

The first challenge here would be her finding the documents, especially if Stuart didn't want her to find them; the next challenge would be deciphering the financial gobbledygook to find out if anything was amiss. They'd need help with that. Most of the time Ambler couldn't decipher his own bank account.

TWENTY-TWO

That evening Ambler checked in with McNulty at the Library Tavern to find out how things went with Dr Barnes. It was late and only a couple of hangers-on were draped over the bar at the far end.

McNulty was in his element; he loved telling stories. 'For the first couple of minutes he acted like I'd walked in with dog shit on my shoes. Kind of a pompous ass . . . too important to talk to the likes of me, until I did like you said and told him I was a book hunter with a specialty in crime fiction and was searching for very specific and very valuable books that I learned might be in the Trinity College Library collection. Then, his ears perked up.

'He told me about you. But when I said we paid top dollar, he let it be known you weren't so important in the sum total of things. He wanted a list of the books I was interested in. I told him I couldn't do that. If word got out about how valuable they were, bibliophiles would descend on the place like prospectors during the gold rush.

'He wanted to show me a database or spreadsheet or whatever, with the books from the collection listed on it. I told him – like you said – that wouldn't work. I had to see the physical book because the condition of the book was important.

'He got cagey and wanted me to verify who I was, so I gave him one of the cards I'd picked up from the rare bookstore on Madison Avenue. While he thought about that, I picked out the book you told me to look for, the Rex Stout book that wasn't about Nero Wolfe, and told him what I might give him for it.

'As we know, greed beats out caution every time. He told me he'd gotten it from one of the faculty members who'd stored away a few of the more valuable books from the crime fiction collection for safekeeping. He'd need to contact him and get back to me on the next steps.' McNulty glanced around the nearly empty bar, the two leftover tipplers staring vacantly into their almost empty rocks glasses, and then settled back on Ambler.

'I knew there would be a problem if he called the phone number on the business card I gave him, since the person who answered would say they didn't know what he was talking about. I didn't want to give him my cell phone number because sometimes I can't take the call and the voicemail thing would say, 'Leave a message for McNulty', which would give him pause since Stevenson is the name on the card.'

Ambler was sure McNulty had found a way out of this dilemma. But he'd have to wait to find out. McNulty the actor had a good sense of dramatic timing, so he paused for a long moment.

'I told him I'd be out of the office for a few days,' he said when the moment was right. 'So he should call my assistant who manages my appointments. I gave him Adele's cell phone number. You'll need to straighten her out on this. She asks too many questions when I try to tell her something.'

After the Library Tavern, Ambler stopped by Adele's apartment. He wanted to talk on the phone but she insisted she should change the bandages on his bullet wound so it didn't get infected. When she finished dressing the wound, he told her about McNulty's adventure and her role in the scheme. 'It worked out better than I'd hoped,' he said. But she was perplexed.

'How does knowing who stole the library books, if anyone did, help you find out who murdered that student? Which is the only thing you should be worrying about, so your son doesn't go back to prison.'

He couldn't really tell her how the unfolding events he put in motion – McNulty putting one over on Barnes to find out who stole the books, and Florence Randolph getting access to the faculty senate's financial records – fitted into a plan, because he didn't know if they did. What he did know was he'd be in a different place than he was now if he knew who stole the books and if there were discrepancies in the faculty senate finances. Knowing these things might not tell him who killed George Olson and Walt Nichols, but it might tell him where to look next.

The next afternoon, Adele found Ambler in the 42nd Street Library's crime fiction reading room. She'd gotten a call from Barnes's office. 'I told her I needed to check with Mr Stevenson and get back to her. I called McNulty. He said to ask you.'

'Is the meeting with Barnes?'

'The girl who called – I think a student – basically read from a script. She didn't know anything. When I asked her whom he might be meeting, she told me exactly what she'd already told me. Pick a time tomorrow afternoon between 2:00 and 5:00. And she gave me a room number in Baker Hall, whatever that is.'

Ambler wasn't sure whether McNulty should go alone, or whether he should go with him. He thought for a moment about bringing John also, but decided he wouldn't. He'd told John to lie low and stay away from the Trinity campus, and was surprised when John was fine with that. He'd hardly seen his son or grandson since John got out of jail. Last night he found out the boys had been spending the last few evenings at Sarah Hastings's house in Westchester.

Adele wanted to come with him, but they decided – given her condition – that too much excitement wasn't a good idea. The confrontation, if this was what it became, was unlikely to be violent . . . though you could never be sure. He decided he should go with McNulty.

The appointment was for 3:00 and they arrived a little early. On the way up, they decided McNulty – known for the time being as Maxwell Stevenson – would enter the room first and Ambler would arrive a bit later, once McNulty had ascertained that the principals were in the room and texted him. This happened not too long after McNulty went in. The text was simply: 'Now.'

Ambler didn't know what or more precisely whom to expect, but wasn't much surprised to see Doug Stuart sitting at a table across from McNulty.

The same couldn't be said for Stuart when Ambler came through the door. The protector of the environment and voice of the Trinity faculty stopped speaking in mid-sentence; his quick, irritated glance toward the door became the dead-eyed stare of a corpse. After another moment, his facial expression crumpled and his eyes grew moist. Beyond the upheaval of his facial muscles, he didn't move; nor did his stare leave Ambler, though it continued to be an unseeing stare.

Stuart waited for someone besides him to speak first. Ambler waited, too. McNulty broke the silence.

'My guess is you know one another, so no need for introductions. I'd also guess that everyone in the room – including you, Professor – now knows that I'm an imposter. And since both of you know more about book collecting than I do, I'll let you carry the ball from here. I do need to be at work by 5:30, so I'd appreciate it if you'd get down to business rather than pussyfooting around.'

Neither Ambler nor Stuart spoke, though by now Stuart was glowering rather than staring.

McNulty didn't wait long. He flicked his wrist in the direction of Stuart. 'You, Professor, could start by standing up in a huff and saying, "What's the meaning of this?" If you don't like that approach, you might try something more conciliatory, "This isn't what it looks like." Or "You've got me all wrong."'

Stuart gradually regained his senses, some color returning to his face. Still, it took a couple of tries for him to get his voice fully under control. When he did, he said to Ambler, ignoring McNulty, 'You may think you've pulled a fast one, but don't be so sure.'

Ambler held his peace. It was better to let Stuart try to explain his way out of whatever predicament he thought he was in without helping him out by asking questions.

Stuart continued to glower at Ambler. You could tell by how he worked the muscles in his face that he knew he shouldn't say anything more, but he just couldn't help himself.

Because college professors essentially talk for a living – call it lecture, if you want – they tend to think they can explain most things and solve most problems with talk. So this, Ambler believed, was what Stuart would do. And, sure enough . . .

'Our faculty squabbles mean the world to us but are of little consequence to the world at large.' He produced a weak smile. 'They say of faculty controversies, the less consequential the issue, the more bitter the battle.' He added a bit of energy to the smile and flashed it first at McNulty and then at Ambler.

By the time it reached Ambler, it had weakened considerably.

'All of this about the prized first editions missing from Sam Abernathy's dust-covered assemblage of forgotten books would have amounted to nothing more than a practical joke if it hadn't been for the untimely death of our colleague.' No longer smiling, he shot a glance at Ambler to gauge how he was doing. Ambler had yet to say a word.

'Despite your subterfuge – you're more resourceful than I gave you credit for; I suppose you could say I walked into a trap – you haven't uncovered anything criminal . . . if this was your intention. The first editions I was talking with your co-conspirator about were moved from one place on campus to another. They don't belong to Sam; they belong to the college.

'You may think Edward and I planned to sell them to . . .' His nod toward McNulty was disdainful. '. . . this charlatan for personal profit. But you misjudge us. The proceeds of any sale were to be used to benefit the college's foundation.'

His tone bordered on triumphant. 'So, despite your elaborate deception, you haven't caught us – me – at anything more than a mean prank I played on Abernathy.' Stuart's smirk reminded Ambler of Barnes's smirk, and he again wanted to smack him. 'If you planned to have me arrested, I guess you're out of luck.'

Ambler didn't mind that Stuart found a way to avoid criminal charges. He got what he came after. Though he didn't tell Stuart this, his self-satisfied smile might have.

'Not having you arrested might be disappointing. But it's not the most important thing. You took the books from the collection so you or someone else could accuse Sam of pilfering or embezzling, a character assassination that would help you keep your faculty senate position. Dirty campus politics, nothing more, am I correct?'

Stuart's imperious stance didn't last long. He was unnerved by Ambler's lack of interest in having him arrested. So he began fidgeting, unsure of what Ambler was after and so not sure what he might do or say next.

He needn't have worried. Ambler didn't have anything else

up his sleeve for the time being. He told Stuart to return the books to the library, to leave them with Rebecca. He could work out with Sam how to explain their disappearance and return.

On the way back downtown on the Number 4 train, McNulty was grumpy. 'What did we do all that for? What did we get out of it?'

There wasn't a good answer. What happened was a shifting of the pieces. Another part of the puzzle became clear. 'For one thing, we got Sam off the hook for the missing books.'

McNulty rolled his eyes. 'Right. Who cares about two more corpses in the Bronx as long as you got the books back in the library? You can rest on your laurels.'

Ambler ignored the sarcasm. 'If Stuart has anything to hide, the good professor has to be uneasy. The same goes for Barnes. They've been found out. Not for anything disastrous *yet*. But they know we know they're crooks. Stuart wouldn't be meeting you in an off-the-beaten-track unused classroom if everything was on the up and up.'

McNulty's eyebrows went up and down a couple of times. 'So the money from selling those books would go in their pockets after all, not the college foundation?' He shook his head. 'I'm slowing down in my old age. I gave the slimy bastard the benefit of the doubt. I let my guard slip and didn't suspect the worst. I'm proud of you for having so little faith in the good intentions of your fellow man.'

'What happens with someone who has a guilty conscience is they're afraid they screwed up; that you're on to them,' Ambler said, talking as much to himself as to McNulty. 'They keep going back over what they did, worried they made a mistake somewhere. They might have left a glove at the scene of the crime. There might be a record of a phone call they made to the victim. Someone saw something. Someone heard something. When you're under that kind of pressure, the kind guilt produces, you can think of a hundred things someone might discover that link you to the crime.

'Let's take Stuart. He pilfered the books; he thought he'd got away with it, covered his tracks; no one would suspect him. But we found him out. Now, if he's a murderer – and

I'm not saying he is – he thought he'd got away with that, too. Now, he's got to worry.

'First, we found out Walt Nichols killed George Olson. If Stuart hired Nichols to do the killing – and I'm not saying he did – he must have figured Nichols would never be caught because he had no motive, no reason on earth to kill Olson. But we tracked Nichols down. There's no way we should have been able to do that. So he's got to worry.'

McNulty followed along and caught up. 'Worried about it enough to kill the guy. Kill the killer.'

'The truth is we shouldn't have been able to track Nichols down. It was an accident. We set out to find a deranged student and found a hired killer.'

McNulty nodded. 'Like when a scientist is trying to find a cure for measles, runs a couple of experiments and accidentally finds a cure for athlete's foot.'

TWENTY-THREE

The next shoe dropped the following afternoon. Ambler had returned to his desk from the Lenox and Astor room, where he'd given a lunchtime lecture on the holdings of the crime fiction collection to a small group of mystery aficionados and tourists, when his phone rang.

'I've got them! . . . or at least the records for the past few years.' Florence Randolph was as excited as a little girl in an ice-cream parlor. 'The work-study student knew where the passwords were. Doug has no idea I can get to the accounts.' She said this with a conspiratorial chuckle. After a pause, she added, 'This may be a silly question. But what do I do now that I've gotten them?'

Ambler felt like the dog chasing the car when the car finally stops. He didn't know what to do with the accounts either. He told her he wanted to check with a couple of people who knew more about this kind of thing than he did – he had in mind his cop friend Mike Cosgrove and David Levinson, John's lawyer – and he would call her back shortly. 'I think we'll need someone more expert in financial crimes than either of us is to take a look at the accounts.'

Another break, he told himself. Things were falling into place. Getting hold of the senate accounts had to be a positive development. But maybe it wasn't. Nothing was certain. The opposite was true: everything was far from certain. His suspicion that Stuart – or possibly Barnes, or Barnes and Stuart acting together – conspired in George Olson's murder and killed Walt Nichols had less substance than a conjurer's illusion.

Stuart liked money and had an unknown source of income – unknown at least to his ex-wife – that allowed him to live beyond the means provided by a college professor's salary. That, and his close association with Walt Nichols, made him Ambler's suspect. There was more proof that the Easter Bunny was real.

It would be great if someone had seen Stuart entering or leaving Nichols's apartment the evening of the murder, or if he'd left his fingerprints at the murder scene. A pattern of emails between him and Nichols before George Olson was killed would also be something he could hang his hat on.

His reasons for suspecting Barnes were even flimsier. Barnes was ambitious and appeared to be unscrupulous and dishonest. So you could believe either one or both of them to be unethical or, to put it bluntly, crooks. This didn't mean they were murderers. Most crooks weren't killers, certainly not cold-blooded killers.

Having the faculty senate's financial records could easily turn out to be a bust. He didn't know how to find evidence of fraud or embezzlement in a set of books, and he doubted Professor Randolph did either. And in the unlikely event they found fraud, this might tighten the noose around Stuart's neck. But it wouldn't prove he hired Walt Nichols to kill George Olson, or that he killed Nichols.

Ambler could see all his effort come to nothing. George Olson's death and Walt Nichols's death could have nothing to do with Trinity College. Olson could have owed money to gangsters or got on their bad side for any number of reasons. So they'd hired Nichols to kill Olson and then killed Nichols because he talked too much or they didn't want any witnesses. They'd get away with those murders, as gangsters often do, and John would rot in prison for a crime he didn't commit.

A few minutes after their first conversation ended, before he had a chance to call either Mike or David Levinson, Florence Randolph called back. 'I solved our problem,' she said. He started to ask which one but held his tongue.

'I called Lew Montgomery and he's anxious to help.' She was excited, talking in a rush, and went on about how she came to think of Lew, and how luckily he was in his office because she didn't have his home phone or cell number, forgetting Ambler had no idea who Lew Montgomery was or what he might help with.

He interrupted her. 'Could you slow down a little, please? I'm not following you.'

She took a deep breath. 'I've never been involved in anything like this before. I think I'm overexcited.'

Lew Montgomery, it turned out, was a young accounting professor who'd studied forensic accounting in grad school and thought he'd remember enough of it to recognize any irregularities in the senate accounts.

'I remembered Lew,' she said, 'because he'd told me after I'd been elected secretary-treasurer to call on him if I needed help getting the senate's books in order. He was one of the junior faculty members complaining about how the travel and conference funds were allocated.'

For a few seconds, Ambler – distracted by his own made-up explanation for the murders – entertained the possibility that Montgomery was part of a group of upstarts who killed Olson because he was keeping their conference money from them. He dismissed the concern, deciding to pursue one promising lead – or half-baked idea, depending on how you looked at it – at a time.

Randolph would set up the accounting professor on the computer in the faculty senate office that had the accounting software while Stuart was in class, and then again when he left for the day. Ambler had no idea how long it would take Lew Montgomery to find out anything, but said he'd come up to the campus the following morning.

When the phone rang that evening, he didn't know what to expect, but a sixth sense told him it would have to do with the murders. It was Sarah Hastings. She spoke in a whisper. 'John isn't there, is he?'

Ambler said no. John and Johnny had gone to a movie. Since John had gotten out of prison, he went to a movie theater any time he could. Going to an actual theater was one of the things he missed most when he was in jail.

She knew John would be out, she said. She didn't want him to know she called. 'I want to help,' she said. 'There must be something I can do. I know he didn't kill that man. I know better than anyone.' The intensity in her voice gave what she said significance he wasn't expecting. He waited.

'It's my fault he won't say where he was . . . It's because

of Rebecca.' She told him about Rebecca Dawson's dilemma, most of which Ambler already knew, but he didn't know the most important part. Rebecca had been with Sam Abernathy on the night Walt Nichols was murdered. Her husband was supposed to be away, but he came back early and found the kids with a babysitter. Sarah Hastings had been with John, but to protect Rebecca from her bullying husband she had lied for her and said they'd been together.

'You were with John the entire evening?' He knew she hadn't been, because John had been with Oscar and his pals at the time of the murder. He asked the question because he wanted to know if she was making up a story to cover for him.

She hesitated and then said 'yes', sounding so tentative he smiled.

'From when until . . .' This time he was the one who hesitated. He'd asked another busybody question. He didn't need her to say John spent the night with her. 'Forget it,' he said. 'I know you're trying to help. But it won't work. Not telling the truth is too risky. John wasn't with you at the time Walt Nichols was murdered. I know where he was and why he won't say where he was. We need to work around that.'

'But he was with me. He just couldn't say that because of Rebecca—'

'I told you: that's not going to work!' he thundered.

He didn't mean to sound stern, to lecture her like he was her high school principal. Doing so was wrong. Sarah was trying to help. She'd called because she wanted to help John. She of all people didn't deserve to be yelled at. He pictured her shrinking away from the phone.

'I'm sorry,' he said.

'I'll do anything I can to keep John from going back to prison,' she said. 'I shouldn't have brought up Rebecca. She's in a terrible situation. She did ask me to say she was with me. She's trying.' Her voice shook. 'Sam is trying. That night – the night of the murder – they had an appointment with a domestic violence attorney. They're trying to find a safe place for Rebecca to go where her crazy husband won't find her.' She choked on the words.

He waited for her to collect herself. It was about to get worse; she didn't know yet how much worse. They'd talked enough about dangerous husbands for the time being. He didn't know how she'd react when he told her he suspected her ex-husband of murder, so he decided not to tell her. He'd wait until he had proof, if he ever did.

Instead he said, 'I'll be on campus tomorrow afternoon. Can we meet late in the day? I should know more about how you might help by then.'

Lew Montgomery's appearance was reassuring. He carried himself – and dressed – the way you'd expect an accountant would. Unassuming in manner, wire-rimmed glasses, thinning hair, a brown tweed jacket, he seemed mildly distracted in the way some men have of being so focused on their work that anything else happening around them seems an imposition.

He told Ambler and Florence Randolph what he'd found, but first told them about the accounting software, as if this would mean something to them – that the system was an ancient, desktop version when almost all accounting software was based in the Cloud now. After that he told them about the method he used to examine income and expenditures, including a critique of the accounting method used by Doug Stuart, the only person who'd accessed the accounts in years. Stuart's method, he said, was haphazard and sloppy and designed to hide transactions.

Montgomery took off his glasses and pointed with them, first at Ambler, next at the computer. 'Usually an embezzler knows something about bookkeeping, so they can cover their tracks. Our colleague's approach was so obvious a child could see what he did. He simply wrote checks to two companies that don't exist. I imagine he thought by keeping the checks he wrote relatively small, no one would think twice about them.

'Of course, it might have drawn less suspicion if the distinct companies didn't have consecutive account numbers in the same bank.' He put his glasses back on and stared at the computer for a moment.

'He did something else I'll need to check further to be sure.

He wrote reimbursement checks to himself for conferences he attended, or senate-related travel that I can't find receipts for. The ones I have found are illegible, faded print or smudged, so that dates and amounts are unreadable. If I had a suspicious nature, I would think the smudging and such was done by design.'

Although what he'd heard was clear to Ambler, Randolph wasn't so sure. 'Are you saying that Doug was pilfering?'

Montgomery's tone was solemn. 'Pilfering would be a gross understatement. When we've done a full accounting and know how long this has been going on, I think we'll find Professor Stuart has misappropriated tens if not hundreds of thousands of dollars over a period of years.'

He returned to the computer for a few minutes. 'What would be most helpful,' he said when he'd pulled himself away from the screen and removed his glasses again, 'would be to get access to the bank accounts for those fake companies. Since I don't see how we can do that, the best course of action now would be to turn the matter over to the police.'

Randolph thought that over for a moment before saying, 'The next step should be to tell Dr Barnes what we've learned.'

This gave Ambler a start. He didn't like either idea, as his interest lay quite a way down the road and involved using what they'd learned about Stuart's pilfering to help solve two murders. Explaining this to his collaborators would not be easy.

'I'd rather we didn't take either of those steps just yet.' He watched what might be storm clouds gathering in the questioning faces of his companions. 'First, Barnes and Stuart are close allies. We don't know how Barnes would react, or if he'd believe us. We have to assume he'd want to get Stuart's side of the story first . . . which would warn him.'

He turned to Lew Montgomery. 'The police might not think we have enough evidence for them to do anything without Stuart's bank account information. I have an idea how we might get that, and I'd like to try that before we take the next step.'

He didn't want to tell them he suspected Stuart of murder, nor tell them his plan for getting to Stuart's bank accounts. He didn't know what would happen in either case, so he asked them to give him a few days to see what he could find out.

'Nothing much will change in a couple of days,' he said, although in truth he hoped a lot would.

He met Sarah Hastings in the cramped Mystery Writers collection reading room. It was in an out-of-the-way part of the library; a quiet place, despite all the excitement and problems it had generated lately. She waited for him seated at the small library table against the wall at the end of a row of shelves. Her face drawn, the expression in her eyes anxious, she appeared already overburdened. He was sorry to add to her troubles.

Without any preliminaries, he told her that Lew Montgomery had found discrepancies in the financial accounts of the faculty senate. For a moment she seemed puzzled, waiting for an explanation. Before he could give her one, she caught on.

'Money is missing?' She tilted her head as if she'd heard something. 'Stolen . . .' Whatever she heard was in her head; she spoke words to put her thoughts together, to come to a truth she was reluctant to arrive at. 'Stuart stole money from the faculty senate?'

He didn't answer because she wasn't asking him. After another moment, she'd put her thoughts together. 'I guess I'm not surprised . . .' And then. 'No . . . No, that's not true. I am surprised. I'm shocked. Devastated.'

The whites of her eyes reddened, her lips trembled, and her face wrinkled like a child's in the few seconds before she began to cry. She faced Ambler, determined to talk to him through her tears. 'I shouldn't have married Stuart. He was a god to me when I first knew him. You worship gods. Gods may love you in their way; they don't worship you. Stuart is a genius. He has a calling . . . he's brilliant; anyone would see that . . . a genius. Yet . . .' Her gaze was beseeching. 'An Achilles heel, a fatal flaw, a weakness that destroys you. His is avarice . . . one of the seven deadly sins, I think.'

Not many tears fell; two or three trickled down her cheek; no sobs. 'His career is destroyed, isn't it?' Her voice was strained. Again, she wasn't looking for an answer.

But this time Ambler gave her one. 'It's worse than that.'

She stiffened, sitting ramrod straight in her chair, as if she would now hear the damning verdict.

'He's been stealing from the senate for a long time.' Ambler sucked in his breath and pulled himself up as straight and stiff as Sarah, though he was standing. 'I'm almost certain George Olson caught on to what he was doing.'

He tried to soften his words, which was no use. 'George confronted Stuart with what he knew, and I think that's why he was murdered.'

She took a moment to understand this. She would fear the worst but with a hope that it might not be the worst, and slowly that small hope would be extinguished. 'A thief? A murderer?' Her shrill voice had an edge of unreality to it, a voice from the depths where horrors lived. Ambler was afraid she'd become hysterical.

She came around though. By a tremendous force of will, she came to terms with her new knowledge. Ambler wished his pal McNulty was there with his bottle of Irish whiskey.

'How long have you known this?'

The truth was Ambler didn't know it; he'd suspected and now he'd come to where he accused. Yet he didn't have proof. 'Once I realized Walt Nichols had been hired to kill George Olson, I looked for something that made sense. People are usually murdered by someone they know . . . Do you remember talking about your ex-husband's lavish spending?'

She nodded.

'It was out-of-character for him, you might have said, or I might have thought. He's intelligent enough to have pursued any number of more lucrative fields than college teaching. Yet he became a college professor because he is sincerely concerned about the environment. He cares about shaping young lives. He's one of those people who want to save the world and who those of a more selfish bent make fun of.'

Ambler wasn't sure he should say this, but he went on anyway. 'Yet his avarice wasn't out of character. It was fully part of his character, as was his inability to connect with you. A narcissist isn't capable of love. You mentioned a secret income stream.

'Some professors – even in a socially conscious field – make a discovery or invent something, devise a computer program and become wealthy, like the University of Florida professors who invented Gatorade.

'A friend of mine at the library checked every possible way Stuart could have created a profit-making venture. She checked grants from the government and foundations. She checked speakers' bureaus and book publishers. It's possible she missed something. He might have had some other source of outside income there's no public record of. But it's unlikely.

'I talked to George Olson's widow soon after his death. After Walt Nichols's murder, when I realized he'd been hired to kill Olson, I talked to her again. The first time, I needed to talk to her about the argument Sam and her husband had before he was killed. I wanted to know if there was bad blood.

'This time I wanted to know about a different problem. I asked if she knew why Sam said George was going to support his campaign for senate president – if George had had a falling-out with Doug Stuart.

'She told me it wasn't a falling-out. They were never really friends. George was vice-president of the senate as a token nod to the senior faculty. It was a do-nothing position. Stuart had all the power. George didn't have a say about anything. Didn't have a role and didn't care.

'Just recently, George discovered Stuart had abused his position, had been abusing it for years.' His tone of voice changed, as if he needed to get something extremely important across to Sarah.

She seemed to sense this, watching him intently. 'So why now, all of a sudden? Doug had been abusing his position for years.'

'Exactly.' Ambler felt like he was making his closing summation to the jury, a jury of one. 'Right after that conversation which left me puzzled, I learned of something else. Because of a complaint about unfairness from the junior faculty, Olson had been preparing a report on how the senate allocated travel and conference funds. This meant, for the first time as far as I could tell, someone besides Stuart examined the faculty senate finances.'

Sarah wasn't being defensive; she was trained to be

perceptive and to think logically. 'Wouldn't the faculty senate accounts have been audited by the college?'

This had occurred to Ambler also. But embezzlers at banks and businesses had gotten away with their schemes for years, despite yearly audits, before eventually being caught. 'I guess. But the faculty senate budget is a tiny part of the overall college budget. Stuart would submit a report or a balance sheet or whatever. In any event, the college never found any problems.'

She thought about what he'd said for a few moments. Her expression was placid, as if she were doing something she was used to, thinking, analyzing, putting pieces together, weighing the validity of one contention against another. She was considering the validity of the claim that a man she'd known intimately, admired, at one time loved, was a thief and a murderer. She'd neither accept nor deny the contention until she was sure.

TWENTY-FOUR

t took a while. She asked quite a few questions until she got to the fatal flaw in Ambler's allegation. 'What you say happened makes sense.' She spoke calmly, her hands folded on the desk, as if she might be speaking to her class. 'I find it believable. Yet from what I've heard, you don't have proof.'

Ambler wasn't trying to put anything over on her. She was right. 'I don't have proof. That's why I came to you.' He told her about Lew Montgomery, the accountant, and the lapping scheme he'd discovered. 'The case would be stronger if we could find the bank account into which the siphoned-off money went. I hoped you might be some help with that.'

'And the murder?'

'The murder is different.'

He'd wracked his brain over this and, no matter how he approached it, he ended up in the same place. 'Someone might have heard Stuart planning George Olson's death with Walt Nichols. Nichols might have told someone what he'd done. There's almost nothing else that can tie Stuart to George Olson's murder. The possibility of finding evidence in the other murder is a little bit better – fingerprints, witnesses, if anyone looked for them – but not much.'

If the sadness and despair he felt showed when he thought about the hopelessness of the position his son was in, she didn't let on. She was surprisingly matter-of-fact. 'Doug isn't a cold-blooded murderer. If he did these horrible things, I don't know how he could live with himself.' She wrinkled her brow, looking intently at Ambler, as if he were a student not trying hard enough to understand what she meant.

'I don't mean that figuratively.' She said this as if Ambler had not understood or disagreed with her. She was right; he hadn't taken what she said literally. 'How could he live with himself?' was something one might say about anyone who'd committed a murder.

'Doug, despite his narcissism as you called it, is a sensitive man. He's not a sociopath. He has a conscience; he can empathize with others.

'I know this . . . I've seen him commiserate with homeless men on the street, shooting the breeze with them like they were golfing buddies. He used to go to the Seven-Eleven, pick up fifty dollars' worth of cold cuts and snacks and such, take them to a homeless encampment, and hang out with the hobos for an hour or so. He never physically threatened me, never came close. He hated killing. He hated war.'

She'd become slightly deranged, wild-eyed, as she talked about her ex-husband. Ambler thought she was asking forgiveness for him. But she wasn't.

'Having done these horrible things – having committed murder – will eat at him. Even if he was so diabolically smart that he's never convicted of the murders, the fact that he committed them, knowing that he took a person's life will haunt him; that plus the mortification of the embezzling charge, the reality – or even the possibility – of exposure will destroy him. He'll pay the price for his sins.'

For Ambler, Stuart paying for his sins wasn't enough. If he wasn't charged and convicted of murder, John would be. He considered telling this to Sarah. But what difference did it make? She didn't have the evidence to convict Stuart.

Yet she understood more than he thought she did. 'The way out of this, the only hope for John, is that Stuart confesses to what he's done.'

Ambler took a moment to understand what he was hearing. People do confess to crimes. That's why cops interrogate suspects. That was where the third degree came from. In the old days, cops would beat confessions out of suspects. Some still did. They call it an interview now rather than an interrogation. Whatever they called it, he knew Mike had persuaded more than one murderer to confess to his crime. He wondered if he could pull it off.

Cops had to tell suspects they were entitled to a lawyer, that anything they said could be recorded and held against them. He wouldn't have to do that. Cops lied to suspects, letting them think they had evidence they didn't have, or telling one suspect that their partner had confessed to being at the crime scene but had fingered the other suspect for the actual murder.

What if he confronted Stuart with the evidence of the theft and lied to him about what he'd learned from George Olson's wife? He could say George told her he'd caught Stuart stealing. He could also say he found Walt's girlfriend, who knows more than she's saying; it will be just a matter of time until she talks.

He didn't fully trust Sarah. Would she really turn against her ex-husband? Or, when it became a question of sending her ex-husband to jail for the rest of his life, would she lose her nerve? How would he know the answer?

Maybe she read his mind. 'Your son has become very important to me. John and his son. I've never met anyone like them.' She scrutinized Ambler for a moment. 'He told me you and he are only now coming to know one another. You didn't know him when he was growing up.'

Ambler felt the accusation like a stab in the chest. He could tell by her expression she didn't mean what she said as an accusation, and realized now how he'd taken it.

'He said he's forgiven you, but you feel tremendously guilty—'

'For deserting him,' Ambler said bitterly.

'For being absent,' she said. 'He was very angry at you. He said for a while in prison he blamed you for what he did.' She was trying to sound comforting. 'He said he thought as long as you blamed yourself for what happened to him, he might as well blame you as well.

'He's never been able to tell you this. He came to an under-standing of himself in prison.' Her expression was bright. 'Don't tell him I told you this. He decided he was in the mess he was in – that the fight that put him in jail happened – because he'd been living the kind of life his mother led.' She glanced away and then back at Ambler. 'He told me about her, too – dragging her out of bars, the revolving collection of men she wanted him to call Dad.

'He never did, by the way. What I'm getting at is that he decided in prison he wanted to live the kind of life you lived, and not the kind of life his mother lived. He was through with that.'

Ambler was stunned. First, because his son wanted to be like him. But also by the realization that Sarah Hastings, in the short time she'd known his son, knew more about John than he did, knew him many layers deeper. He wanted to ask about that, what was happening between her and John. He didn't because he didn't think he had a right to. She answered the question he wanted to ask anyway.

'I think I'm in love with your son, Mr Ambler, and I think he's in love with me. It's not a good idea for him to get involved in this kind of head-over-heels thing right out of prison when he hasn't truly found himself yet. It will take a while before we know it's a sure thing. But don't be surprised if it is.

'Meanwhile, I meant what I said. I'll do anything I can to keep him from going back to prison.'

He believed her. He didn't need to tell her the consequences to her ex-husband of her helping him. She might be a bit starry-eyed at the moment about John, but she was clear-sighted about what they were up against. He told her he was going to question Stuart, pretending he knew more than he did, lying about what he knew if need be.

She was skeptical. 'Doug won't be fooled easily. He's the smartest man I've ever known. His weakness, if that's what it is, has to do with who he thinks he is. He not only thinks – with some reason – he's smarter than everyone else. He also thinks he's morally superior to everyone else. You need to confront him with the crimes he's committed, with his moral failure. He has to be made to confront himself, not be allowed to hide from himself what he's done.'

Ambler was fully committed now to Sarah Hastings as his ally. They talked for another hour about how to bring Doug Stuart face to face with his conscience. The first question was when and how to confront him. It would have to be soon because Florence Randolph and Lew Montgomery weren't going to wait long to tell the world, or at least the campus, that Doug Stuart was a thief.

There was no telling what would happen once that news

broke. White-collar crimes – skimming, kiting, lapping, embezzling – can often be settled quietly without bringing in the
law, a resignation, restitution. The reputation of the institution
isn't tarnished; everything is swept under the rug. If that
happened, he'd have lost a lot of leverage with Stuart.

And then Sarah told him something else that altered the
landscape. She continued to stay in touch with Stuart. Their
divorce had been more or less amicable. They attended faculty
meetings and campus functions without running afoul of one
another. She even took care of his dog when he was traveling.
'It was my dog, too,' she said.

'You have access to his house?'

She nodded.

'Does he have a safe?'

She watched him quizzically. 'I don't think so. He didn't
when we were married.'

'His bank records. Do you think you could find them if
they're in his house?'

She was puzzled for another moment and then caught on.
'I bet I could.'

He looked at her meaningfully. 'It would be stealing. You
could be charged. Even if you weren't charged, when Stuart
finds out, which he most likely will, whatever friendship you
have with him would be over . . . It also could be dangerous.
He might take revenge.'

She shook her head. 'I never in my wildest dreams thought
I'd have this kind of intrigue in my life. I don't say I like
it. Meeting John was crazy enough, a former prisoner, a
convicted killer. And now I'm going to help prove a man I
was married to committed murder . . . It's all so unreal. But
I can handle it.'

She stared at Ambler for a moment. 'And you've done this
before? Many times. I don't understand how you can do it,
how you immerse yourself in the worst kind of conduct humans
are capable of.'

'I don't know myself how I do it . . . Since I first learned
to think for myself, I've been opposed to killing of any kind.
Like your former husband, I'm opposed to war. I don't accept
the idea of revenge killing. I don't like good guys killing bad

guys any more than I like bad guys killing good guys. If I had my way, no one would kill anyone. Yet here I am, in the middle of another mystery involving murder: one that may end up ruining my son's life.'

Late the next afternoon, Sarah called Ambler at the library. 'I've got them, I think,' she said. 'I knew Doug was going on an overnight field trip, so I told him I wanted to take Samantha to be groomed and keep her overnight. He was fine with that; he wouldn't have to kennel her.

'It took a couple of hours but I found a bunch of bank statements. He has two banks. The one I knew about – the one we had together – and another I didn't know about, from the National Bank of Dominica.

'I found folders of the statements the bank sends every month to a mailbox in Manhattan, with a record of deposits and withdrawals. It doesn't look like he keeps careful records; the stuff was in a pile way back in the bottom drawer of a wooden file cabinet.

'I'm sure it's his bank account, but the records are for money market accounts in the names of two companies, DS Environmental Services and Sustainable Enterprises. I've never heard of either of them. Maybe your friend at the library can find out about them.

'I took a dozen or so of the statements the bank sends every month from each account, a couple from each year going back seven years.

'Most of the deposits are for a few hundred dollars, some for two or three thousand dollars, none larger than three thousand.' Her voice went up a couple of octaves. 'But holy crap, there are a lot of them; a dozen or more deposits a year for years.

'I don't know if these are his only secret bank accounts. I had to leave to pick up the dog at the groomers. The bank stuff is such a mess, I doubt he'll miss anything. Did I get enough?'

'Definitely enough . . .' He was going to say 'to hang him', but didn't. 'I'll get them from you tomorrow and we can talk about what happens next.'

When he finished the phone call, it was near enough to quitting time that he left the library and went over to the Library Tavern to sip a beer and think about what he would do with the incriminating information he now had. He sat for quite a while watching McNulty make drinks and not coming up with a plan. It was like a chess game, in which a good player would think many jumps ahead of what was happening at that moment on the board.

So far, he hadn't been able to think more than one jump ahead. He'd tell Stuart what he'd found and see what he said or did. He had to admit this wasn't much of a plan. Other possibilities and ideas floated around in his head, but he couldn't figure out a plan until he knew how his nemesis would react when he was confronted with the evidence of his financial crimes.

He kept coming back to the reality that proving Stuart embezzled from the faculty senate didn't connect him to the murders. No matter how he looked at things, he ended up clutching at the very thin straw Sarah Hastings had offered him: Stuart's guilt over the murders might overwhelm him with remorse and lead him to confess.

After the cocktail-hour rush had slowed – like for most bars with an after-work crowd, almost all of the tippers arrived within a few minutes of one another as if they'd all arrived on a bus that pulled up in front of the bar at 5:45 – McNulty sauntered over, refreshed Ambler's beer, and drew himself a short one into his coffee cup.

'We're on to the next phase of Operation Doug Stuart,' Ambler said. 'The problem is I don't know what to do.'

McNulty made sure everything at the bar was attended to and leaned closer. 'You want the guy to hear footsteps getting closer. He thinks we're on to him, so you keep acting like we know all about what he did, and pretty soon he starts believing we do.'

'We've got more than that.' Ambler told him about the embezzlement and the purloined bank statements.

McNulty's reaction was subdued. 'So you can ruin his digestion for a few days with that, but it doesn't get you any closer to pinning a murder on him. Those embezzling things are tricky; a lot of times, the boss just says tsk-tsk, get the fuck out of here and never come back. That's it; they don't want the cops to investigate because the cops might uncover their own shady doings. The trick with stealing is if you steal a lot of money and do it quietly, you get away with it. Not like if you steal a few bucks; that happens they throw the book at you.'

'Getting back to "pinning a murder rap on him".' Ambler waited while McNulty tended to the service bar. 'However much we pretend we're on to him, when push comes to shove, we don't have anything. And he's smart enough to know that. What we have is his conscience.' He told the bartender Sarah Hastings's take on her ex-husband's belief in his moral superiority and how that might work on his conscience.

McNulty's forehead wrinkled and his eyebrows narrowed. 'I always thought the morally superior types were haters beneath it all. I'd bet on a lot of things before I'd bet on that fucker's conscience.' He nodded, almost like he was rocking in a rocking chair while he thought about something.

'This is something I thought about when you told me how that murder of this guy Walt they charged your son with happened. They wrestled for a gun and the Walt guy lost. Same thing happened with your son years ago when he went to prison; he got slammed for it. Same kind of thing happened with you.' His voice softened and he took on this expression of sympathy he took on sometimes that would almost make you cry. 'Sorry to bring it up . . . and you walked. The reason you walked was the guy you tangled with had already killed someone.'

Ambler caught on.

'So you make out you're dead certain you know what Stuart did. Maybe he doesn't believe you. You haven't shown him any proof. But he doesn't know for sure you don't have proof. Like you said before: he can't be sure he didn't make a mistake, leave something behind; maybe someone saw him. The Walt guy talked to someone. A million things that could incriminate you run through your mind. I can tell you that happens, even when you didn't do it and the cops think you did.'

He tucked his coffee cup under the beer tap again and took

Ambler's mug and topped it off. 'I'm telling you, you need to act like you're certain . . . That's no easy thing, you know.' He spoke sharply.

Ambler knew how much pride McNulty took in his training as an actor. He'd worked on it for years, still worked on it. Despite hundreds of auditions, small off-Broadway parts, years without success, you might say, he knew he was a good actor, a real actor. He took his art seriously.

'You don't just pretend like you did when you were nine playing Cowboys and Indians. You gotta go home tonight and practice . . . and then practice again tomorrow morning. If you work at it, practice enough, you'll be convincing. Lucky for you, you don't have to memorize any lines.'

'Once you got him – not convinced; you won't convince him – but doubting . . . Once you got him doubting, you offer him a strategy he hasn't thought of – a way out. This covers the growing doubt he has that he'll be found out.' McNulty raised and lowered his eyebrows. 'And it gives him the chance to make a deal with his conscience though, as I said, I wouldn't bet the house and barn on that one.'

That night, after Johnny was asleep, Ambler told John what he'd found out about Stuart and that he would confront him. He didn't tell him about Sarah's help because she didn't want John to know she was helping.

As he listened, John was pensive. He asked a couple of questions about the embezzlement. But he didn't say anything when Ambler told him he didn't know yet how they would prove Stuart was the killer they were after. Ambler didn't want to tell him about the plan to try to get Stuart to confess, because Sarah was tied up with that, too. And because it might not work.

Surprisingly, John didn't press him. But after a while, John said, 'This might be hard on Sarah . . . Professor Hastings. She was married to him, you know. When she was young,' he said hurriedly. 'She was really young . . . and he was older, a kind of rock-star scholar, so she fell for him, I guess.' He stopped and was pensive again.

'I don't know why I told you that . . . She said marrying him was a bad idea; it's over. But they're still friends, and she talks about him like he's a genius. Now he's going to take a fall, right? You're going to get him on the embezzling, even if you don't get him on the murders, right?'

Ambler heard the resignation in his son's voice. 'We're going to get him on the murders, John. I promise you that.'

John's smile was world-weary and resigned. 'Thanks, Pop.'

TWENTY-FIVE

Lew Montgomery examined the bank statements from Doug Stuart's fake companies and matched the deposits from the bank statements with the withdrawals and checks from the senate account. 'It's all we need,' he said.

Ambler took the bank statements and told Montgomery he'd get them back to him by the following day, telling him he had one more thing to work out but needed to keep it to himself for now. After a bit of thought, Montgomery agreed to wait.

Stuart returned from his field trip the next afternoon and Ambler called on him unannounced at his office later that same afternoon, armed with a representative sample of bank statements, canceled checks, photocopies of withdrawals and deposits – and McNulty's strategy.

McNulty wasn't far away, in case the endeavor went off the rails, although he didn't expect that sort of confrontation. He hoped the encounter would be of a moral and ethical nature. He'd also armed himself with a copy of an article Stuart wrote for the *Journal of Environmental Studies*, 'The Moral Imperative of Sustainable Living'.

Stuart was sunburned, cheerful, exuberant, as someone might be after a brisk walk or an afternoon swim. If he felt the walls closing in on him, he didn't show it, greeting Ambler with the open, friendly smile that made him seem both vulnerable and approachable, despite his arrogance, and would help explain why students were drawn to him.

'I'm surprised to see you.' He glanced at his watch. 'You barely caught me. I was about to head out.' Letting on perhaps without meaning to that he'd rather Ambler hadn't caught him. But he bounced back. 'I've just returned from a field trip so, as my students would say, I'm dipping out on my office hours.'

He noticed Ambler's expression for the first time, perhaps an expression Ambler was unaware of.

'You look down in the dumps.' He said this in a kind of

'buck up, old man' tone, but caught himself. 'Of course you would be, with all you're dealing with.' He sat down and gestured toward a chair in front of his desk for Ambler.

'I have to say, being out in the field with a group of students – we visited a sustainable farm in Dutchess County; among other things, we weeded an asparagus patch by hand – energizes me; reinforces my connection to the natural world, helps me forget, at least for a little while, the atrocities man has perpetrated against man and the natural world. Helps me forget about cruelty, injustice, senseless murder.

'I didn't realize how much George's tragic death and then Walt's death weighed on me. I'm usually an upbeat guy . . . but these last weeks have devastated me.'

His glance at Ambler once again showed that vulnerability and openness, but this time it was colored with sympathy. 'I know it's worse for you . . . especially because of your son.'

'I killed a man once,' Ambler said; not something he'd planned on saying at all. 'Strangely, it was under the same sort of circumstances as when my son killed a man, and even more strangely, similar to the circumstances of Walt Nichols's death – a struggle over a gun belonging to the other man. In my case, the man was a murderer, so I wasn't charged or jailed like my son. The prosecutors determined the shooting to be accidental and justifiable.'

He let this sit with Stuart for a moment, and watched his reaction which was barely perceptible, not much more than a twitch of heightened interest.

After a pause that was too long not to be disconcerting, Ambler continued. 'Even though I was exonerated, I've never gotten over it, never forgiven myself for having a hand in someone else's death. For weeks after it happened, I suffered panic attacks and sleepless nights.

'I still wake up from nightmares – often the same nightmare in which I have the opportunity to not pull the trigger, to not kill the man, but in each nightmare I pull the trigger. That wasn't what happened. I didn't have a choice on whether to pull the trigger when it happened; the gun just went off. But that doesn't change the nightmare.'

Stuart's expression had frozen in place and was impossible

to decipher. It might be guilt; it might be denial; it might be accusation.

They sat in silence for another long moment until Ambler said, 'Taking another person's life isn't natural to humans. It might have been as we developed from whatever we're descended from into what we are today. When humans fought to survive against predators who would kill them, killing would have been a natural response. But wouldn't you say it's been bred out of us over the centuries of civilization and is an aberration when it happens?'

Stuart stared in disbelief. Whatever his expression had been before – guilt, denial – it was now incredulity, as if Ambler had levitated and was floating above the desk. Ambler let Stuart stare and entertain his thoughts, though Ambler couldn't fathom what they'd be.

After a moment, he prodded the professor, 'What do you think? Would a sustainable world include murder?'

Stuart closed his eyes, as if to avoid an unpleasant sight. 'What a strange thing to say.' He frowned, deep wrinkles forming in his forehead, and watched his hands as he folded them on the desk in front of him. When he looked at Ambler again, his mouth wrinkled with distaste, as if he might spit something out. 'Maybe because you do what you do – this sick obsession with murder you have – you can ask questions like that . . . I don't think like you.'

'Suppose you murdered someone.' Ambler wasn't sure what he was trying to get at, or even what he might say next. He wanted Stuart to remember the murders, to picture them, to be unable to not think about them. 'You're an ethical person. You do good in the world. You care about your students; you care about the world we live in.

'What if circumstances arose that threatened your very existence – not a life-and-death situation, but one in which your life would be changed utterly, your life as you planned it and lived it would be destroyed?

'To preserve that life – let's say a life devoted to doing good – you murdered a person, or perhaps persons, who would destroy it. Would you feel remorse afterward that was unbearable? Or would you think it justified because you had no choice, that person's life for your life? You might tell yourself you'd find a way to make amends – you'd devote the rest of your life to serving humanity. Would that be enough?

'It might. But what if there were another wrinkle? Would you allow an innocent person to go to prison, to suffer the consequences of what you did?'

Stuart shifted in place, his glance darting every which way, every few seconds sneaking a peek at Ambler, unable to sit still, squirming uncomfortably like a person with a desperate need to get to a bathroom. After a moment of this, he stood, backing away from his desk and Ambler, pressing himself against the windowless wall behind him as if he were warding off Hamlet's ghost.

'You're insane.' His voice cracked. 'You don't know what you're talking about . . .' In a rapid motion, he began a lunge toward his desk and toward Ambler who, as if he'd been waiting for such an attack, instinctively sank into a bow posture to ward it off. But Stuart stopped, not really noticing Ambler's movement.

'Do you think I don't know what you're doing? . . . You're trying to provoke me. You're desperate because of your son, so you're making crazy accusations. Who else have you accused? What do you think you're accomplishing by this . . . this character assassination?'

Stuart took a couple of deep breaths, closed his eyes as if he were making a wish. His tone was less frantic when he opened them. 'I don't have to listen to you.' He spent the next few seconds breathing deeply and calming himself, realizing probably that his reaction was as crazed as he'd accused Ambler of being. He was talking himself down, reminding himself it didn't matter what Ambler said; nothing connected him to any murder; Ambler had only conjecture – a guess – and he was foolish to have let it bother him.

For those moments, Stuart's friendly vulnerable expression had become a mask of hate. Calmer now, he tried to break through the mask with what became a wan smile. 'You really have gone off the deep end . . . implying I'm a murderer. Why? . . . Why would I kill Walt? He was like a son to me. I rescued him. I was helping him turn his life around . . .

'What would I have to gain by George's death? He was my partner. We were a team. George was affable and unassuming, a threat to no one . . .' Stuart faltered, as if he caught on from Ambler's expression that something unexpected and damning was coming.

Ambler tried to keep his tone neutral. 'I was getting to that.' He dropped the financial documents on Stuart's desk and stepped back. Stuart's eyes went to the documents and glued on to them, transfixed, so Ambler could have levitated and he wouldn't have noticed.

Stuart pondered the documents without touching them. You had to believe he was searching for a way to make them disappear, or to say they weren't his, or they weren't what they appeared to be, or there was a simple explanation. You could tell because he appeared to be shaking. He hadn't come up with anything.

With no reason to hurry, Ambler waited and watched. He'd never confronted a person with evidence of his guilt quite like this before. Mike must have done it hundreds of times. He should have asked his detective friend how he handled such a thing; he should have prepared himself better for this showdown. He was sure Stuart didn't know what to say. The odd thing was, Ambler didn't know what to say either. What he wanted was simple enough. He wanted Stuart to confess to a murder he committed, so John wouldn't go to jail.

When Mike did this sort of thing he'd have evidence – or if he didn't have evidence, he'd pretend he did – and he'd confront the suspect with it. The suspect would sooner or later confess after stalling for as long as he could, once he saw for certain there was no way out.

Sometimes Mike might say it would go easier on the suspect if he admitted his guilt. This wasn't always the truth. But the suspect would be grasping at straws. This was what Ambler needed to do now, convince Stuart he was at the end of his rope; there was no way out. This was where the plan he worked out with McNulty came in.

After what seemed like a long time, Stuart met Ambler's gaze with what Ambler thought was a look of defiance, certainly not surrender. 'What is this? . . . How did you get

your hands on my bank statements? You stole them!' He
tried for a tone of high dudgeon but couldn't pull it off; he
spoke without conviction; trying for indignation, he fell short.
Before he got to whatever point he'd thought to make, his
face betrayed him; he looked to Ambler like a penitent, asking
for mercy.

Despite having the high hand, Ambler had a difficult time
bearing down; sensing Stuart's abject humiliation, he had to
force himself not to feel sorry for him. He went ahead. 'You
know as well as I do – better – what you're looking at and
what it means. You've been stealing money for years and you
got caught. You panicked and – desperate to save yourself
from exposure – you got rid of the man who caught you
stealing. You're smart enough – arrogant enough – to believe
you could get away with murder.

'How would anyone discover you killed George if someone
else committed the murder? How could the killer be caught
if he had no connection to George, no reason to kill him?

'You had too much faith in your own cunning – you were
seduced by hubris – believing you could engineer a foolproof
murder. In a way you did; we found George's killer almost
by accident. Working from the wrong assumption, by happen-
stance we wound up in the right place. And then our suspect
was murdered. Fate took away what it had given us. My son
was charged with Walt Nichols's murder. The second murder
you committed.'

While Ambler was speaking, Stuart's mind must have been
running a mile a minute. By the time Ambler had had his say,
Stuart had regained some of his composure. 'I don't want to
talk with you anymore. Maybe you think you've got a case
against me because of some financial irregularities. But I can
explain any discrepancies you've found.

'I'm not a lawyer. Neither are you. What appears to you to
be misappropriation of funds might be bookkeeping errors. In
any event, I suggest you turn your findings over to the college,
to Dr Barnes, which would be the aggrieved party, if there is
an aggrieved party. If there are charges to be made, Barnes
can make them.'

It appeared now Stuart might be the one gloating. And he

might have considered doing so if he hadn't sensed Ambler wasn't finished.

'Actually, I'd already considered that. I don't know if Barnes will want to prosecute and bring another scandal to the college. He might instead work out something with you. Restitution. A resignation. A recommendation letter to a less prestigious college, maybe a community college. You'd lose your standing in the field. Colleagues would know something went wrong, there'd be a hint of a scandal, but they wouldn't know what it was. You might even over time rebuild your reputation. Make your way to the top of your field again.'

Stuart watched Ambler, his expression reflecting distrust one moment, hope the next moment, leaving him looking mostly confused, unsure how to take what he was hearing.

Ambler continued blithely. 'My friend McNulty, the bartender.' He smiled at his embattled and bewildered adversary. 'You met him – the fake bookseller who tricked you into selling books you didn't own. McNulty has noted more than once that you don't get into bad trouble if you steal a lot of money. It's only when you steal a little bit that they bring the hammer down on you.

'The fact is your embezzlement isn't important to me. I cared about it because I wanted you to know I knew. Just as I wanted to get on the record that you removed the books from the crime fiction collection to frame Sam Abernathy and ruin his chances in the faculty senate election. And while we're at it, I plan to debunk your "a witness saw Sam Abernathy in the library" ruse. I've been going down the list of ex-cons you gave me and found one who thought he saw Professor Abernathy. But now that Walt's dead, he's no longer sure.

'To sum up, I exposed your efforts at subterfuge because I wanted you to know I was on to you, so you'd pay attention when I got to the most important thing. As I said, it's what happened after the embezzling came to light that I'm concerned with. I don't need to tell you what that is.'

While Ambler pressed on, he feared that at any moment Stuart might make a dash for the door or make a charge at him. That Stuart didn't do so reinforced his confidence in Sarah Hastings's belief that her ex-husband might be betrayed by his guilt. So Ambler would play Porfiry Petrovich to Stuart's Rodion Raskolnikov.

Stuart again found his tongue and made another attempt to regain his arrogance. 'I don't know what you're talking about. And I'm willing to bet you don't know what you're talking about either. I made some bookkeeping mistakes. Some money might have ended up in the wrong account. I'll explain all that to Barnes . . . and take my lumps. I don't hide from my mistakes.'

Ambler, who'd been standing since Stuart stood up, sat down again. 'Murder is more consequential than financial crimes. Barnes can't sweep that under the rug. Yet there's hope. Some murderers do make amends and regain their reputation.'

'I'm not . . .' Stuart started to say but stopped.

Ambler again worried he'd bolt for the door, and again he didn't.

'You know and I know that you hired Walt Nichols to murder George Olson and then murdered Nichols when you realized he'd been found out, by me if not yet by the police. So you killed him to keep him from implicating you in a murder conspiracy.

'You don't have to admit it; all you need to do is listen. I'm trying to help you. Don't overreact. You can disregard what I say but wait until I finish.

'If you confess before a warrant is issued, you have a good chance for a plea.'

Stuart's nervous laugh was a chilling cackle, a fractured sound that had its roots in agony. 'A warrant for what? . . . There's no warrant.'

'Not yet. If I've figured out you're the killer, the police will, too. The case needs to be bulletproof before they'll bring the charge. Another witness, possibly two.'

'What wit—' Stuart caught himself, but knew it was too late.

Ambler didn't acknowledge the slip. Instead he watched his adversary like a doctor might watch a patient he'd told was very ill. He hoped his expression was kindly and sympathetic, offering some hope to offset the fearful expression of his patient.

'The important thing is what you confess to. The important thing is you create the narrative of what happened before the police put a different narrative together.'

Again Stuart started to protest and again Ambler cut him off. 'You might not want to hear what I'm telling you. At the moment, you don't have to admit that it's true. Later, when you've thought about it, you'll realize I've given you a way out of a dire predicament you might have thought there was no way out of.

'I told you about the similarity and the differences between the situation in which my son killed a man and the situation in which I killed a man and – for the sake of argument,' he held up his hand to hold off Stuart's protest, 'the situation in which you killed a man.'

Stuart had a puzzled expression, as if he was trying to follow, not too successfully, a complicated argument.

'Putting aside what I know happened, I'm going to present an alternate version of history. You may wonder why but you'll understand by the time I finish.

'In this version of history, a concerned professor realized that a student he mentored, a young man who was like a son to him, made a tragic mistake. The student discovered – possibly the professor told him of the dilemma – that his beloved professor was about to be exposed as an embezzler. We'll put aside for a moment the truth or falsity of the accusation against the professor. The fact was the exposure would ruin the professor's life.

'We should note here that the student in question was a violent offender who'd served time in prison and had been released into a reentry program that included admission to the Trinity College program for former offenders.

'The student, Walt Nichols – having not yet outgrown the propensity to violence that had been part of his life since childhood – took it upon himself to protect his mentor and solve his problem in the best way he knew how: by getting rid of the accuser.

'The mentor-professor had no way of knowing Walt would murder his accuser. In fact, he had no idea that this was what happened when his colleague the accuser was killed. When

he did realize with horror what had happened – this part is a
bit fuzzy; I don't know when or how he found this out. But
you can work that out later.

'Once the professor knew his student had murdered his
colleague, he went to him to persuade him to turn himself in.
The student – having reverted to his violent ways; the bit
between his teeth, so to speak – would have none of it. They
argued.

'The professor told his student, who'd turned into someone
he no longer knew, that unless he turned himself in, the
professor would turn him in. The professor saw the gun and
realized Walt hadn't really turned a corner in his life. He may
have tried, but he'd lost the battle for the young man's soul.
The hardened criminal, the cold-blooded killer, had displaced
the student working to turn his life around, and the professor
was faced with a life-and-death situation.

'He tried to wrestle the gun away from Walt; he had no
choice. Walt would shoot him unless he got the gun away
from him. So he tried. They fought. The gun went off. Walt
was dead. And then as he looked in horror at what he'd done,
the gun went off again. The professor ran.

'For a while, he kept quiet. No one knew he'd killed Walt.
Since George was dead, no one knew about the financial
irregularities. He thought he might get away with everything.
But guilt and remorse over what he'd done caught up with
him. He couldn't live with himself. He couldn't face his
students knowing he was living a lie, so he turned himself in.'

Ambler wondered if Stuart had been holding his breath
while he listened, because he let his breath out now in a loud
sigh and buried his face in his hands.

'I should've listened to Walt and let him kill you when we
had the chance.' He spoke into his hands. 'I said if he put a
bullet in you, it would be enough to scare you off; he didn't
have to kill you. I should have known better.'

This wasn't the response Ambler had hoped for. Stuart had
shifted himself into a different gear and sounded like he'd
given up the professoriate for Mob life.

'Why wouldn't I kill you now and not have to worry about
confessing to the other crimes?'

With some effort, Ambler kept his voice steady. 'I'm not the only one who knows what you've done. If you killed me, you'd get caught and sentenced for three murders. If you follow the strategy I'm giving you, at worst you'd be charged with manslaughter and serve a couple of years. With a good lawyer, you might not get prison time. The man you killed unintentionally and in self-defense was a murderer.

'Either way, you'll have a good shot at redeeming yourself . . . a bit tarnished but a star professor seeking redemption, a tarnished but unbowed champion of the environment.'

As they talked, a kind of bond grew between them. Ambler could see Stuart come to believe – a bit of a stretch – Ambler was on his side.

'Talk to Sarah,' Ambler said. 'She's your friend. She believes you're a better person than you think you are yourself.'

'We're divorced. That's over.' And then a pause. 'She knows?'

Ambler nodded. 'She's still on your side.' Another stretcher. 'A person doesn't have to be in love with you to be a friend, to care about you.'

Stuart went back into his own thoughts for a moment. When he came out, he asked, 'Why are you doing this? You're telling me how to get away with murder. Why would I believe you'd do that? How do I know this isn't a trap? Why would you go against what you stand for to help me?'

Stuart's tone was belligerent, but it didn't bother Ambler. 'You've got me mixed up with someone else. I've never thought of what I do as a battle of good versus evil. If you get away with this, I don't see you killing anyone again. I think you're sorry for what you've done. You've taken the lives of two people because of your greed. There's more to you than that. You'll feel more remorse as time goes on and you come to realize your fancy car, your expensive watch, whatever trinkets you've acquired weren't worth it.

'For me, what do I get out of doing this? My son is exonerated. Sam Abernathy is cleared of suspicion. That doesn't solve all of his problems. But it takes care of a big one. Two people are dead who were alive when I first came to this campus. I'm sad about that. If I'd come here that first day, recognized what was going on and prevented them from dying, I'd feel I'd accomplished something. Returning things to the status quo leaving two dead behind isn't much of an accomplishment. But I'll have to be satisfied with it.

'Think it over. It's the best way out.' He gave Stuart David Levinson's card. 'Tell him the version of history I told you. He doesn't need to know any other version. He'll work with what you give him.'

TWENTY-SIX

McNulty served Ambler and Adele their hamburgers, Ambler his beer and Adele her seltzer water. He put the seltzer water down gingerly, as if the glass was something he didn't like touching.

'Women for years had a beer or a highball now and again when they were pregnant and the human race continued to propagate,' he said.

'Scientists learn new things; new data show what they thought was true wasn't true, so they change the advice they give.' Adele smiled beatifically; nothing anyone could say would dampen her new secret happiness.

'Like the ads in the old days when the doctor on the back cover of *Life* or *Look* was telling you to smoke Camels.'

'Something like that,' Adele said guardedly. 'Scientists discovered cigarette smoke was harmful, so they recommend people don't smoke.'

'So why should we listen to the scientists now,' McNulty said smugly, 'if in a few years they're going to tell us they were wrong and we should do something else?'

'That's ridiculous, McNulty.' Adele's feathers were ruffled.

'Here we go again,' said Ambler.

McNulty laughed. 'Just messin' with you, Adele. You take good care of that little baby.' He addressed Ambler. 'So I hear the professor turned himself in. David finally has a paying customer. He got the guy out on bail and tells me he'll walk on the murder charge. Some crime fighter you are.'

'I told Stuart your idea on copping a plea. I hope you didn't tell Levinson that.'

'Bartenders are noted for their discretion. Secrets are safe with me. The good thing is I got Sam out of my apartment. God, what a blabbermouth. He could talk the nuts off a stone statue. He's gone back to the Bronx but not to his wife, I think. He got his girlfriend into some kind of battered woman

protection program. She and her kids are gone. Sam doesn't
even know where they are.

'A couple of days after Sam left, the battering husband came
to my apartment looking for her. I told him Sam took her and
the kids to Schenectady but to be careful . . . both Sam and –
Rebecca is her name – were armed.'

'One good thing—' Ambler started to say before McNulty
interrupted him.

'And Adele told me your son is shacked up with a lady
professor up in the Bronx.'

'I didn't say anything of the kind.' Adele snapped at
McNulty. 'I told him Sarah, the pretty and charming professor
Raymond likes so much, helped John get an adjunct position
teaching guitar at a college in Westchester.'

Again to McNulty, 'What you so crudely misinterpreted
was Professor Hastings has a big house all to herself and she
invited John and Johnny to stay with her on the days he teaches.
He can also give lessons on the side while he's in Westchester.
And he's almost as close to Johnny's school as when they're
here in Manhattan.'

The final piece of the puzzle Ambler had so far kept to
himself. Harry had told him a day ago the fate of the New
York Mystery Writers collection. How that came about, Ambler
told Adele later that evening after she changed the bandage
on his shoulder for the last time.

'It's healed,' she said.

Doug Stuart took some of Ambler's advice but not all of
it. In making his confession, he left out the part about George
Olson discovering irregularities in the faculty senate's
finances. In its place he concocted a story about George
threatening to disclose an embarrassing romantic indiscretion
from his past that could cost him his faculty position and
ruin his reputation.

The police didn't care much about that part anyway; they
were interested in the murders. And more than happy to let
Stuart take two of them off the books, even if he didn't end
up doing time for them.

Florence Randolph and Lew Montgomery took their case
to Barnes and, as Ambler predicted, Barnes worked out a

hush-hush deal with Stuart but also with Randolph and Lew Montgomery. Stuart would resign his faculty senate position and, as the last officer standing, Randolph would become president and Montgomery vice-president.

The term 'misappropriation of funds' would disappear from the conversation. Stuart would be reprimanded for 'financial mismanagement' and 'fiscal irresponsibility', resulting in substantial monies with which the college had provided the faculty senate being unaccounted for. Stuart agreed to restitution.

While it was generally thought Stuart repaid the college over $250,000 by borrowing from his TIAA-CREF retirement account, the truth was he had that much money and more stashed away in his offshore bank accounts.

The most surprising turn of events, however, caused Ambler to admit he'd misjudged and mischaracterized Dr Edward Barnes. Shortly after Harry told him about a new donation to the crime fiction collection, he found a letter in his mailbox. The letter, on embossed stationery with the logo of Trinity College of the Bronx, was short and gracious, thanking Ambler for his service to the college and telling him the college was providing the Trinity College New York Mystery Writers collection to the New York Public Library on permanent loan.